FAIR WARNING

"If you can get away from here, you will have a chance to live a happy life again."

"Meaning what?"

"Why, meaning that you could go back to drifting… no fighting…taking things easy…never worrying. That was what made you very happy, Melendez."

"Aye," said the younger man, "you seem to know me pretty well! And if I stay here?"

"You'd have to be on your guard every moment of the day and the night. You'd have to have your head turned to look over your shoulder, never knowing when a bullet would come at you from behind."

—from "Bad Man's Gulch"

B.S.

MAX BRAND®

BAD MAN'S GULCH

LEISURE BOOKS   NEW YORK CITY

A LEISURE BOOK®

March 2007

Published by special arrangement with Golden West Literary Agency.

Dorchester Publishing Co., Inc.
200 Madison Avenue
New York, NY 10016

ISBN 0-8439-5832-4

The name "Leisure Books" and the stylized "L" with design are trademarks of Dorchester Publishing Co., Inc.

Printed in the United States of America.

Visit us on the web at www.dorchesterpub.com.

BAD MAN'S GULCH

TABLE OF CONTENTS

THE ADOPTED SON

"The Adopted Son" was Frederick Faust's seventh published work of fiction. It appeared in 1917 in the October 27th issue of *All-Story Weekly* under the pen name Max Brand. The story was featured prominently on the cover by way of a photo of Francis X. Bushman and Beverly Bayne, who starred in the film version of "The Adopted Son" that same year. "Read it all here. See it on the screen," announced the caption. From the beginning Faust was seen as a gifted writer who was marketable to a large audience.

I

WAYLAID

If he had confined his attentions to Mexicans, it would have been all right, for those were days when guns were very popularly worn in Texas and almost as popularly used. In fact, his little affairs with Mexicans helped to make Lazy Purdue pleasing to the populace of several towns in southwestern Texas, and they led to no further result than a brief interview with a sheriff who would half playfully insist that such things must stop.

For the rest, people refused to take Lazy seriously, except when he was angry, which happened very, very seldom. Under the influence of the peculiar caress of his eyes, his voice, and his smile, his man-eating past was forgotten.

Besides, he was very young, and many things are forgiven one under thirty. He had floated irresponsibly for several years between boyhood and manhood, absolutely refusing to work more than a fortnight at a time. Because of this, and also because he generally replied to all questions that he was "just lazyin' around," he had acquired his uncomplimentary nickname.

But when Lazy Purdue shot young Colton in Calamity Ben's saloon, public sentiment changed. Even the sheriff forgot to smile.

Lazy got away from Averyville to a good start because nobody in town felt equal to following him single-handedly, and it took nearly half an hour to organize a posse. He maintained his lead because he had won one of the best horses in those parts gambling with Jimmy Bixbee the week before. He rode that horse to death thirty miles east of Averyville, and then "borrowed" a mount from the corral of the Double X Ranch.

After he made the loan, Lazy knew that he was done with Texas for good. In those days the brand of Cain could fade from a man's forehead and be forgotten, but the horse thief was damned through eternity.

So Lazy took a deep cinch on his new mount and rode for life. He made the railroad station an hour and a half ahead of the posse and took an eastbound freight. After that he kept on east. He had no plan. He merely felt that he wanted to get as far east and north as possible. He had dreams of Canada.

At New Orleans he shifted north after working his way across the river. With the Mississippi behind him, he began to feel more careless. He had shifted from freight boxcars by this time, and was riding the rattlers, when on a clear, moonlit night the train came to a stop and Lazy felt someone beating on his feet and shouting: "Get out of there!"

He was quite aggrieved. He had not noted the lights of a station and thought that the train had merely stopped to take on water. Therefore he worked his way off the rods with some irritation and stood before the conductor.

"You worthless swine," shouted that official,

"you can't get by with this sort of stuff on my train! Beat it!"

"My," sighed Lazy, "ain't you rough."

Something in his soft voice made the conductor raise his lantern to look over his tramp more carefully. At the same time he took several backward steps. "It's all right," said the conductor, "but you can't travel on my train. Wait for the next one. There's a freight due in a few hours." He continued his backward progress, still with his lantern held high and shining into Lazy's eyes.

"Wait a minute, old pal," said Lazy, "I reckon I've traveled quite a ways from my old stamping grounds. Just what part of the country may this be?"

The conductor laughed somewhat uneasily. "This is eastern Tennessee," he said. "Don't you see the mountains?"

With that he swung himself onto his steps, waved his lantern, and the train went swirling out into the night, leaving Lazy, rapt and motionless, staring the other way. He might have caught one of the rearward coaches, but he had quite forgotten the existence of the train. He had almost forgotten what mountains were like, so long had he been conscious only of the white, shining levels and flat monotony of the Texas plains.

Now he remembered. Now a thousand things came back to him. He felt the full force of the velvet-black masses rolling and leaping up to the cool blue sky. And a light May wind touched his forehead with a remembered gentleness and laden with forgotten scents of unseen, growing things.

He was fresh from the vast arching horizons of the desert. He was fresh from space filled only with terrible heat or formless night, a space wherein man's thought grows into a meaningless monody of commonplace. But here was space more impressive because it was partly filled. There was the sense of life in every movement of the air. The sky was framed between the muscular upthrusting arms of the hills. He let his eyes move softly from one familiar outline to the next.

Lazy Purdue removed his shapeless hat and stretched his arms and legs where they still ached from the continuous jar of the rods. "Lazy, my friend," he murmured, "I reckon you've been a tolerable long time coming back home, but you've arrived here at last."

He started up the road that wound dimly up- and downhill, beside woods where all the leaves were murmurously astir, beside rolling pasture land where the bells sounded faintly as the cattle moved, browsing. He could see them sometimes in the moonlight. And once on a hilltop, black against the skyline, a great bull paused and turned his head and gazed at him in sullen, bovine inquiry.

He did not know how far he had walked when he heard a beat of galloping hoofs behind him. He turned to stop the rider and parley. The horseman came to an abrupt halt before his upraised arm, and Lazy found himself looking up into a handsome, boyish face, above which a broad-brimmed hat flared cavalier fashion. A cravat was folded loosely about his throat.

"Who might you be?" queried the boy, frowning curiously at him.

"I'm a stranger," began Lazy Purdue's soft voice, "and I'm looking for work. Can you tell me where I'm apt to find it in these parts?"

The boy considered him a moment, rubbing his chin as if in thought. "Sure," he said after the moment's pause. "I reckon there's two places where you'd find work. One's over to McLane's. I don't know as I'd advise anyone goin' there."

Lazy Purdue started. The deeper shadow of the night concealed a frown that stirred his forehead. "An' what's the matter with the McLanes?" he queried.

"They's a tolerable lot that's wrong with 'em," stated the boy. "For my part, I never heard anything good about them. If you want work, you better go up to Conover's. That's my name."

Lazy Purdue started so perceptibly that young Conover leaned down from his saddle to look more closely at him.

"Are you George Conover?" asked Lazy Purdue.

"I reckon I am," said the boy, "but who might *you* be? How did you know me?"

"I didn't know ye," answered Lazy Purdue in a murmur, "I jus' heard a little about you when I come first into these parts. I reckon I'll go along up to your place."

"Can you find the way?" asked Conover.

"Sure," said Purdue. "I reckon I can pick it out from what people have told me. It lies to the right from that forking of the road right ahead, doesn't it?"

"Right," said Conover. "Hope you land a place. I'm thinkin' Pa wants another man."

He spurred down the road, drowning the sound of Lazy's thanks with the rattle of hoofs. Lazy looked after him with a strange chuckle. "*Me* go to the Conovers?" he murmured. "I reckon not. Will a cat go into a dog's house? The McLanes is no good, eh?" He broke off with a sudden laugh. Something in the idea struck him as irresistibly humorous.

In the meanwhile, young Conover whirled out of sight behind the trees at the fork of the road ahead. At the same instant two shots struck through the quiet of the night, followed by a choking shout, then a moment of silence, and a horseman, bent far over his mount's neck, raced down the left side of the fork.

Lazy ran toward the forking of the ways. He found young Conover propped against a rock by the roadside with his horse standing motionlessly beside him. Lazy cursed softly as he leaned over him.

"Where's you hurt?" he asked gently as he raised the fallen head to the light.

The boy smiled feebly up at him in the moonlight. "I reckon I'm hurt all over," he answered in his drawling voice.

"That dirty dog that rode down the road did it?" whispered Lazy fiercely. He had seen many a death, but this helpless body that a few moments before had ridden so strongly and bravely to be shot down without warning—Lazy Purdue struck the back of his hand against his forehead.

"Tell me," he demanded, "was it one of the McLanes?"

Conover looked up at him with a dim wonder. "You seem tolerably familiar with things in these parts for a stranger," he answered. "Yep, it was one of the McLanes. I don't know which one. I didn't get a good look at his face, but I know it was a McLane. It's the old feud. I reckoned it was dead years ago when old Henry McLane was driven out of the country for killin' two Conovers. The feud's come again. You tell Dad it was a McLane. I ain't goin' to last long enough to tell him myself."

"I'll remember it till I'm dead," breathed Lazy Purdue. "Where're you hurt, partner? Maybe it ain't so bad!"

"Aw, I'm done for all right," said the boy faintly.

"He got me clean with both shots. One high in the chest. One's lower down. That one'll do the work."

Lazy was already stripping his shirt into long pieces. He tore off the boy's upper garments and saw against the white skin two purple patches from which ran the telltale trickle. He used up the shirts with his hasty bandages.

"It ain't much use"—the boy sighed—"I'm tol'able sleepy already, and . . . and it hurts like . . . like hell!"

"Steady, old pal," commanded Lazy Purdue, "we're goin' to pull you through yet . . . or God help the McLanes!"

"Maybe you c'n get me home," whispered Conover. "I kind of hanker to get home before . . . before . . . My, I'm awful sleepy."

The horse shied twice before Lazy could lift his helpless burden to the saddle. Then he climbed on behind and started the horse at a walk up the road. Young Conover's head fell back limply against his shoulder. He talked feebly with little silences between his words.

"I dunno why they wanted so powerful bad to get me," he said. "I ain't never done anything to harm 'em except that I'm the last of the old line of Conovers. Think o' that. The very last one, 'ceptin' Pa, who ain't due to live much longer. My, ain't it a terrible chilly night for May time?"

Lazy said nothing, but urged the horse to a faster walk. He felt an almost brotherly urge of affection for the dying boy. A peculiar gritting sound reached his ear. It was a moment or two before he realized it was the grinding of his own teeth.

Young Conover was beginning to rave. He repeated bits of remembered conversation, and terms of fishing and hunting. By the time they reached the long avenue of trees at the end of which the old Conover house rose, white and tall, he fell silent, and his breath began to come in great, hoarse gasps.

"Faster," he urged. "Faster. I'm goin' quick. My Gawd, ain't the trees powerful dark an' powerful high?"

They came to the verandah, and Lazy halted, dropped to the ground, and exerted all his unusual strength to gather the boy into his arms. The verandah was dark, but through the open door came a glow of lights down the steps. As he put his foot on the lowest of these, Lazy felt the body in his arms stir convulsively. He ran up the steps and entered the open door, but, as he did so, the body fell limp. Something told Lazy that he had carried death into that home.

"Hello, there!" called Lazy Purdue in loud tones. "Yoo-hoo! Come here, someone!"

An old Negress ran into the hall. She came to an abrupt halt when she saw the light from the pendant lamp white on Lazy's strong, naked torso and glimmering ominously on the limp body in his arms.

"Oh, my Gawd!" she screamed. "Marse Conover! Oh, my Gawd, come quick!"

A white-haired little man appeared in the door that she had left ajar. Lazy Purdue thrilled a little as he studied the face.

"I think this is your son," he said quietly.

The old man showed no signs of emotion. His lips straightened somewhat, but, otherwise, his face was calm as he bent over the body. He pressed his ear against the boy's heart. Then he stood to his full height, stiffly erect. "Will you carry the body this way?" he asked courteously, and waved toward the room that he had just left.

Lazy Purdue entered a high-ceilinged room and strode across it with his burden, dimly conscious of oval-framed portraits of trim-whiskered gentlemen and lace-shawled ladies. He laid the body on a sofa and stepped back with nervously unoccupied fingers. The boy lay easily, as if asleep, a faint smile on his lips, and his head fallen slightly to one side. The stained bandages showed darkly against his body.

A step sounded in the room, and Conover and Lazy Purdue turned their heads with one accord. It was a little, grave-eyed lady with iron-gray hair.

"My dear," began Conover, raising his hand in warning.

She motioned him aside and leaned above the body. Outwardly she betrayed no more emotion than her husband had done, but as he watched her, Lazy Purdue shrank inwardly. Then she crossed the limp arms one above the other, straightened the head, closed the eyes, and, leaning a little farther forward, touched the colorless lips with her own. Lazy prayed heartily to himself that she would weep or cry out. This deathly silence in the presence of death made him cold and sick at heart.

She turned to him at last, and her eyes lingered on a great red stain that crossed his forehead and another that marked his naked breast. He straightened under her glance as a soldier straightens under the eye of his captain.

"Who has done this thing?" she asked. "Can you tell me?"

II

RESURRECTION

The blood turned to ice in Lazy Purdue's veins. It seemed to him as if that question cut the thread of his old life and brought him face to face with something new. He closed his eyes and shook his head. Then he saw in a vision that swiftly fleeing horseman riding into the night with the murdered boy left behind him. A trace of color came into Lazy Purdue's face.

"It was one of the McLaneš," he said in a strange, hushed voice. "It was one of the McLanes what done this here murder, so help me God!"

She walked to him and stood inches away. He felt as though she were suddenly grown tall, and as if her eyes had grown into points of fire that burned into his heart.

"Who was it?" she demanded. "Give me his name!"

"I dunno," Lazy said as steadily as a soldier answers a roll call. "He only told me it was a McLane when I found him. He was waylaid at a forking of the road, just below here a couple of miles, and shot by surprise. I saw the man ride away into the night."

She turned from him to her husband. "John, dear . . . ," she began.

A voice broke in from above: "Pa, oh, Pa!"

The two old people started apart and looked at each other with suddenly stricken faces.

"Keep Marion away!" he pleaded to his wife.

"I . . . can't speak!" she said. "John, you must go an' keep her from comin' down!"

"Oh, Pa!" called the voice in a higher key.

"We . . . we'll go together," said the old man, and he took his wife by the arm and they went together to the door that opened into the hall.

Lazy Purdue followed them, and with them he looked up the broad and winding stairs that led from the hall into the second floor of the house.

She stood at the upper bend of the staircase, leaning somewhat to look the better upon them. She had evidently been in bed when the cry of the old Negress disturbed her. She was dressed in a dressing robe of bronze, tinted green, and, above the place where her left hand gathered the robe at her breast, the fluffy white of her nightgown peered through. From the sidewise-tilted head, a tide of golden hair poured past her throat and over the white arm to her waist.

She seemed to Purdue to have passed the wistful beauty of girlhood, and yet she was not a woman.

"Pa," she was saying, and the half-lisping murmur of her dialect ran like a flow of water in the heart of Lazy Purdue, "what has happened? I heard a cry like old Dinah a little while ago. Something has happened!"

"Honey, dear, there ain't nothin' the matter. You go back to yo' bed and sleep."

But her eyes had widened as they fell upon the

grim and dark-stained torso of Lazy Purdue standing, towering, behind her parents. She ran lightly
down the steps, pressed aside her parents, and stood
bravely before Lazy, but he could see her glance
growing full and steady with premonition. He
pressed his lips hard together and returned her gaze.

"What have you-all brought into this house?" she
pleaded. "Stranger, what terrible thing have you
brought heah, and what's that blood on yo' breas'?"
A desperate meaning came into her eyes, and she
caught the hard muscles of his naked arm with her
hands.

"It's George!" she said. "Oh, my God!" She
whirled and faced her father. "Father!"

He strove to meet her eyes, but a tremulousness
came on his face and his head sank.

"Father!" She was beside him now, and her arms
were around him, and she was kissing the old and
wrinkled face. "Pa," she said, "poor ol' Pa, take me
where he is!"

He led her silently into the room, but, when she
saw the body, she cried out—a sharp, hurt sound
with a little drawling moan at the close. She broke
away from his arms and ran to the body and knelt
beside it.

Lazy Purdue was conscious of a cold sweat on his
face and a terrible faintness in his heart.

The girl rose slowly and faced them with a hard
and changed face. "Pa," she said softly, in a tone
that belied the hard-clenched hands and the narrowed eyes.

Her father took a step forward and faced her, but
made no answer. She pointed dumbly to the move-
less figure behind her.

"Aye," said Conover, "don' I know what it means?
Dear God, don' I know? There must be blood paid

for this . . . an' I . . . an' I can hardly shoot a rifle from a rest."

There was a moment of grim silence. The girl's finger still was pointing and the question was still in her eyes, but there was no further answer.

"Marion," said the old man at last in a calmer voice, "they's some way out of this, an' I reckon I'll find it. Now, you-all go to bed. I reckon I got to think. Marion, you-all go to bed."

She hesitated, and then walked slowly from the room with bent head.

The old man turned to Lazy Purdue. "An' you, suh," he said gently, "I know you will honor us by sleeping under my roof tonight."

Lazy Purdue shuddered. He could not meet Conover's eye, but he spoke lowly: "I . . . I have no right to stay in this here house . . . least of all on *this* night."

"You will hurt me, suh," said Conover, "if you leave. His room is ready for you, suh . . . I beg you to use it. It's a long walk to any other place, and the night is late. Come with me."

He led the way and Lazy Purdue, after a moment of hesitation, followed him with bowed head as the girl had gone a moment before. He followed up the stairs, and the old man opened a door and lighted him into the room.

Old Conover pottered about the room, lowering window shades, drawing back the sheets of the bed, and turning on the water in the bathroom, and then he laid out a suit of clothes on a chair.

"You an' George," he muttered half musingly, "mus' be about the same build. I reckon these will fit you tol'able well."

But Lazy Purdue could not answer for a strange choking in his throat.

"Good night," said Conover, "an' God bless you for the kindness you done my boy when he was dyin'. Good night."

He closed the door softly, and Lazy Purdue looked grimly about the room. From every corner the thought of the dead boy looked out at him. Upon the wall hung brilliantly colored photographs of girls, evidently cut from calendars. Lazy Purdue recognized one of these as the inviting advertisement of a prominent breakfast food. Her hair fell down in two braids in front, and between her smiling lips lay a strand of heavily headed wheat straws. A brace of strong fishing rods stood slant in one corner of the room with a riding crop and two pairs of spurs near it. Another side of the wall bore a rack in which were three shotguns of the latest make, and below them the gray, shining barrel of a repeating rifle.

It seemed to him that the boy had come back to life and was moving about the room with him as he made ready for bed. He could imagine the topics of the conversation from girls to hunting, and all in the whimsical drawl of the mountaineers, a remembered and delightful music to the ear of Lazy Purdue.

The soothing touch of the warm water of the bath drew the ache from his body, and afterwards he sat a while near the window wrapped in a dressing gown and alive with thought. Then came a light tapping on the door. He opened the door cautiously and peeked out. Marion stood in the hallway. She was dressed in the robe still, and he glimpsed the white of her feet in their bedroom slippers.

"I must speak to you," she entreated. "Father and Mother have gone to bed, an' I must speak with you for just a little minute. Will you let me in?"

He opened the door silently, and she slipped past

him. When he turned slowly from the closing of the door, he found her standing in the center of the room, facing him, her eyes wide with resolve and fear. They faced each other silently for a long moment; he with a certain sadness and she with a peculiar eagerness.

"I have come on a strange errand," she said somewhat breathlessly.

He made no answer.

"I have come on a strange errand," she repeated, gathering courage and determination as she went on. "An' when you hear what I ask, I'm only a-hopin' that you won't laugh. Oh, I *know* you won't, for when I leaned over the rail o' that stairs and looked down and met your eyes, I knew they was a man's eyes, an', when I went down an' spoke to you, they was no waver in them and they looked through an' through me. Will you-all hear me now?"

He clenched his hand as the note of pleading came into her voice, and a shock of premonition as to the nature of her request made his forehead cold.

"Go on," he said somewhat hoarsely, "I'll listen to the end."

"Stranger," she said, "you brought a death into this here house, an' the blood o' that death was on your shoulders when you carried the body in. Stranger, it ain't a common murder in your life. It ain't something you c'n shake away from your mind after you leave this here part of the country. I know by the way you-all look that you been many places and you've seen many strange things, but there ain't nothin' that'll ever stay with you the way this night will."

With an instinct for protection against the steady searching of her eyes, he dropped into a chair and covered his face with his hands. "Go on," he whispered, "I'm hearin' it all."

"Stranger," she said evenly, "you done heard my father say that he c'n hardly shoot a rifle from a rest. Stranger, I reck'n *you* don't need no rest for a rifle."

He heard the slip of her feet on the carpet as she went to him rapidly. Her hand fell lightly on his shoulder.

"Will you-all take the place of the boy you done carried into his home dead? Will you-all be a brother to me till this here death is washed out in blood? Oh, suh, you're a man, an' a man's man, an' I c'n ask this thing of you, an' I know you'll say yes to me!"

He rose and turned half away from her. She went grave with wonder, seeing the agony on his face, but, when her eyes ran down to the tight-clenched hands, her thoughts changed and she stepped a little away from him. "You ain' afraid?" she breathed. "Oh, *don'* say that you're afraid!"

"God help me," he said, keeping his eyes away from her face by a great effort of will, "there don't seem no way I c'n help myself. Oh, if you could only dream jus' how many reasons I've got for not doin' this thing, you wouldn't talk o' fear."

She stepped to him again and drew him facing her with a soft pressure of her hand upon his shoulder, and he could feel the light touch of her body against his, so intent was her pleading.

"You're goin' to do it?" she begged. "Oh, I know you will! It's a terrible lot to ask o' a man, an' you may have lots o' reasons for not doin' it, but, when I've lef' you to yourself an' you get to thinkin' it over, you'll see the dead boy again an' you'll make up your mind. Oh, he was such a nice boy, suh, an' so gentle to me, an' clean in his mind and clean o' heart! Suh, *he* would never have killed a man by layin' in wait for him an' shooting him down with no warnin'! Even a snake makes a noise before it strikes. I ask you, stranger, are these McLanes as good as snakes? Think o' that and answer me in the mornin'. Good night, an' . . . an' God bless you."

He heard the door close behind her, and suddenly the room seemed cramped and small to him. He went to the window and threw it up and leaned out into the cool, fresh air. By degrees the little noises of the night floated in upon his consciousness as if the silence grew into a nearer reality—the hushed whisper of the stirring trees about the house, the distant *hoot* of a far-away prowling owl, and the light incessant *chirping* of the crickets.

He turned away and stood a long moment leaning against the wall with closed eyes, for he saw her clearly then as she had stood at the bend of the stairway with the tide of golden hair running by her throat, and the deep question of her eyes.

"There's one thing thicker than blood," he groaned to himself, "an' this is it, Lazy Purdue." He opened his eyes and clenched his hands and made a great step into the center of the room. "An' what do I owe to *them?* Didn't they do me dirt when I was a kid an' never hurt none of them? An' I comin' back to them after they turned me out?"

He went to bed with his resolve, and, when he woke the next morning, his mind was clear with purpose and he felt even a return to his usual spirit of careless gaiety. He rose early and went downstairs dressed carefully in his new clothes, store clothes of far more luxurious material than any he had ever worn.

He found Conover on the front verandah and went to him immediately. He had determined to speak the thing out while his mind was made up.

"It ain't easy for me to talk much," he began, after they had exchanged their good mornings, "but last night I got to thinkin' about the boy that's lyin' dead in the room, there. He died in my arms as I was carryin' him through this here door, sir." He paused a moment and swallowed hard. "I don't mind sayin'," he went on, "that I have killed men myself. But I never killed a man that wasn't looking me straight in the eye and doin' his damnedest to kill me. I never shot a man from behind a tree."

He started to walk uneasily up and down the verandah. Old man Conover watched him with an emotionless face.

"Well, sir," said Lazy Purdue, "I heard you say that you could hardly shoot a rifle from a rest. I don't need no rest, Mister Conover. Will you use me like one of your own family to fight them McLanes?"

The old man eyed him without changing a muscle of his face. "I reckon you said my boy died in your arms while you were bringin' him through the door?" he queried.

Lazy Purdue clenched his hands and opened them slowly. "Yes," he said.

"An' you c'n shoot straight?"

The shadow of a smile touched Lazy Purdue's mouth. "It's the only thing I can do well," he said.

"The McLanes shoot powerful straight," said the old man dreamily.

"If you have a hammer an' some nails an' a revolver," said Lazy Purdue, "I'll show you what they call shootin' in my part of the country."

"They's a post there, just off the verandah, wher' you c'n drive them," said Conover slowly, "an' I'll get you a hammer an' nails, an' here"—he reached to his hip pocket as he spoke—"is a gun."

In an old hitching post a few yards away Lazy Purdue drove six nails, one below the other. Then he took the revolver, tried the action with a smile of content, and whirled the chambers.

"I'm goin' to walk away from this here post," he stated, "an', when you holler fire, I'm goin' to turn and shoot. You see I haven't my hand on the gun. You watch that bunch o' nails." He commenced to walk rapidly away from the post, his arms swinging carelessly and the revolver bulging slightly in his hip pocket.

"Fire!" called Conover.

Lazy Purdue whirled, and, as he whirled, the six shots rang out, one report blending with the other.

Conover walked to the hitching post. He examined the post carefully. "The first shot was a hair's breadth to the left," he said, and, as he turned, he sighed heavily. "I don't know what part of the country you come from, my frien', but, oh, I wish to God that my boy had been raised there."

As they crossed the verandah, old Mrs. Conover met them at the door, her face somewhat paler than before. "John," she queried, "what was that shootin'? Has there been some more devil's work this mornin'?"

The old man laid his hands on his wife's shoulders. "Mary," he said, "I c'n hardly shoot a rifle from a rest. But here's a man who don't need no rest. Mary, our boy died in this man's arms, an' he wants to make that death good on the McLanes."

She eyed Purdue coldly, and once more he straightened as if about to receive an order. "That death can't be made good by anyone but a Conover," she stated. "Have you forgotten that, John?"

Old Conover turned almost fiercely on Lazy Purdue. "Will you change your name to George Conover?" he asked.

"My first name hasn't ever been anything but Lazy," said Purdue, "an' my last name . . . well, I reckon I have pretty strong reason for wanting to change that name right now, or leastwise forget it. I reckon George is a lot better name than Lazy, an' I don't know any better other name than Conover."

III

THE FAIR

As they walked into the breakfast room, Marion Conover entered. One glance at the faces of the three evidently told her all that she wanted to know. She walked to Lazy Purdue and shook hands with him silently, but the brightness of her eyes left him ill at ease as they sat down at the table.

There was no restraint among the other three. With that fine instinct of hospitality that always enables them to put a guest at ease, they forgot their own great sorrow and commenced to talk casually of casual things. But they had not sat long before a Negress appeared in great agitation at the door.

"Marse Conover," she said in a shaken voice, "they's a visitor heah! His name is McLane. Oh, my Lor', it's Marse Tom McLane!"

Old Conover rose. "Send Mister McLane right in," he said calmly.

She stared at him for a moment with wide eyes of wonder before she turned to do his bidding.

A moment later, Lazy Purdue saw a great, broad-shouldered man standing in the doorway. He must have been close to sixty, but from his square-toed riding boots to the top of his iron-gray head he appeared one of those rock-like men who defy time. His rough black beard was untouched with silver. He seemed to fill the door in which he stood, and he towered even above Lazy Purdue when the latter rose at that sight.

"Will you sit down an' have some breakfas' with us?" said Conover in a soft voice. "They's some tol'able good bacon this mornin'."

Tom McLane made a step farther into the room. "I can't eat in your house now, John Conover," he said. "I've come to find out if you're goin' to call in the law."

"Aye," said Conover, "the same law that there has always been between the Conovers and the McLanes."

McLane passed a blunt-fingered hand across his forehead. "I knew that would be your way," he said, and his rough voice shook, echoing through the room like a chorus, "but time ain't been too gentle with you, John Conover. You're an old man, John, and you ain't nowise fit to fight with the guns, an' I'm still strong, an' my boys are tolerable strong, and now you're alone ag'in' us. Harken ye to me, John Conover, an' you, Mary Conover. I know the thing that's happened last night. I know that a man of the McLanes killed George Conover, but what man that was I c'n tell no more'n ye can tell. But another man's death won't bring the first dead man back to life, and blood ain't never washed out blood. Oh, I know it wasn't a fair fight, an' it makes my heart's blood cold to think o' the waylayin' by the night. Things wasn't that way when you and I was boys. But you ain't in a way to hit back at us now, John. Tell me some way to make up to you for your loss, an' I swear I'll do it."

"I c'n answer that," said Mary Conover fiercely. "Oh, I c'n tell you what you c'n do to make up for the loss we have, Tom McLane. You c'n take out o' my heart the longin' for a man-child. You can take out o' my memory the pain an' the woe o' bearin' that child. You can take away the thought o' the first time I looked on him, pink an' red and helpless. You c'n take out o' my ears his first cry o' life, an' the thought o' the years an' the years o' care an' trouble an' love, an' the nursin' through sickness, an' the singin' to sleep, an' . . . oh, all the glory o' givin' a fine, clean strong man to a man's world. That's all you got to do, Tom McLane. C'n you make up that loss, Tom?"

John Conover dropped a tremulous hand on his wife's shoulder. "You was always a man," he said, "you was always a man, Tom McLane, an', supposin' I was as naked o' help as you're thinkin', I might listen to ye now. But I ain't naked yet. My boy George lies in the next room smilin' so's I can't forget how he looked when he was a little sniper. When my boy George died, he was carried home by this here man, an' his blood was on this man's forehead an' over this man's heart, an' so now he has taken this here blood debt on his hands and he is my son. Look him over. Do you reckon he's worthy o' the guns o' your tribe, Tom?"

There was a long pause while Lazy Purdue braced himself to the shock of McLane's stare.

"An' this man is your adopted son, John?" asked McLane.

"I'm goin' to town today to bury one son," said Conover, "and then I'm goin' to the courthouse to get another son in the eyes of the law."

McLane strode to Lazy Purdue and caught his hand in a great grasp. "I reckon you're goin' to bring more blood into this feud," he said, "for you've looked considerable on death, I'm thinkin'. But here's a man's hand. It's the last time you'll ever take it in friendship."

He turned back to Conover. "But I'm tellin' you, John, blood will never end this here feud. It ain't in the power of guns to make justice and quiet."

"Aye," said Conover, "but there's a tolerable old law that ain't in any book. Blood calls for blood, an' new blood may not wash out old blood, but it'll go a long way to cover it up. It covers a heap o' things, Tom McLane."

"So be it," said Tom McLane. "I reckon we ride armed from now on. But I'm supposin' that on the day o' the fair, there won't be no fightin', leastways up till midnight o' the dance. Am I right?"

"I reckon that's the custom," said Conover.

"Good mornin', suh," said McLane. "Good mornin', madam." He strode to the place where Marion Conover stood by her chair and he tilted back her face between his rough palms. "An' I hope to God that this here feud don't bring no more trouble to your face, my sweet girl," he said, and, as he went to the door, he turned and paused again. "Oh, folks, I'm fearful sick at heart over this night's work!"

He left the room, and the heavy beat of his feet passed from the house and left a waiting silence.

That day Lazy Purdue and John Conover rode to the town, with the two women, behind the wagon that bore the coffin to the churchyard, and when the burial was completed, the men rode on to the courthouse, and, when they came out, Lazy Purdue bore the legal name of George Conover.

"An' here I am," mused Lazy, as they walked arm

in arm down the steps of the courthouse, "an' I've sure come home at last, and here I am in the wrong house."

Indeed, he felt a perpetual strangeness about the place, for he knew that he had been taken into that home as a killer of men, and all his heart revolted against the work that lay before him.

The days passed calmly enough, but there was no doubt that the storm would break sooner or later.

A little interim of Arcadian quiet came to Lazy Purdue. The duty that he had taken upon his shoulders rested lightly there. He was with Marion constantly until he came to be half bodyguard and half escort to her, riding with her or walking over the mountain paths.

But all that while the shadow of trouble followed them, even when they knew it not, as the hawk circles high in the air above the barnyard, a real danger although flying out of sight. It was Henry McLane who lurked about the mountains with his rifle, alert, soft-footed, dangerous as a stalking panther, and as silent. A dozen times he had seen them walking or riding together at a distance, but only once did he come close enough to stalk them effectively.

He had seen them walking at some distance away from them, and he hurried after them as fast as he could through the brush at the side of the road. Once or twice twigs crackled under his feet and made the pair halt to listen, but they went on again. He could hear them talking and laughing, and it infuriated him.

When he came within close range at last, they had paused at the edge of a small stream that foamed about the shoulder of a hill and went on noisily down the valley. They were considering some method of getting across the water without wetting

Marion. Lazy Purdue had proposed to carry her across, but she demurred. The faintness of her demurral angered Henry McLane. They were standing well apart. He was in no danger of striking Marion with his shot. So he knelt upon a log and carried his rifle to his shoulder for a careful aim. But the log, which was rotten save for the outside shell, crushed under his sudden weight.

At the sound, Lazy Purdue swung Marion into his left arm and whipped out his revolver, keeping it leveled at the place where McLane crouched unseen. In this manner he backed across the stream and disappeared around the bushes on the farther side.

They could guess at the cause of the sound, but they had seen nothing. The hawk had crossed their path unseen.

From the Negroes, who form the wireless news agencies of the Southern states, the Conovers heard tales of the actions of the McLanes. They were preparing for the worst. The boys practiced with their guns incessantly, and, whenever they appeared on the roads, the three men rode together. So it was when the day of the fair came and Lazy Purdue announced in the morning at the breakfast table that he was going to the town to take part in the sports.

"I hear there ain't no fightin' of the old feuds on fair days," he said.

"There never was in the past," agreed John Conover.

"That's not sayin' there won't be none now," interjected Mary Conover. "Boy, don't be foolish. There's no trustin' the McLane boys. If they'll fight from behind trees, do ye think they will respect the old laws of the feud?"

Lazy Purdue ticked the spoon lightly against his

coffee cup. "I'm powerful curious to see the folks of this here town," he stated, "an' I think I'll be goin' there today. Besides" he continued, "ain't Marion goin' to be queen o' the fair?"

"Aye," said Mary Conover, and she flushed slightly with pride as she spoke. "She had to start for town early before breakfast because she has to see how they fix up her throne and see that all is all right an' that her court is already in their costumes, an' all of them silly, pretty ways they have at the fair."

"Aye," said Conover, "this is the first time there won't be a Conover to shoot for the queen of the fair."

"Shoot for the queen?" exclaimed Lazy Purdue. Then he remembered. He remembered far back to his childhood when he had seen these fairs that made the month of May the wished-for time by every mountaineer within thirty miles of the town. The fair itself consisted of exhibitions of riding and cattle and horse shows and sports, and at the end of the day the youths of the gathering were privileged to shoot for the queen of the fair. Having won her, the successful man claimed her for his partner at the dance that closed the festivities of the day.

The singular part of the shooting was the nature of the mark at which the men fired. It consisted of ten strings suspended from a crossbar and kept taut with pebbles tied in the end of the strings. The idea was to fire at the strings, and the man who, out of ten shots, cut the most of the ten strings received the queen of the fair as his partner.

"Well," said Lazy Purdue, "I reckon we can all go. I reckon they don't think men shouldn't follow where a woman is brave enough to lead in these parts, do they?"

Old Conover laughed to himself. "You're right," he said. "An' I'm thinkin' I'd like to go down an' watch, myself, jus' to point out the sights an' the people to you, George."

IV

THE SHOOTING

It was late in the morning before they reached the fairgrounds, a large meadow near the town. People had evidently driven from miles around to see the events of the day. For at every post and tree near the grounds were hitched carriages and wagons of all descriptions. Framing the open square of ground where the exhibitions and games were held stood a line of flag-bedecked tents and booths where girls displayed all manner of edibles and wearables.

It was unquestionably the event of the year, this May Day fair. The young gallants strutted slowly around in the unaccustomed splendor of tight-fitting trousers and high-crowned hats and brilliant neckties. The girls flaunted, in the main, homemade dresses cut after nearly Parisian patterns, and here and there one of the more adventurous appeared in elbow gloves twirling a gay-colored parasol behind her head.

It was very garish, but there was no jarring note for Lazy Purdue. After the sun-burnt girls of Texas, these blooming cheeks were dreams of beauty to him, and the whole picture came to him as being

colorful, richly satisfying, and astir with the pulse of
young life.

Old Conover took his arm and they strolled from
place to place to watch the various sports and ex-
hibits.

Everywhere people gave way a little before them,
and Lazy Purdue was conscious of many a whisper
running about them and many a steady stare, but,
when one has met the eye of gambling cowboys in
Texas saloons, even the boldness of the Tennessee
backwoodsman has no terrors. He returned their
stares with manifest indifference, measuring the
men with lackluster eyes, and letting his glance
linger with its natural careless caress when he found
a pretty face among the girls.

"They're talkin' fast enough about you," old
Conover commented, chuckling, "but I reckon the
new Conover will stand 'em off pretty well."

He had, in truth, grown into an almost parental
pride over his new boy. From the corner of his eye
he considered and approved the lean figure by his
side, suggestive at once of alertness and strength.
Lazy's clothes sat well on him, and the carefully
wrapped cravat lent a touch of distinction.

He urged him to take part in the various sports,
but Lazy Purdue replied that he wished to learn the
habits of that part first. When it came to the horse-
back riding, he was stirred a trifle, but he relapsed
into his accustomed silence. A lean, black stallion
pitched off two riders before the third mastered him
amid loud plaudits.

"In my part of the country," drawled Lazy Purdue, "a ten-year-old boy would be ashamed of that
sort of ridin'."

The time came for the shooting, and the crowd
surged forward across the field, fighting for places

and leaving only a dangerously narrow lane for the shots. From a crossbar, ten pellets of rock were suspended by white strings that hung glimmering and almost invisible at a short distance. Opposite the crossbar stood the bunting-covered throne of the queen of the fair. She sat, smiling and chatting with the girls who stood grouped about her tinsel throne. Her dress was light blue, and a parasol of the same color shaded her bare head, save when the sudden sunlight touched her hair to fiery gold. She appeared to Lazy Purdue regally indifferent to the hungry eyes that now and then fastened upon her from the crowd of upturned faces.

"Somehow," muttered Lazy, "that don't seem to be Marion Conover."

Old Conover shook his head and smiled. "Aye," he answered, "she's a right pretty girl. Put any woman on a throne an' she commences to look different. But look, now. Here starts the shootin'."

A group of young men had gathered in front of the throne and faced toward the dangling strings.

"That big fellow with the short, black mustache, he's Henry McLane, Tom McLane's son," muttered Conover, "an' the smaller chap with the smooth-shaven face beside him is his brother Luke." His hand closed on Lazy Purdue's arm. "Henry McLane won the shootin' last year," he said, "by cuttin' six strings, which is more'n anyone ever cut since I seen the shootin'. I reckon he'll dance with Marion tonight." He turned his face up to Lazy Purdue with a faint appeal. "Unless you shoot, my boy."

Lazy shook his head and smiled. At the moment, his eyes were otherwise occupied than with shooting. In fact, his eyes were fixed in one direction so steadily that finally the queen turned her face and returned his gaze. It seemed to trouble her. He had watched her scan the mob of many eyes without a tremor, but, as her glance crossed his, it shocked to a pause and held there for a moment, and he thought he saw the beginning of a flush as she turned her head again.

In all the days that had passed since he went into the Conover home as a part of it, he had seen her, of course, every day many times, but the thing that is near us is ever the thing that we fail to prize. And so it came that after that first vision of white and gold that startled upon him from the curve of the staircase that first night, she had grown back into his thoughts. He took her for granted, just as he imagined she had come to take him for granted. But now that she was sitting so near to him, he still felt as though the consciously expressed admiration of all these hundreds of men had set a barrier between them.

Once more her head turned and her glance crossed his. Lazy's heart jumped in his breast. After all, it was going to be a good game.

He raised his hat as if in acknowledgment of the unspoken greeting, and smiled slyly up to her. He could see her bite her lips to keep back the smile, and then her head turned, but not with the slowness of absolute self-possession.

In the meantime, the shooting had commenced. One after another the men took a position on the ground and told off their shots slowly. One cut four strings and there was applause. Another cut five and received an ovation. Still another, toward the close, cut six and the crowd shouted with excitement.

"You're tied, Henry McLane!" shouted a man in the crowd, as the tall figure of Henry McLane strode out to take his position in front of the target.

"That was what I did last year," he answered

scornfully as he dropped to the ground and poised his rifle. "Watch this year's score."

"Aw, I reckon you was only a boy a year ago!" yelled a humorist. "Waal, you got a full man-sized job on your hands today, Henry boy."

A loud guffaw greeted this remark.

"George," said Conover, "do you think you could hit them there strings? It ain't any usual mark, an' I know the boys around here practice it all year, gettin' ready for this one day. Do you think you could hit any of them? Just one hit wouldn't be any disgrace, an' there's always been a Conover at these here shootin's before."

"I don't know," said Lazy Purdue. "I'm not interested in the strings, not a bit."

The old man turned away with a sigh.

Henry McLane had commenced to shoot. He cut five strings in as many shots, and the crowd stood rapt over such unprecedented marksmanship. On the next two tries he missed, but his eighth shot cut the sixth string and tied the highest mark of the day. He waited until the cheering had died away before he shot again and missed, but on his last trial he cut the seventh string.

A crowd swirled around him with noisy congratulations, but Lazy Purdue had eyes for only one face. She was leaning forward with parted lips, a face flushed with excitement, and one hand was caught to her breast. Her eyes had found him in the moving crowd, and he turned with a sigh from the appeal in her eyes.

"Wait a minute, boys," called the heavy voice of Henry McLane, "don't go to bustin' my hand shakin' it this way! I reckon there ought to be one man in the crowd willin' to shoot ag'in' me. There's never been a shootin' before where a Conover didn't take part. There's a new Conover here today, I hear. Will he shoot?"

The crowd gave back between them and left McLane and Lazy Purdue face to face. Their eyes met and held.

"I sure appreciate this," remarked Lazy Purdue, "but I ain't used to any such marks in my part of the country."

"It must be a terrible long ways off!" called a voice.

A suppressed titter ran through the crowd, and Lazy Purdue saw one face, high above the rest, go pale. He took off his hat and bowed to the throne. "I'm goin' to beat your score," he remarked calmly to McLane, "not because winnin' gives me any pleasure in particular, except that I got a sort of hankerin' to dance with Marion Conover tonight. It'll make this here fair a sort of family party, you know."

"By the Lord," called a man, "he may not be a real Conover, but he's a Conover in spirit!"

Old Conover offered Lazy Purdue his rifle as the latter stepped toward the firing position, but Lazy waved him away.

"I don't take to them sort of shootin' irons," he remarked quietly. "In my part of the country we use a different kind." As he spoke, he drew from each hip pocket a long, shining Colt and stood balancing them in either hand and facing the target, which had been renewed. The crowd caught a breath of suppressed excitement. Never in the history of the backwoods had a man been known to prefer a pistol to a rifle.

"Here's where you lie down," directed the umpire of the shooting.

"I reckon I don't care to get my clothes all dirty."

Lazy Purdue smiled. "They're such nice clothes. I'll do the shootin' standin'."

He raised the revolver in his right hand and fired one shot. The ten strings still hung glimmering. He fired once with his left hand, but still with no result. By the rules of the contest he must now beat McLane's score of eight shots. Lazy Purdue lowered the guns calmly and turned to where old Conover stood in the crowd.

"I reckon that these guns are a little cold," he said casually.

"That's like a Conover all right," said a voice, "blamin' a bad eye onto a good gun."

Purdue turned and met the sneer of Henry McLane. Then he smiled and turned back to his shooting. The crowd was snickering softly now and talking behind their hands. He could visualize the pale, intent face of Marion behind him. Suddenly Lazy Purdue went cold and on his face came a look that few men had seen and none cared to see twice. The hands rose as steadily as springs with the revolvers. One after another he told off the shots with alternate hands. One by one the bits of string snapped in two. Five—six—seven. He lowered the revolvers and turned to Henry McLane amid a chill silence.

"It isn't what you do"—Lazy Purdue smiled—"it's how you do it." He turned to the throne behind him. "Lady," he said, "will you give this shot luck for the sake of the dance we shall have together tonight?"

She made no answer, but sat with staring, incredulous eyes.

Purdue laughed softly and turned back toward the mark. The right-hand revolver rose, a stream of fire leaped from its muzzle, and the eighth string parted.

Physical skill is dearer than religion to the hearts of the backwoodsmen, and, at the sight of such shooting, the mountaineers forgot, at least for a moment, all their prejudices against this calm-eyed stranger. They crowded about Lazy Purdue, slapping him on the shoulder and calling out the clumsy terms of familiar praise. He had become the hero of the day. It was something to tell over on winter evenings. It was a tale to remember for one's children.

After a while old Conover shouldered a way to him through the crowd. "Oh, boy," he said softly, "I'm desperate proud of you! *Desperate* proud! I c'n hardly wait to tell Mary about this."

But Lazy Purdue had turned and stared up to the figure on the throne. She had dropped her head with a noticeable flush on her face, and her fingers were interwound in her lap.

Lazy Purdue sighed. He was content.

V

THE DANCE

The dance began that night at nine o'clock. The signal for the opening of the grand march was a wave of the hand from the queen of the fair, whose throne was by this time removed from the field and placed at one end of the huge barn that served as a dance hall.

In the upper reaches of the hall the wavering light of the host of lanterns at times showed great cobwebs, tattered and fluttering in the uncertain breezes from many cracks in the wall, but this upper region of gloom was, on the whole, shut off from the attention of the dancers by the throng of streamers and flags that hung from the lower rafters on the barn, and it was further obliterated by long streams of twisted papers of bright colors that were strung from side to side.

A double row of chairs on each side of the great room accommodated the dancers. In the first row sat the youths and girls who still retained any claims to youth and agility, and in the back row the gossiping parents sat. For the two-step and the waltz were

still in their heyday, and the time was long before
white-haired elders should perambulate dancing
floors to the easy measure of the one-step.

The girls and the young men still sat somewhat
stiffly aware of their best clothes, and conversations
were, on the whole, still formal. Remarks upon the
weather still vied with remembered bits of dialogue
from popular magazines. Laughter was low and
controlled, and the men were still wriggling their
necks uncomfortably in the high, white collars.

The scene was fairly familiar to Lazy Purdue, but
he had never seen to his remembrance such a collec-
tion of flashing eyes and ardent cheeks. In Texas,
things moved with more abandon, perhaps, but also
with a certain easy good-fellowship that destroyed
half the lure of a party, which set the men almost too
much at their ease, and destroyed that enchanting
aloofness upon which the country girl depends, as
the city cousin depends upon an elaborate toilet.

But the time came when the queen, seeming very
white and far away under the light of a cluster of
lanterns about the throne, waved her hand, and Lazy
Purdue rose to claim her. He experienced a feeling of
elation as he strode across the floor to her glittering
throne. The thought that this shining beauty would
be in a moment walking on his arm at the head of the
long line of the grand march and that in a few moments more she would be whirling with him through
the mazes of a two-step was almost too dazzling to
be true. But the very consciousness that all eyes were
upon him nerved him to a super-nonchalance.

He handed her down the steps of the throne with
the ease of a Louis XIV courtier, and he proceeded
with her at the head of the grand march as if this
were an ordinary after-dinner formality of his life.
But all the while he was aware of the light touch of

her hand upon his arm. She in turn, who had resolved to maintain her part in that inevitable dance with an ice-like calm, why was it that her breath came shorter and quicker as the march proceeded, that her lips parted to what was almost a smile, that her eyes shone, that the hand upon his arm increased its pressure?

Gods of the eternally lifting spirit of springtime, and all ye gods who preside over the uplifted faces of youth, explain it. I cannot!

But when they heard the change of the music, and when they whirled into the rapid two-step, she gave to the pressure of his arm about her, and they danced as one body filled with one spirit. And he looked down to the flushed face and to the indescribable curve of throat and shoulder and white breast, and she looked up to eyes that had lost their usual indifferent caress and were now flaming with a light about which she trembled at the thought of question.

So when the dance ended and she knew that he was asking her when he might dance with her again, her thoughts were far away, and she looked at him through a mist. She promised him, after much urging, a waltz far on in the evening, and then she was free.

Free? No, for his eyes followed her and held her. She found herself grown absent-minded in the midst of her conversations, and, whenever she raised her eyes, they fell as if fate directed them upon the steady eyes of this new George Conover.

It was maddening. It was strangely and sweetly thrilling at the same time. And when the time came when he stood in front of her and claimed his second dance, she rose half willingly, half afraid of herself and of him.

"We are not goin' to dance this," he stated. "I've got a lot to say that can't be said while we're dancing. We're goin' outside to talk."

She stopped to protest, but the silent compulsion of his arm through hers forced her on, and, as they walked, her heart commenced to beat a tremendous tattoo so loud that she looked at him fearfully to see if he had heard. But he strode on unconsciously with his eyes straight ahead.

They crossed the brilliant entrance to the hall; they stepped out into the soft, May night, and down the path from the barn, and through the orchard, which gave a keen sweet scent of apple blossoms to the air, and at last to the stream that bubbled and played over its rocky course through the orchard. He pointed to a rock.

"Let's sit here," he said, "and then you listen to me."

She sat down obediently—yes, thrilling to the fact that she should be obedient to his command—but she clenched the hand he could not see to recall her self-possession.

He sat for some moments beside her, frowning, his chin resting on his clenched hand and his eyes straight forward.

"Ain't it tolerably queer?" he began at last. "In there under the lights an' with the noise and the movement o' the crowd, an' all that, I reckoned that I had about a thousand things to say to you, Marion Conover. But when I come out here, with just the beat o' the music comin' to us like the hummin' of a bee, and the purlin' of the stream here, and the smell o' the apple blossoms . . . say, these here apple blossoms are powerful sweet, don't you reckon, an' . . . an' strange-like?"

She eyed him swiftly and smiled away into the

shadows under the trees again, the softly mottled shadows that the moonlight cast from the stirless branches.

"I reckon they's powerful sweet, an' . . . an' strange-like," she agreed.

He was still studying out his thoughts with a frown. "I reckon that there was never any McLane had any use for a Conover, an' no Conover ever had any use for a McLane?" he queried at last.

"No," she said faintly and angrily because her voice was weak.

"I reckon this feud's about as old as these here hills," he continued in a soft drawl, different from the mountaineers' harsh guttural or piercing nasal whine.

"I reckon it must be about as old," she agreed.

"I reckon the feud has jus' naturally broke loose again an' is goin' to raise hell with everyone?" he continued.

"I reckon it is," she said with a peculiar closing of the heart.

"Then if a McLane should get to like a Conover 'round about now, he'd be nothin' better'n a fool?" he inquired. He turned his glance and regarded her anxiously as he asked this.

She had to drop her eyes and clench the hand he could not see harder before she could manage an answer. "I reckon he'd be a tolerable big fool," she agreed, and then: "Are you comin' to like one of the McLanes, George?" She hesitated softly over the name.

"No," he said fiercely, "but I have come to like . . . Oh," he broke out in a different tone, "ain't it terrible hard, ain't it terrible hard to want to say something, and know you should say it, an' not dare say it because you know that, if you did, you'd lose the thing you want more'n all the world, somehow? Oh, God, how I hate all this feud!"

She drew a little back and stared at him, surprised by his sudden violence, and yet attracted by it. He had gone back to staring miserably before him.

"But after all," he went on in a hard voice, "they's only you an' I to consider in this here matter. Feud or no feud, they's only you an' I. If they was a thousand feuds, it couldn't change me. If they was a thousand feuds, it couldn't make your hair any more like gold or your lips any redder, could they, Marion?"

She sheltered her face from his inquiry with one hand and shook her head in mute agreement.

"Now I'm goin' to ask you a queer sort of question," he said. "I'm goin' to ask you if anything sort of strange happened to you today?"

"No," she breathed, "not a thing that I can say."

"Well," he pondered, "it's mighty queer, that's all. But something happened to me while I was standing in the crowd at the fair today, and I thought you might have noticed it." He was silent again, frowning heavily. "Somehow," he said deliberately, "I reckon you're an almighty big liar when you say a thing like that."

"I . . . I . . . What do you mean?" she stammered.

He turned to her swiftly and caught her hand. "Honest to God, Marion Conover," he said, "didn't you notice nothin' while I was standin' in that crowd?"

She dropped her head and shook it faintly. He turned and sighed.

"It sort of appeared to me," he continued, "that, when my eye crossed yours, something clicked, and then my eyes went wrong . . . and, when they looked at yours, they was seein' way deep into them. Did *you* feel it? No, I reckon you didn't, because you didn't see yourself. An' here I've been all these days at your house and seein' you every day, an' yet all these days I never seen you the way I seen you today, with all the crowd around, an' you so far away, an' lookin' so powerful pretty and white and sunshiny, Marion girl, that I reckoned half the time you might just up and blow away in the wind. Doesn't that sound funny for a chap who hasn't touched a drop of whiskey all day?"

"It sounds powerful funny, I reckon." She smiled under the shelter of her hand.

"You see, Marion Conover," he went on, "I never seen any girl just like you. Would you believe that?" He turned again with frank inquisition in his eyes.

She strove to meet his glance for a moment, but a choking in her throat forced her to turn her eyes away again.

"Down in the parts I come from," went on his soft drawl, "they simply ain't no girls that ain't all sort of browned up like the desert on a winter's day. You know that funny tan color? No, I reckon you don't."

The petal of an apple blossom from the tree above them came in a fluttering pause upon the back of his hand. He examined it with strange interest, and then captured it with his other hand. Then he caught her arm and drew her gently closer.

"You see this here petal?" he said.

"Yes," she said, and prayed that he would not be able to tell the beating of her heart.

"I stood there an' looked up to you, an' I kept a-thinkin' of all the tan and dim-lookin' people down there where I came from, an' every one lookin' tired most of the time . . . and there was you!" He paused with a smile of breathless reminiscence. "You was like this petal," he said. "Yep, I reckon you're a lot like this petal now."

Here he leaned to peer inquisitively up into her hidden face. "All your forehead," he murmured, half musing, "is like the tip of the petal, and your cheeks . . . well, they're like the pink of the heart of the petal. Can you see what that meant to me?"

There was no answer, and, as the silence grew, he could feel a slight tremor through her body as if she were chill in the night. He raised her face boldly, the strong tips of his fingers under her chin.

"And your hair in the light," he went on, "was like another sun, like the sun that gives the color to the heart of the petal, and the blue of your eyes . . ." He caught his breath and tilted her face farther back. "My God," he whispered, "the blue of your eyes was like another heaven for me to look into and forget myself! Honest, I never seen anything so deep."

She caught his hand away from her face, but the fingers that held it were weak and tremulous, and the lips with which she spoke then were quivering, and her voice was uncertain. "Don't talk like this," she said. "It makes all my blood weak like water, an' . . . an' strange like the wind o' this night with the scent of the apple blossoms on it . . . an' . . . an' . . . ." Her eyes wavered away from his until they became a shadow, and the quivering lips parted to a half sob. "What does it mean?" she cried desperately. "Oh, go away! I . . . I *hate* you! An' . . . an' I feel as helpless as a child with you so near!"

He caught her into his arms with an instinct stronger than any reason, and truer, and he bent back the curve of her soft body as he drew her to her feet, rising himself.

"I reckon I know," he said at last, and his lips

crushed down on the warm curve of her mouth. "Oh, I reckon I know at last. It's love! Marion sweetheart, this is love. It started when I first looked up to you standin' on the curve of the stairway, with your hand holdin' your dressin' gown together at your breast. An' it has grown like a seed, but faster'n a hundred springs could make seeds grow. An' today the seed grew in an instant into a tall flower and busted wide open from a bud, all in an instant. Why, the whole world would go wild if they could see that flower, an' the whole world would go drunk with the dizzy sweet of the smell of it, for the flower's love, sweetheart. Listen . . . I c'n hear your heart a-beatin' here, right under mine, an' your eyes don't dare look into mine for fear they'd be a-sayin' too much, or let me look deep, too deep, an' right on down into your heart, Marion!"

He felt her whole body give to him, felt the tremor of her breath against his cheek.

The stream ran shining and whispering in the moonlight; the wind hushed through the fragrant boughs of the orchard; the moments passed like the fluttering fall of the apple blossoms, one and one.

She drew away to arm's length, her hands still resting on his arms, her eyes meeting his in flashes and falling away as quickly in confusion, and the smile playing furtively about her lips: "There was something else you was about to tell me a little while ago, before . . . before . . . can you tell me now, dear? You was talkin' so funny and sort of broken about the McLanes and the Conovers, and having something to say which you wanted to say and yet was afraid to. Can you say it now?"

His face altered swiftly, and his lips moved as if to speak. Then he shook his head. "I can't say it yet, honey," he answered, "an' I won't say it till the

preacher has done all that anyone c'n do to make
you mine forever. An' then I'll tell you, an', when I
say it, I reckon this ol' feud'll go off an' hide its head
an' laugh itself to death."

The dull, slow *clanging* of a bell broke in upon
them, and at the sound she grew pale and still.

"Listen," she said. "It's midnight. An' the truce
for the feud has ended now, an' we are not home.
An' Pa'll think that you have taken me home, and
he'll go home an' find we're not there, an' go mad
for thinkin' things. Oh, honey, how'll we get back?
The McLanes'll be waitin' for us sure along the road,
an' . . . an' . . ."

He laughed softly. "If they's any McLanes waitin'
in the road for me," he said at last, "I reckon it'll be
about the last waitin' they'll do for anyone. Why,
honey, these McLanes an' the rest of these people
around here don't know no more about gun play
than women! They ain't never been up against the
real thing, an' they're sure goin' to have some fun if
they tackle me in the night. An' with a clear moon
like this!"

He loosened a pistol in his hip pocket as he spoke,
and she, remembering the shooting at the fair that
day, was silent, half in dread and half in content.

VI

TO END THE FEUD

They found their horses in the long line hitched in front of the dance hall, and started home at a sharp gallop. It was a typical backwoods road, winding helter-skelter up- and downhill and around many a sharp curve. If there were any lying in wait, they would have found a dozen places to secrete them in every half mile.

But they had come within two miles of the Conover house before it happened. The spirit of the backwoods is one spirit, and she had guessed their plans accurately.

As they swung around a sharp bend, two shots rang out in close succession. The first clipped past the hair at Lazy Purdue's forehead. The second knocked off his hat.

His return fire came like a flash on the heels of the second report. Firing a revolver from the saddle does not lead to accuracy or results, but Lazy Purdue had lived all his life on a horse, and, while he checked hard on the bridle, he whirled in his saddle, saw a shadowy horseman in the shade of a tree, and fired at the flash of steel in the horseman's hand.

The answering *clang* of metal told that he had shot the pistol out of the waylayer's hand, and the next moment the other was spurring hard down the road, bent far over the pommel of his saddle.

"Shoot!" screamed Marion Conover. "Shoot! Shoot! Oh, the coward, the yellow-hearted cur! Oh, you've lost him! Why didn't you shoot?"

For Lazy Purdue sat his saddle with his horse half turned on the road and the pistol poised in his hand. But his face was drawn and bitter.

"An' that is what the McLanes have sunk to," said Lazy Purdue. "My God, they ain't men . . . they're varmints!"

"Why didn't you shoot?" she pleaded, shaking his arm in her excitement as she rode up to him. "You could have killed him six times while he was riding the first twenty yards."

He slipped the pistol back into his pocket and looked at her for a long moment before he replied. "My pistol jammed, I reckon," he said. "I simply couldn't pull the trigger."

"Did you see his face?" she continued.

"No," he answered, "I didn't see his face very clear. I reckon he must have been a McLane."

"You *reckon*?" She laughed bitterly. "I tell you, I seen him as clear as day, an' I'd swear it before God. That was Luke McLane, an' he was tryin' to get even with you for beatin' his brother at the shootin'!"

Lazy Purdue dismounted and picked up the revolver that he had shot from McLane's hand.

"At least," he said, smiling slowly as he examined the battered weapon, "Luke McLane won't be pulling the trigger with his right hand for quite some time."

He refused to speak of the affair again on the way

home, and, when he kissed her good night, he seemed to have forgotten the incident. But the next morning he ordered his horse saddled, and rode out without giving a destination. He rode north from the house, so that anyone watching him might not suspect his destination, but, as soon as he was out of sight, he took the first crossroad and cut straight south. He had never ridden that way before, but he seemed to know the roads by instinct, and took every turn certainly.

His mind was busy as he rode, and it was busy with the feud. There was some way out. He felt for the six-shooter in his pocket and smiled. He thought of another thing and frowned. Then an inspiration came to him. It was a desperate thing to attempt, and a dangerous one, but he had seen it work once in a barroom in southwestern Texas, and he was confident that, if it worked there, it would work here. He checked his horse for a moment, and emptied his gun's chambers at the side of the road.

In ten minutes more he was before the McLane verandah, his horse tethered to the hitching post, and was knocking at the door of the house. A Negro opened it, and then half closed it when he saw the visitor.

"I wish to see Tom McLane," said Lazy Purdue.

The Negro bobbed his head hastily and disappeared down the hall. A moment later Tom McLane appeared, followed by the hulking figure of his son Henry.

"Suh," said Tom McLane gravely, "will you do me the honor of entering my house?" He bowed the way in with clumsy but careful courtesy.

In a moment more the three men were alone in a room. It was plain that Henry McLane carried his suspicions of this visit, for he lurked at a distance with his hand ever near to his hip pocket. But his father was a different type, or a better judge of men.

"I don't want to be irritatin'," began Lazy Purdue in his usual drawl, "but I'm powerful curious to know how Luke's trigger hand is this mornin'."

Henry McLane cursed softly, and his father stiffened and turned somewhat pale, but his eyes held steadily to Purdue's face.

"That was a dog's trick my boy tried to play on ye," he stated. "An' I'm glad out o' my heart that ye shot the gun out o' his hand. He won't use a gun for many a day, suh . . . an', when he does, he'll know enough to use it in a man's way."

Lazy Purdue smiled gently upon him. "Down my way," he murmured, "if a man tried a thing like that an' didn't pull the trick, the boys would be laughing yet. They'd be laughin' so hard, suh, that they wouldn't hardly have the strength to string him up to the nearest tree and shoot him full of holes. I'm askin' you to look at the funny side of it, suh. Heah's a man an' a harmless girl a-ridin' down a road, an' heah's another man waitin' under a tree, with his gun ready an' everything, set to shoot this first man full o' holes. An' then the first man comes 'round the bend, an' the second man shoots twice . . . an' misses . . . an' then gets his gun shot out o' his hand. Yes, suh, it was very funny!"

"Suh," said old McLane earnestly, "I dunno jus' how I can tell you how ashamed I am o' that boy, but I'm not ashamed o' the way he missed you. I'm only powerful glad he didn't have black murder on him after that night. An' one thing more, suh. When that boy had his gun shot out of his hand and rode on down the road like hell was behind him, why didn't you shoot ag'in, suh? He was your meat then, an' no one could've blamed you for drilling him through the back."

The caressing chuckle was still in Lazy Purdue's laugh as he answered. "That's where you show you ain't highly developed on your humorous side, Mister McLane," he asserted. "Why, suh, I was so busy laughin', an' my arm was shakin' so with that laughter, that I simply didn't dare fire at him, suh. I might've hit the girl what was ridin' with me, suh."

For a moment McLane frowned, and then his face cleared suddenly. "Conover," he said, "for I reckon you've got a right to that name now, there's somethin' about you that strikes me mighty familiar. I dunno what it is. Seems as if I seen you somewhere a long time ago."

A faint flush appeared on the face of Lazy Purdue. "I got somethin' to say about that," he answered, "but it's somethin' I can't say now . . . an', when I do say it, I reckon it's goin' to have a powerful lot to do with this here feud. But what I've got to say now is that they's a powerful lot to settle between the Conovers an' the McLanes jus' now, an' I come here to suggest a way o' doin' it.

"Now, down my way o' the country, when a man is a bit angry with another man, he don't lay for him behin' trees an' shoot at him like he was a yowlin' cat in an alley. He jus' sends him a word that he's goin' to get him the next time they meet face to face, an', when they do meet, they pulls an' shoots, an' they's an end o' the thing without endangerin' any girls that can't use guns."

He drew his revolver from his hip pocket and at the movement the two men started, but he stepped to one end of the room with the revolver hanging quietly by his side.

"Now," he went on, "I'm talkin' to you as man

talks to man in my part of the country. I reckon you're pretty much of a man's man, Tom McLane. I know what people say about you in this here part of the country, and I reckon you'd feel pretty much at home in my part. This here is my proposition." He was speaking slowly and carefully as if he had to feel for his words. "Sir," he said, "what you call a feud here is what they gen'rally call murder where I come from. Down there, they shoot at a man while he's a-lookin' at the man that shoots, an' they don't wait for him behind a tree.

"I propose that we end this here feud," went on Lazy Purdue, "but I propose that we end it in a man's way. I'm goin' to stand up here at this end of this here room, and one of your sons, preferably Henry, is goin' to stand at the other end of this here room, and we're each goin' to have a revolver in our hands, and you're goin' to stand in the middle of the room against the wall there and you're goin' to have another revolver in your hand. An' then you're goin' to count up to ten, slow and deliberate-like, and, when you reach ten, we're goin' to raise our guns and shoot, and the quickest shot is the man what's goin' to live. But if one of us raises his gun and shoots before ten is reached, you, Tom McLane, are goin' to shoot that man down, even if he's your own son. Is this fair an' square? An' then if I'm done for, I reckon there's a pile of people won't care a lot. An' if Henry's done for, I reckon the feud will be called square. Blood covers up blood, don't it, Tom McLane?" He stopped, breathing somewhat heavily from his own oration.

Tom McLane turned on his son. "Well," he said, "what do you say to this? Does the game suit you?"

"No" burst out Henry, his lips twitching while he

spoke. "This here game is murder, that's what it is, an' it doesn't give a man a fair chance, it . . ."

"Silence," roared Tom McLane, "are ye a son of mine? By God, I say the game suits me! What? Will ye turn down a fair an' square gamblin' chance, an' you the best shot in these parts, Henry McLane? Stand up at that end of the room, I say, an' get out your gun, and, if you make a stir to shoot before I count ten, I'll shoot and shoot straight if you were ten times my son. Get over there! This here feud has raised hell with two fine families long enough. I lost an uncle an' two cousins. It's goin' to stop, an' there ain't no better way than the way that's put up to you now. Stan' over there!"

With reluctant feet and backward glancing eyes, as if the spot he had just left were the only safe one in the room, Henry McLane took up his position and looked toward the calmly smiling face of Lazy Purdue. The sight seemed to infuriate him suddenly beyond all self-control. "Sure I'll play the game," he cried through tense lips, "an', by God, I'll blow your head offen you, George Conover, jus' as I blowed the head off the other George Conover! You ain't no spirit come back with another man's name. I reckon you're flesh an' blood. Pa, you c'n begin to count."

He stood leaning forward as if poised to run, with the pistol clenched so tightly in his hand that his fingers went white about the knuckles. His eyes ate hungrily into the face of Lazy Purdue, who stood opposite, quite at his ease and hardly glancing at his opponent. His eyes bore the casual caress, which was their customary expression.

"One, two, three . . . ," began Tom McLane, his pistol moving to keep time to the slow measure of his count.

"Four, five, six," he went on, still in the same calm voice with the heart-breaking pauses between every count.

The whole frame of Henry McLane seemed to wince and grow weak, but he ground his teeth and remained steadfast on his mark with his eyes narrowing.

"Seven, eight," continued the steely voice.

Henry McLane moistened his lips with his tongue, and his eyes wavered sidewise.

"Nine!"

The revolver of Henry McLane exploded into the floor, and he shrank back suddenly against the wall.

"Begin . . . begin over again," he cried uncertainly. "I . . . I . . . my finger moved."

"Henry McLane," pronounced the hollow voice of his father, "I'm beginnin' to doubt whether or not ye're my true son. If that pistol had been pointin' a bit higher, God might've had mercy on you, but I wouldn't!"

Henry braced himself again to the mark as his father recommenced the counting. His eyes were held as if by a fascination to the sinister and mocking smile that curved Lazy Purdue's lips.

"One . . . two . . . three!"

A strange wavering began throughout young McLane's figure as he stood crouched on the mark, and a noticeable pallor crossed his face.

"Four . . . five . . . six!"

His lips were working now, and his eyes shifted from point to point on Lazy Purdue's confident figure as if he were uncertain where to take his aim.

"Seven . . . eight . . . nine . . ."

Henry McLane dropped in a huddled mass upon the floor, and the revolver went spinning out of his hand.

"For God's sake don't shoot!" he screamed. "This is murder! Don't shoot! I . . . I . . ."

It seemed to Lazy Purdue that he would rather have taken a bullet in his heart a thousand times over than have looked once upon the sudden horror that came upon old McLane's face.

"My God," he was saying over and over as if to himself, "*this* ain't what I'm seein'! This is some damned dream. *This* ain't no son of mine. *This* ain't what I reared an' packed in my arms when he was sick, and loved before he was half a man . . . oh, my God, this ain't real!"

VII

FOREWARNED

Henry McLane rose shudderingly and cowered against the wall. His large form seemed to have shrunk strangely in size. Lazy Purdue replaced his revolver in his hip pocket.

"Harken ye to me," said Tom McLane, "ye've showed me my own son with new eyes, but I reckon ye ain't goin' to live a tolerable long time to talk o' it, or I ain't goin' to live a powerful long time to hear o' it. Do they give ye a warnin' down in yo' part o' the country? Then take my warnin' now."

"Don' go runnin' away with yourself," protested Lazy Purdue. "I reckon me an' your family have had quite a little doin's lately all between us. An' what do ye say now to a little sort o' truce between us? This here is the fourth of June, an' on the ninth o' this month me an' Marion Conover is goin' to get married. After that there marriage, you c'n go ahead with your little game. I'll meet you halfway."

"Good," said Tom McLane. "They's peace between us till the tenth. Then get all your Conovers together, for on the tenth the McLanes are goin' to be in Willoughby Hollow, the whole tribe o' them, an' they're goin' to start for the Conover house to wipe this feud out once for all, an' you along with the rest of 'em, my frien'. When midnight o' the ninth passes, you c'n be ready for us with all your tribe behind you, fo' they's goin' to be mo' rifle play that night than they's been since this heah feud started."

It was a fair enough warnin' and a man-to-man speech, yet Lazy Purdue made no report of it to the Conover family.

The next day the Negroes of the household brought word that the McLanes were gathering from all directions, a score of them at least. Old John Conover was deeply alarmed and proposed half a dozen times a day that they send for their blood relations to meet this formidable preparation, but Lazy Purdue laughed these thoughts aside. He had taken complete command of the situation and relegated John Conover far into the background.

More than this, the household was too busy during those few days with preparations for the marriage to pay much attention to the outside world. If Marion objected that it was too soon after the death of her brother for her to marry, she was overborne by the quiet insistence of Lazy Purdue, and in this he had the backing of the two old people. They had seen enough of trouble; they saw in this marriage the chance to perpetuate the old Conover name, and they rallied behind Purdue when he declared for an early marriage.

It was decided to make the wedding a strictly family affair with no outsiders to surround the event with the noisy rejoicing that generally characterized the backwoods' marriages.

One thing bothered Lazy Purdue. As the days went on, he came to notice on Marion's face, when she sat watching him and thought herself unobserved, a peculiarly mocking smile. He knew it could not be mockery, but it was something so akin to it that he was deeply worried. He questioned her about it one afternoon, but she broke into laughter and refused to answer.

They were married late on the evening of the ninth, and, after the minister had left, the family sat a long while on the verandah, silent for the most part, listening to the vague noises of the night with the stir and rustle of the warm June air about them. The old folks went off to bed in time, and Lazy Purdue sat with Marion, talking little and thinking deeply.

He knew that this was the crisis of his life. As he looked at the pale profile of his wife's face and to the vague smile that altered her lips, he commenced to wish profoundly that he had gathered the Conovers around him to fight this last battle in the night. But in a moment the thought left him. Blood ties are strong in the backwoods, and they lay strong in the heart of Lazy Purdue.

A *clatter* of hoofs came up the path, a horseman halted on sliding hoofs before the verandah. The horseman leaned far to one side and peered into the face of Lazy Purdue in the clear moonlight.

"You're the man what calls himself George Conover?"

"I am."

"Then here's a note from Tom McLane." He tossed a little white pellet to Purdue and galloped off, clattering into the night.

Purdue unfolded the note and read:

This'll reach you about midnight. We're down in Willoughby Hollow an' we start for the

Conover house when the tenth begins. Is this a warning?

Lazy Purdue pulled out his watch. It was five minutes before twelve. He rose and stretched himself and yawned. "Marion," he said, "I'm goin' into the house for a minute, an' then I'm goin' to leave you for a little while."

She made no answer as he went into the house, but, when he returned onto the verandah, he found her standing and waiting for him, and saw her eyes calmly noting his two holsters and the double belt of cartridges that ran about his waist.

"You're goin' down to fight them in the night?" she asked quietly.

"No," he said, "I reckon it won't get to fightin'. I'm merely goin' down to talk to 'em. I got something to say that ought to end this here feud. If they won't listen, then we'll have some gun play . . . something of a kind they never dreamed of before."

She remained passive while he kissed her. "Honey," she said, "I reckon I know what you're going to tell them. Can't you . . . can't you jus' send 'em a messenger to tell 'em what you've got to say?"

He laughed shortly. "No," he said. "You don't even dream what I've got to say, an' I've got to take this here message myself."

"They'll be twenty to one," she said slowly, "if it comes to fightin'."

"Twenty rabbits don't scare one dog," he stated, and laughed gaily back to her as he strode down the path.

Willoughby Hollow lay nearly a mile away from the house, and he commenced to run as soon as he was out of hearing of the house. He feared that he was too late and that the McLanes would start their move on the house before he could reach them to parley.

But when he reached the Hollow, he heard not a sound. In the middle of the Hollow, there was a long and narrow clearing between the wooded slopes that ran up on either side, and Purdue paused at his side of the clearing to watch. It was not long before he noticed a shadowy figure behind a tree, and then another, and another farther away. The McLanes had evidently delayed their advance, perhaps because some of their clan had arrived late on the scene.

"Tom McLane!" shouted Lazy Purdue, "a truce! I got something to say to you."

"There ain't no more truce!" called the voice of Tom McLane. "Have you got your men behind you, George Conover?"

"Aye," said Lazy Purdue, "I've got my men behind me, an' they're enough to wipe all the McLanes that ever were off the map. But listen to me. Tom McLane, I got something to say which you an' all the McLanes ought to hear. There won't be any more feud when you hear it."

"Damn you an' your words!" shouted Tom McLane. "I've heard too many of 'em before. The time has come for rifles to talk. I've got a bead on you now, George Conover, an' I'll give you twenty seconds to get back into cover with your men!"

Purdue realized the significance of McLane's tone. They were out for blood, and they meant to taste it. He leaped back into the shelter of the tree trunks, and in a moment more than half a dozen rifles exploded in swift succession and a volley of singing messengers of death whirred around him or splintered against the branches.

They were not long unanswered. Lazy Purdue commenced to fall back up the hillside, but in long and slow zigzags from side to side. The McLanes, believing that the Conovers were out in force, advanced slowly, firing at every shadow. Purdue, picking his shots, landed man after man.

The odds were not so much against him as would have seemed. The riflemen required a long time, comparatively, to get their sights set and draw their bead on their target. Moreover, they could not secure a fair aim at the shadowy figure that fled softly from tree to tree. The light of the moon, never very good for rifle shooting, was almost impossible in the patchy and uncertain light of the woods.

But it hardly bothered Lazy Purdue. As he moved rapidly from tree to tree, he fired at every flash of steel and at every exposure of a figure. Quite accustomed to firing by simply pointing his revolver and without any effort at drawing a bead through the sights, the dimness of the woods hardly bothered him. By the time one of the McLanes had drawn a bead on his moving figure, he was already in shelter behind a tree trunk and taking pot shots at the flashes of rifle fire.

Such was the rapidity of his lateral movement and so slowly did he draw back up the hillside that it must have seemed to the McLanes that they were opposed by an almost equal number of fighters, and every one a dead shot.

Purdue was not shooting to kill. He fired at the flash of reflected light from the weapons themselves, or at the exposed legs or arms, and that he scored frequently many a brief outcry and following burst of sincere cursing attested.

As he drew farther up the slope, the pursuit behind him grew slower and the fire less intense. Two shots had nipped the sleeve of his left arm, but, otherwise, he was unharmed.

VIII

THE END OF THE FEUD

At that moment he heard someone crashing through the brush behind him. He thought at first that it must be some of the McLanes in a flanking movement, and, whirling where he crouched, he poised his revolver ready to fire. At the same instant a dark figure blundered out of the shadows higher up the slope and ran toward him.

"George!" called the figure.

Lazy lowered his revolver hastily, for it was the voice of old Conover.

"Get down and crawl!" he ordered. "The McLanes are here . . . thick."

The old man came rapidly toward him. "George," he said, "there's no use fighting any longer. Life an' death don't matter much now. Marion's gone. I seen it from the window, but I couldn't do a thing. By the time I ran and got my rifle, they was gone."

"Talk slow," said Lazy Purdue, taking Conover hard by the arm. "Who went with her?"

"Henry McLane," breathed Conover tremulously, "an' he carried the sun o' my life away with her. She was on the hillside down by the house as plain as day in the moonlight. She was listening to sounds we heard from here. And then I saw big Henry McLane ride on her out of the shadow of the trees and pick her up as a hawk picks up a chicken. I saw her struggle and strike at his face. I heard him laugh and saw him kiss her. Then he spurred out of sight. It seemed to me he headed for the river. God knows where he has taken her now. It may be too late for pursuit!"

"But not too late to find him," Lazy said through his teeth. He raised his voice to a shout. "Tom McLane," he called, "if you're a man of honor come out and talk to me like a man! Here stand I, George Conover, with my guns on the ground beside me, and my hands in the air. I want a truce to talk."

He tossed his revolvers to the ground as he spoke and stepped out into the open. A rifle barked, but the voice of Tom McLane followed the sound swiftly as the *hum* of the bullet went close by Lazy's head.

"Stop firing," he ordered, "or I'll account for the next one who shoots with my own gun." He stepped out from the shadows, a great patriarchal figure. "What do you want with me, George Conover?"

"It's I that wants something of you," cried old Conover. "How long have the McLanes taken to warring on women, Tom?"

"They never will," answered Tom McLane.

"But they have!" cried Conover. "Tom McLane, your own son Henry has carried my daughter away."

"And my wife," said Lazy Purdue. "There's an end to this feud while I go to bring her back, is there not, McLane?"

Tom McLane went up to Lazy and caught his hand. "Boy," he said, "I'll ride with you on the way, if you want me to. He's no son of mine . . . and the feud's done till you come back."

Lazy Purdue was already halfway to the shadows, running for his life up the hillside. When he reached the Conover house, he raced to the stable and saddled a horse. It seemed to him that all his fingers were thumbs before he had drawn the girths and filled his cartridge belt again, but in a moment he was in the saddle and thundering down the road.

He cut across the fields at the first opening. There was but one shallow place in the river where Henry McLane could have crossed the ford. Otherwise, he must have ridden around by the bridge, and Lazy knew he would not waste time to do this. He headed straight for the river, and, on the sand by the edge, he saw deep hoof prints. They stirred him on with a sudden warmth of hatred, and he sent his horse splashing into the water.

It was a steep grade up the other side, and his horse went slowly. He did not urge him, for he knew that a desperate ride lay ahead of him that night and he wished to save strength for the final race. McLane's horse carried two, and the burden must tell before long. So he worked his way up the hillside until he came again to the road where it topped the very crest.

Below him the road wound whitely in the moonlight down the other side of the ridge, and, as he looked, breathing his laboring horse for a moment, he saw a black speck swing out onto one of the lower stretches of the road.

It must be McLane.

He crushed one hand over his eyes and thought quickly. He could not possibly overtake McLane by following down the road. At the foot of the ridge it branched into several forks. It would be a matter of guesswork as to which one Henry would take, and the chances were seven to one that Lazy would follow the wrong trail.

There was a chance, however, that he could cut down to the foot of the graded road by going straight down the mountainside and avoiding the long curves.

Yet it was desperate work. The mountainside was thick with second-growth saplings and underbrush, and in several places the mountain dropped almost perpendicularly. Still it was the one possible chance, and Lazy dismounted to tighten the girths again. Then he started the wild ride downward.

He never stopped. He could not. The impetus that the horse gained in the first few moments carried him resistlessly onward, whinnying with terror. Half a dozen times Lazy thought they must inevitably crash into some large tree or rock that jutted up suddenly before them, but each time he managed to swerve the horse sufficiently to one side.

It was a sure-footed mountain horse. Otherwise, they would both have been crushed to death within the first 100 yards of the swift descent. As it was, the horse laid back on his haunches and they slid crashing on through brush and over pebbles, many times near death but always averting it.

It seemed a century to Lazy Purdue; in reality, it was only a few desperate moments before they slid out into the road at the foot of the mountain. Before him rattled hoofs, and he saw a dark figure whirl around a curve.

Lazy shouted aloud for exultation, for the road that McLane had taken was a blind. It had once been a private way leading to a house that had long ago been burned down. No paths branched from it. It led straight to the side of the house, and there it was effectually stopped by the drop of a sheer precipice.

Lazy drove his spurs into his mount and rode hard. The rattle of hoofs before him drew closer and closer, and at last, in an open stretch, he saw McLane clearly. The fugitive was riding desperately, but Lazy could tell by the sway of the horse that it could not maintain its speed for long. He shouted with triumph and fired his revolver into the air. At the sound, McLane whirled in the saddle and shook his fist back at the pursuer.

While they were riding on the last rise before the house, Lazy drew closer and closer. Again he fired in the air. They swung onto the open space where the burned house had stood. One hundred yards away was the edge of the cliff.

Suddenly McLane flung the limp body of Marion from his horse. Lazy cried out in horror, and, as McLane swung his rifle to his shoulder and fired, Lazy spurred on his mount and blazed away in return. But the motion of his horse disturbed his aim and the bullet struck the mount of Henry McLane. The horse sprang suddenly forward, throwing McLane back in the saddle and racing straight toward the precipice.

Too late for action, McLane saw his destination. He tugged desperately at the bridle reins, pulling his horse's head sidewise, then his despairing shout rang back, and horse and rider plunged outward into the night.

But Lazy Purdue had no time to examine the certain results of that fall.

In a moment he was kneeling by the side of Marion Conover, and at the same time she opened her eyes. She could not speak, but clung to him with eloquent force.

"Where . . . where has he gone?" she whispered at last.

"No man in all the world can tell," Lazy said gravely. He lifted her into the saddle, and then walked to the edge of the cliff. Far below he saw two figures lying on the rocks with the moonlight white upon them. He walked back to his horse with his hat in his hand.

They rode back slowly toward the Conover place, speaking little, and beneath them they could feel the horse still trembling like a human being from the effects of that grim ride. Up the hill they went, and then down to the river, and up again toward the wooded hillside that led to the Conover house. They had no fear now of the McLanes or of any man.

So when a score of voices hailed them on the spot where Lazy Purdue not long before had defied the banded McLanes, they dismounted without fear and awaited results. They came in the form first of old Conover, who ran to Marion and caught her in his arms, speaking broken phrases like a child who has newly learned to talk.

Afterward Tom McLane and his clan strode through the shadows and fronted them. "Two of you have come back," he said, "an' I shan't ask where Henry McLane is now."

"You are right," said Purdue, "for I cannot tell you."

McLane removed his hat. "At least," he said, "he fell by a real man's hand."

"You are wrong," answered Lazy Purdue, "he fell by a surer hand than that of any man. And now, Tom McLane, I want to say what I have tried to say before and couldn't. The feud between the McLanes and the Conovers is at an end."

"That's a lie," said McLane with a slight return of

heat. "I'm tired of bloodshed, but this thing has got to be fought out sometime, and it might as well be fought out now. The McLanes and the Conovers will never rest in peace."

"That's where you're wrong," said Lazy Purdue, "for they're linked together now with blood. There is a McLane that's a Conover and a Conover that's a McLane as far as the laws of God and man can make them. I'm the McLane that's become a Conover."

"How in the name o' God are you a McLane?" breathed Tom.

"Do you remember when Henry McLane, that was your brother, was driven out of the country for killing two Conovers away back years ago?"

"I do."

"An' do ye remember that he took a wee bit of a son along with him when he left?"

"By God, an' you're the boy!" cried Tom McLane. He raised his hand to his lips and gave the long, owl-like cry that had been the rallying call of the McLanes for generations past. "Boys," he shouted, "this here feud is ended! Here's a McLane come home to us an' became a Conover, an' the feud has done run itself into the ground at last!"

Late that night, a little before the dawn commenced, Lazy Purdue sat by the bed of Marion and told a long, long story. When he ended, he was astonished to see that she was laughing lightly up to him.

"Honey," she said, "I knew you was a McLane the minute I looked at you that first night when you stood there with the blood of poor George on your forehead an' over your heart!"

BILLY ANGEL,
TROUBLE LOVER

By the 1920s Faust's output was prodigious and would continue to be so through the 1930s. "Billy Angel, Trouble Lover" was one of twenty-three short novels and stories and thirteen serials to appear in 1924. It was published in the *Western Story Magazine* issue dated November 22nd under the George Owen Baxter byline. What makes the short novel rather unusual is Faust's use of the heroine, Sue Markham, as the point of view character. It is through her eyes that we meet Billy Angel, the rascally hero who finds refuge in Sue's café when he is wounded.

I

SUE TO THE RESCUE

On an October night, Sue Markham saw him first. October nights in the mountains are not the October nights of the plains. In the lowlands the air is crisp, but the frost is not yet in it; in the mountains winter has already come, and on this night the cold was given teeth by a howling wind.

She preferred these windy, biting nights. For, when the trains reached that little station of Derby and paused to put on the extra engine that would tug them up the long grade and over the shoulder of Derby Mountain, the crews darted in for a piece of pie and a cup of hot coffee. For five minutes, she would be kept busy serving like lightning, and the cash drawer was constantly banging open and shut. Sometimes a passenger hurried in to swallow a morsel of food, listening with a haunted look in his eyes for the cry of "All aboard!" She had glimpses of ladies and gentlemen, in this way. She saw their fine clothes, their train-weary faces. And, usually, they left tips.

At first she used to return those tips to them. But she found that it was hard to make them take the money back. So, after a time, she merely swallowed her pride and kept the tips for old Pete Allison, who had lost his right arm in the sawmill and spent his days, since that time, waiting for death and hating the world—hating even the girl and the charity from her that he was forced to accept.

She made a scant living in this way. For three years, since the death of her father, she had kept on with the little lunch counter. It was the only cheerful spot near the station and therefore it was patronized heavily by the train population. She knew, too, that they came into the lunch counter, those oily, greasy, blackened firemen and brakies and engineers, more for the sake of her pretty face than for the sake of the food. So she had learned to smile, as vaudeville actors and actresses learn to smile. Except that she had to put more meaning into those smiles, for an audience of half a dozen is more critical than an audience of half a thousand or more.

At odd moments, when there was nothing else to do, they used to propose to her. It was always interesting, although never important. And they had various ways of going about it.

"I got a raise on the first. Suppose we get hooked up, Sue?"

"Single harness is dog-gone' lonesome, Sue. Let's try to make the grade together."

"You got to marry somebody, Sue. Why not me?"

"Sue, old dear, you're made to order for an engineer's wife."

Almost always there was a note of banter in these proposals, and their eyes remained humorous, no matter how serious their voices might be. She learned that this was because they expected to be refused, and she found out that they compared notes afterward and told one another how she had declined them. It came to be a regular thing. Every youngster who came on the division was expected to lose his heart to Sue and ask for her hand. And afterward he had to tell what had happened. It was a sort of initiation ceremony. She took it as much for granted as they did, of course. But she could never keep from blushing and smiling at them and she usually told them that she intended to be an old maid.

They took these rejections easily enough, and went back into the night to their work, or else they sat down around the stove at the end of the room and let their wet clothes steam out, perhaps. Her life consisted of nothing but men. There was not another woman in Derby. There was not even a girl child. On that side of the mountain she and she alone represented femininity.

On this October evening, a southwester that had been blowing strong but warm all day pulled around into the north and instantly there was ice in the air. She had to send old Pete Allison out for more wood and fill the stove and open the draft until great, ominous red places appeared on the top and along the sides of the stove. Even so, prying drafts continually slid into the room and stabbed one with invisible daggers of ice. The lunch counter, of course, was busier than ever. She burned her fingers with the overflow from coffee cups. Her stock of pie—baked in her own oven in dull times of the day or even at night—was nine-tenths consumed.

Then he came into the place.

There was an arresting air about him. He came in entirely surrounded by a group of four brakies, but she found herself craning her neck at him. He was a big young man, dressed in a lumberman's Mackinaw of a brilliant plaid, but all the looseness of that comfortable garment was plumped out by the swelling muscles of his shoulders.

He took off his hat to her as he went by. The lower part of his face was covered with the stiff, upturned collar of his Mackinaw, but she could see that he was a handsome youngster in his early twenties, with a rather pale face and a pair of bright black eyes. Also, although he greeted her so pleasantly, she knew that she had never seen him before. No matter how thronged the counter might have been, she never could have seen that face before and forgotten it.

He did not pause at the counter, but he went straight back toward the stove and there sat down on an overturned box in a corner so dark that she could not make him out any more, except as a shadow among the shadows.

After a time the others went out. The train was pulling away up the grade. Its stertorous coughing became less thunderous in the distance; the floor ceased to tremble with the vibrations from the ponderous driving wheels. The trucks of the coaches rolled slowly, heavily past the station with a more and more rapid cadence in their rattling.

There was not a soul remaining except Pete Allison and the stranger.

Something like fear came into the girl. She was amazed at herself. Surely there was not a man in all the world she needed to fear. In the pocket of her dress there was a little police whistle that one of the firemen had given her; one blast on that whistle would bring them up to her. Twice she had had to use it; once when a new brakie full of tequila came into the place, and once when a vicious tramp troubled her. And, on each occasion, there had been a rush like a cavalry charge that had ended with her fighting to save the lives of the offenders.

Certainly here was protection enough to have satisfied the most timid of women, but still there was an uneasy feeling in her heart, a sort of tremulous lightness. It bewildered her. As she worked among the dishes, washing them in haste, she found her glances drawn sidelong toward the stranger again and again. He had not moved from his place, except to lean back a little more heavily against the wall. His head had fallen on his breast—perhaps he was sleeping?

She paused with a cup half dried. There had been no rain, and yet she had heard most distinctly the dripping of something on the floor of the room. She listened again, intently. There was no doubt about it—a drop, and then another.

She turned sharply toward the stove, bewildered, in time to see something drop glistening in a dim streak from the hand of the stranger, where it had fallen across his knee.

A little chill of horror crept through the flesh of the girl—and again she could not tell why. She took the lamp from above the counter and carried it to the counter table. The broad, dull circle of its light now covered the lower part of the man's body, his feet and the floor on which they rested, and on the wood there was a little gleaming spot, of a dark color. Of a dark color, but surely not red! Surely not red!

She flashed a glance in terror toward the door. Then she assured herself with a great effort that there was no danger, and she raised the lamp. It showed her the stranger slumped far down on the box, his head deeply inclined, the very picture of a weary man asleep, but at that moment the drop of liquid hung again at the tip of his fingers and dropped once more, a gleaming streak of red, toward the little dark spot beside his foot.

It was blood—was the stranger dead? All the gleaming life in those black eyes—was it gone forever? She put down the lamp and ran hastily toward him. She caught him beneath the chin and rolled back his head. It turned loosely—a horrible looseness. It lay back against the wall, but now the eyes opened and looked stupidly up to her. Surprise showed in them, then alarm. He lurched to his feet and scowled down at her.

"Well," he asked sharply, "what'll you have?"

"Man, man!" cried Sue Markham. "Where are you hurt? You're bleedin' to death!"

He jerked up his left hand at that and exposed the palm covered with a great black clot, while a tiny rivulet ran down on the inner side of his arm.

"The bandage slipped a little, I guess," he said. "That's all. I . . ." He attempted to make a step, and stumbled.

"Sit down!" cried Sue.

"I can't stop," he muttered.

She pointed at him in horror. "Do you see? Do you see? You're all soaked through with blood."

"Stand away, girl. I got to get on."

"You'll be a dead man in an hour if I let you go! Sit down here . . . let me look at that arm."

She caught at him and he strove to push her away. To her astonishment, she found she could master that great hulk of manhood. He was helpless before her, shaking his head, muttering savagely. She thrust him into a chair.

"I'll rest for a little spell longer," he declared, trying to cover up his weakness by scowling at her.

She waved his words away and quickly drew off his coat. The mischief was plainly in view then. A long gash crossed the inside of his left arm, and from the cut the blood was flowing through a crudely made bandage that had been twisted from place.

"What under heaven made that cut?" she cried softly to him. "No knife..." For it was a broad, rough-edged slash.

"A bullet," said the big man finally. "Will you let me get on now?"

"A bullet!" cried Sue Markham. "Who?"

The other leaned weakly back in his chair. "The sheriff," he said. "And there he's comin'!" He jerked his thumb with a feeble gesture over his shoulder, and in fact, through a lull of the wind, she heard the beating of hoofs down the mountainside, sweeping through the little town of Derby.

"Where'll I hide you?"

"Leave me be. This ain't no business for a girl."

"Here behind the counter... they'll never look...."

"I'll see 'em in hell before I sneak behind a girl's petticoats to hide from 'em. You," he added, with a sudden and hysterical return of strength, "what's your name?"

"Sue Markham."

"Sue," he said, "you're as game as there is in the world. But this room ain't gonna be a place where a woman will want to be. Run along outdoors... or upstairs...."

"What'll you do?"

"Set here, easy. Now, run along."

He caught her arm and turned her around. His hand for the moment was iron, irresistible, but in the same instant the strength faded out of it and his arm dropped helplessly to his knees. His whole great body began to sag. But still he tried to keep his head up, and his jaw was set. He apologized, mumbling over the words. "I figgered on goin' straight on. But

I was fagged. I only meant to set here a moment. Didn't think that I'd need to rest more'n a minute. Then . . . I got dizzy. . . ."

"What do they want you for?"

"Something that ain't pretty. Run along, Sue Markham. Leave me be, here."

"You're going to try to fight them when they come. Why, you aren't strong enough to draw out a gun."

"I'll manage myself."

"What do they want you for? Is it serious? Will you tell me? Will you stop staring and tell me?"

His eyes rolled wildly up to her, and something like a hideous smile parted his lips. "Murder," he said huskily.

She had caught him by the shoulders, feeling him go limp beneath her touch. Now she stared down into his black eyes, deep and deep, trying to read the truth about his soul, but finding herself baffled.

"It was a fair fight," she insisted, trembling. "You killed someone in a fair fight."

He shook his head. "Stabbed," he said. "Behind."

A wave of actual physical sickness swept over her. "You mean stabbed in the back?"

"Yes."

"You didn't do it, then."

"Tell the sheriff that," he said, and he smiled again up to her. Even as he sat there on the verge of collapse, that smile gave a touch of something ominous, something alert to his presence. There was a sort of self-sufficient mockery of the world in it.

"I must get you out of the room," she said hurriedly.

He was so near collapse that he talked like a drunkard, with thick, stumbling lips.

"Murder. Y'understand? Murder. Want me for murder. Stand away from me, girl."

"Get up!" she cried, for she could hear the sound of horses pouring up the street.

"Show me the door," he said. "If you won't lemme sit here alone to meet 'em . . . I'll go out. It ain't right you should see what's gonna happen . . . show me the door . . . there's a fog rolled into this room, Sue."

"It will clear up," she told him. "I'll show you the way to the door. Stand up."

He made a wavering effort. She hooked his arm over her shoulder and lifted with all her strength. So he was drawn from the chair. He towered above her, immense, flabby, with his head rolling idiotically on his shoulders.

"Soon as I get to the door . . . the fresh air'll fix me up," he was saying.

"Steady. You'll be there in a minute."

She heard him whisper: "God gimme strength . . . to face 'em." He gasped aloud: "The door?"

"Another step!"

His weight slumped suddenly upon her. His head fell upon hers. She saw his great knees bend. He had fainted. And the rush of the horses filled the street just before the old saloon with thundering echoes, empty, thundering echoes.

It was like having a sack of crushing weight, but only half filled, thrown upon her. She could never have lifted this weight. Even now that it was propped against her, she went reeling beneath it, and his legs trailed out, and his feet dragged side-wise behind her.

So she got him to the counter and lowered his length behind it just as the door from the street was cast open. Had they seen her and her burden?

II

THE SHERIFF CONDEMNS

She stood up from lowering the wounded man to that shelter in time to see young Tom Kitchin, the sheriff, stride through the door with half a dozen men shouldering after him. They came stamping their feet for warmth, their heavy coats powdered with snow. But there was an eagerness in their faces that made her heart shrink. Surely they had seen. Their first words reassured her.

"The boys tell me that they seen a chap that answered his description come in here ... Billy Angel ... we want him, Sue."

She leaned on the counter, resting both her elbows on it. She took all her courage in her hands, so to speak, and she made herself smile back at handsome young Tom Kitchin.

"I've never met anyone called Billy Angel. Is this a joke, Tommy?"

He shook his head, too serious for jest. "A great big chap. Looks strong enough for two. Wore a heavy Mackinaw. Got a devil-take-the-next-man look to him. Couldn't mistake him once you set eyes on him. Old Pete Allison says he was here and that he ain't seen him leave."

"Did Pete say that?" said the girl, silently registering a grudge against the old man.

"He did."

"He went out the back door about fifteen minutes ago."

"Back through here?"

"Yes."

"We're off, boys!" cried the sheriff. "We'll run the dog down in an hour."

"Wait a minute, Sheriff," said Jack Hopper, the engineer, who was the rearmost of the party. "Wait a minute. If he cut back through the back door, he's headed for the hills."

"Weather like this? You're wild, Jack," answered the sheriff. "He'll cut for cover!"

"What's weather to him? He's got something inside him that'll make him warm."

Another broke in: "You'll never get him. It's blowing up a hundred-percent storm. Let him go for a while, Sheriff. After he's run around through the snow all night, tryin' to keep his blood goin' . . . he'll be spent pretty bad. We'll go out and ride him down in the morning."

The sheriff, growling deep in his throat and scowling, stepped to the back door of the room and cast it open. A great white hand of snow struck in at him. The flame leaped in the throat of the lamp, and the fire roared in the stove. He closed the door with a bang and turned his head down, shaking off the snowflakes.

"You're right, Jack," he said. "He's gone for the hills. And we'd never find him in this weather. Maybe he'll freeze before morning, at that. I hope not. I want to see the hanging of that rat." He came back to the lunch counter. "Coffee all around, Sue. We're cold to the marrow."

Her heart sank. Under her feet lay the wounded man. Perhaps at this very moment he was dying! His face was a dull white, his eyes were partly opened, and showed a narrow, glassy slit. She could not repress a shudder. But there was nothing to do except to obey the order. She went about it as cheerfully as possible.

From the big percolator, the polished, gleaming pride of the counter, she drew the cups rapidly, one after another, and then held them under the hot-milk faucet until they were filled. She set them out; she produced the sugar bowls and sent them rattling down the counter, where they came to a pause at an appropriate interval before the line.

They were beginning to grow comfortable, making little pilgrimages to the stove to spread their hands before the fire, and then returning in haste. Their faces grew fiery red, and the blood rushed up to the skin. The frowns of effort began to melt from their foreheads.

She was showered with orders.

"Lemon pie, Sue."

"That custard, Sue, under that glass case."

"Some of that coconut cake, Sue. Make it a double wedge."

"When are you gonna leave off cooking for the world and center on one man, Sue?"

"I'm waiting for a silent man, Harry."

"I'm silent by nacher and education, Sue."

"We won't know till you've growed up, Harry."

"Sue, gimme a dash of that Carnation cream, will you? This here milk ain't thick enough."

"It's real cow's milk, Bud."

"The only kind of cows I like are canned, Sue. This here fresh milk, it ain't got no taste to it."

She opened a can of condensed milk and set it before Bud.

"Another slice of apple pie, Sue."

"There ain't any more." This to the engineer, Jack Hopper.

"Didn't I see some back of the counter on that shelf?"

"No, Jack! Really!"

But she spoke too late. He had already leaned far across the high counter, lifting himself on his elbows, and so his glance commanded everything that was behind it—everything including the pale, upturned face of the wounded man who was stretched along the floor.

Her hand froze on the edge of the counter. Before her eyes, the lighted lamp became a long swirl of yellow flame. When her sight cleared again, she found that Jack Hopper was standing back a little from the counter, saying slowly: "Well, Sue, I guess I'll change my mind about having another piece. Let it go." He turned his back and went to the stove, and there he stood with his hands spread out to the blaze. Why had he not cried out? Because he thought that she had some profound reason for wishing to shelter the fugitive—and because Jack Hopper loved her.

The rest gave her a sentimental kindness, but Jack was different. He was no foolish boy, but a grown and hardened man, with a man's firmness, a man's singleness of thought and purpose. For two years he had been campaigning quietly to win her. And in turn, if she did not love him, she respected him as a rock of strength and of honesty. What passed in his mind now as he turned from the counter and stood by the stove?

The sheriff followed him with some question. How calamities rain one upon the other. His foot slipped; he looked down with a cry: "Blood, by the heavens! There's blood on the floor!" Then: "How did this stuff come here, Sue?"

They turned to her, but none with eyes so piercingly intent as those of Jack Hopper. In that crisis she felt herself perfectly calm. There was a stir beside her. She saw from the corner of her eye how Billy Angel was propping himself feebly upon one elbow. He was listening, too.

"One of the brakies off of Three Seventeen was whittling wood by the stove," she said. "He cut his finger."

"Where's the shavings, then?" snapped out the sheriff, frowning at her.

She saw the flush run up the face of Jack Hopper—saw him frown in a belligerent manner at the sheriff.

"He said it would dry up and stop bleeding," Sue said. "He sat there like a fool, letting it drip on my floor until I made him stop."

"Is that it?"

"Yes. I swept up the shavings. But I hadn't time to clean up that mess."

The sheriff nodded. "I'll tell you, fellows," he said to his companions, "I figgered for a minute that maybe that bullet of mine had nicked Billy Angel. He twisted around like it might've stung him a mite. Have you heard about the murder, Sue?"

"I don't want to hear," she said. "These horror stories put my nerves on edge."

"Since when?" The sheriff chuckled. "Well, Sue, you're a queer one. You've always been hunting for all the shooting stories. This was a bad case. Young Charlie Ormond . . . the son of that rich Ormond . . .

he was stabbed in the back by his cousin . . . this Billy Angel. A darned black case, I'd say. Angel was taken in by old Ormond and raised by him the same as Charlie."

She gaped at that recital of horror. "Are you sure he did it, Tom?"

"Wasn't he seen? Oh, there ain't any doubt of it. And he ran for it. An honest man always takes the chance of bein' arrested. This here Billy Angel, he turned and cut for it like a streak." He said to his companions: "Rustle around, boys. See if you can figger it out so's you get the best hosses around the town and have 'em ready by the mornin'. Sure-footed ones are what you'll want after this snow. It's gonna be sloppy work tomorrow if the wind pulls around to the south ag'in."

They went out, calling back to her as they passed through the door, each with some foolish thing to add to what the others said. But she waved to them all with the same fixed, meaningless smile. Then she looked down at Billy Angel.

He was sitting up with his back against the wall. Even while they were calling their farewells to her, he was calmly straightening the bandage on his arm where the bleeding had ceased entirely. Now he looked up calmly at her.

"Well?" she said, feeling that her heart had turned to iron in her breast.

"You could have saved the sheriff a pile of work by pointing behind the counter."

She answered coldly: "They never do things that way in my family. If the dogs were after it . . . I wouldn't show even a rat to 'em."

He watched her quietly. "I understand," he said.

III

HOPPER LEARNS HER SECRET

She would have given a great deal to have recalled that last speech of hers in the face of this perfect poise of the fugitive. For the steadiness with which his eyes held upon her seemed to tell her that, no matter what the sheriff had said, and no matter what the man himself confessed, he never could have been guilty of that dastardly crime of which he was accused. Moreover, there was a sense of a scornful curiosity with which he examined her, and seemed, behind those bright black eyes of his, to be weighing her. And finding her, no doubt, wanting.

Still, she could not unbend at once, and she was full of the revolt that had recently swept over her. There was iron in her voice when she said: "Can you walk?"

"I figger that I can," he said. "Anyway, I aim to try." He laid hold upon the supporting post that held up the counter, and, pulling with the one hand and thrusting himself up with the other, he managed to sway to his knees. There he paused. She could hear his panting, and his breast worked with the cost of the labor. There came to her a disgusting suspicion that he was overdoing the fatigue and acting a part for the sake of imposing upon her. She did not stir to help him. Now he strove again, and came to his feet by degrees, and stood with his big hand spread on the counter, leaning over it, breathing hard.

There was no sham here. She could see a tremor in those large hands, and that was proof enough. No acting could counterfeit the reality so perfectly. Once again there was a sudden and hot melting of the girl's heart.

"Billy Angel," she said fiercely, "did you do it? Did you really do it?"

Even in that moment of near collapse, his caustic humor did not desert him. "Are you aimin' to believe what I say?" he asked her.

"I *shall* believe it."

"Why, then, sure I didn't." He grinned at her again, as though part in mockery and part asking her to step inside a more intimate understanding of this affair. There was no way in which she could come close to him. Still he thrust her away to arm's length and seemed to laugh at her attempts to know him and the truth about him. Something about that grim independence made her admire him; something about it made her fear him. He seemed capable of anything, of facing one hundred men with guns in their hands—or, indeed, of stabbing one helpless man in the back by stealth. She would have paid down without an afterthought the treasures of a Crœsus to have known the truth. She would have paid down that much to win from him one serious, open, frank-hearted answer.

"You didn't do it," she said. "Well, God knows, I

hope you didn't. Now I got to get you upstairs where I can have a look at that wound."

He pointed up and over his shoulder. "Up to your room?"

"Yes."

He shook his head with a half-scornful, half-mirthful smile. "I'll be off."

"You'll freeze to death in an hour. Look at the windows."

They were clouded with thick white, quite opaque.

"Sue," he said, "I dunno but what you're an ace-high trump, but when it comes to hidin' in your room . . ." His smile disappeared; a wild and vacant look crossed his face, and he reeled, holding tight to the edge of the counter while his knees sagged. Only a giant effort of the will had kept him erect, she could see. She caught at him as she had done before, passing his unwounded arm over her shoulder, taking him around the triple-corded muscles of the waist with her free arm.

"Come along," she commanded, and dragged him toward the door that led to the upstairs room.

Then his bravado deserted him. "Sue," he said, "for heaven's sake, lemme go. I don't deserve the good treatment a dog . . ."

"I'm doin' no more for you than I would for a hurt dog."

"Lemme rest one minute more," he gasped out, "and then I can get outside. . . ."

"To die?"

"I'll find a . . . a way. . . ." He reeled, and the weight of his body sent them both staggering.

In that moment she brought him through the door. "Now up the stairs. You've got to work for me, and with me, Billy Angel!"

"Lemme rest . . . one minute. . . ."

She let him lean against the wall, his head fallen back, his wounded arm hanging limply, the other loosely over her, pressing close to him with its powerless weight. She could count the beating of his heart, feeble and fluttering, with pauses in the beats. It seemed that mere loss of blood could not so affect him. In that great bulk of muscle and bone there was only the faintest winking light of life, ready to snap out and leave all cold and dark forever. And it must be she, with an uninstructed wisdom, who should cherish that flame and keep it fluttering until it burned up strong again.

"Can you try now, Billy?"

"I'll try now."

"There's one step up." She lifted him with a fearful effort. "No, the other leg . . . the right leg, Billy. Steady. Now another step. Lean on me . . . I'm strong."

"I got to go. . . ."

"In a little while. When you've had half an hour's sleep."

He muttered with a drunken thickness: "That's it . . . a mite of sleep will set me up. . . . I'll . . . I'll sleep here . . . right on the stairs . . . it's good enough."

It meant all his power every moment of that nightmare of a climb—and more than all her strength when he reeled and wavered—which was at every other step. But at last he reached the head of the stairs, and she brought him safely into her room. When she brought him into it, for the first time it seemed to her a mere corner—so small it was. They reached the bed—he slipped from her shoulder, and the bed groaned under his weight. There he lay on his back with his arms cast out clumsily.

Once more there was that look of death in his face.
The eyelids were slightly opened, and the glazed
pupils glimmered with the suggestion of departed
life. Only, as she watched him with dread in her
throat, she saw a faint twitching of his lips. Then she
hurried about the proper bandaging of the wound.
She brought warm water and washed it. Then, with
care, she closed the rough edges of the wound, still
oozing blood. It was no easy task. The great, twisted
muscles of the forearm were as firm and tough as
the thigh of an ordinary man, but she fixed the bandage in place. She had half a bottle of rye whiskey.
She brought it for him and sat on the bed, lifting his
head. His head alone, limp as it was, was a burden.
It seemed a miracle now that she had been able to
support that tottering, wavering bulk of a man. At
last the glass was at his lips, they parted, tasted the
stuff, and then swallowed it down.

Almost immediately a faint flush came into his
face, and then his eyes fluttered open. They looked
blankly up to her. "What's wrong? What's up?" he
asked, half frowning.

"Nothing," she said very softly.

"Nothing wrong? I thought . . . I dreamed . . . all
right, then. I'll sleep. I got work . . . tomorrow. . . ."
He sighed and instantly he was sound asleep.

She watched him for a moment, and then, hearing
the *jingle* of her store bell, she rose hurriedly. She
passed the mirror, and, catching a glimpse of her
face, she found that it still wore a faint smile, half-
wistful, half-contented.

She was wondering at herself as she ran down the
stairs. In the lunchroom she found the last man in
the world she wanted to confront at that moment—
Jack Hopper himself. She wanted to appear perfectly calm, perfectly cheerful, but, instead, she

knew that she had turned white and that she was staring at him.

"I thought," he said stiffly, "that maybe you might need something done . . . for your friend."

"Friend?" she answered. "Why, Jack, I never saw the poor fellow before tonight."

The raising of his eyebrows stopped her. He quivered with a passion of disbelief and of scorn. "He looked pretty bad hurt," said Jack Hopper. "If there was anything that I could do . . ."

"He's gone, Jack. I only kept him here until the sheriff was gone. . . ."

"Billy Angel is gone?" exclaimed the engineer.

"Yes. Right after the sheriff went away . . . and the rest of the boys."

"Did he sneak out the back way?"

"No," she said, lying desperately. "He walked right out the front door. . . ."

He turned a dark red, and she knew, at once, that he must have been keeping a close watch upon that door and that he was certain no Billy Angel had passed that way.

"Well," said Hopper coldly, "I s'pose that there ain't much I can do then?"

"I guess not," she answered, full of wretchedness, and hating Billy Angel with all her heart for the miserable tangle in which he had involved her.

Twice Jack Hopper turned his hat in his hands; twice words came to the verge of his compressed lips. Then—"Good night!" he snapped out at her, and turned on his heel. The closing of the door behind him seemed to the girl the definite act that separated her from the rest of the law-abiding world.

IV

Delirium

She closed the counter for the night now, then she went up to bed. There was a second room in the story above. It was hardly a room. It was rather a mere corner with a cot in it and a bit of cracked glass for a mirror on the wall, with a tiny dormer window peering out over the roof.

There she lay down, but she had hardly closed her eyes when she heard talking in the building. She wakened and sat up, her heart thundering. It was Billy Angel, then, that they had come for. Jack Hopper, after all, had not been able to keep the terrible secret. She hastened to the door of her room in time to hear the speaking again, and this time she made it out as coming from her own chamber. It was a strange voice, raised high one moment, sinking the next, almost like two men in rapid conversation, yet she could tell that there was only one speaker. It was not Sheriff Tom Kitchin. Certainly it was not Jack Hopper, or any other man she knew. Who could it be, then?

She crouched outside the door, listening. She heard the voice rumble on:

"Take the second road and ride along half a mile . . . talk straight to him. Talk like you didn't fear him none. Talk like you expect to get a square deal, and most likely you'll get one. Steady! Steady! Look here, I've come talkin' business, Charlie. Will you hear me? Go to the second house. Throw a stone up through the window. It'll be open. I'll do that."

The voice died with a groan. It was Billy Angel in helpless delirium. In the silence that followed, she strove to unravel the babbling and bring sense out of it, but she strove vainly.

Suddenly the voice resumed: "Now, Charlie, here we are together, and there ain't nobody likely to step in between us."

At this, a chill of deadly apprehension ran through the blood of the girl. For was this not a rehearsal of the murder scene in which he had struck down Charles Ormond? She had a wild desire to turn and flee, a terror lest she should hear him condemn himself with his own mouth.

"A knife, old son, will do the trick as well. A knife is a handy thing. Look what a wolf can do with his teeth. Suppose that he had a tooth as long as this . . . made of steel . . . and with the strength of a man's arm behind it . . . why, Charlie, he'd crawl into the caves of mountain lions and rip their bellies open when they jumped at him. And the best thing is . . . a knife don't make a sound . . . only a whisper when it sinks into you and asks the soul out of you. If you . . ."

There was no need of anything more convincing than this. To have denied his guilt after this would have been utterest blindness, she felt. But, in the meantime, that voice was rising every moment. Murderer though he was, he was helpless, and, moreover, she had gone too far to draw back now.

She must bring back his strength to him if she could, keeping him secretly in her house.

She opened the door and went hastily in. The lamp was turned so low that only a tiny yellow new moon of flame showed and turned the room into a sea of dark, on which bulky shadows rode and stirred with the flickering of the flame. Only the mirror looked back at her with a dim, ghostly face.

On the bed Billy Angel was a black giant. He was humped against the headboard, his chin on his breast, his enormous arms thrown wide. He spoke not a word, but, while she watched him, filled with terror, she saw one great hand rise and fall, and it seemed to the girl that she was watching the knife driven home into the back of dead Charles Ormond.

She wanted to flee then. The company of a dog, even, would have been a treasure, but she must remain there and do the work that lay before her. If his voice were raised again to its last pitch, it would be strange if someone did not hear it as they passed in the street. And if a man's voice were heard in her house at this hour, every man in Derby would come to the rescue with weapon in hand.

She sat on the edge of the bed. The strength of his hurried, uneven panting made a slight tremor run continually through the room. There was no intelligence in the roving of his eyes. It was the blank, wild glare of delirium that had given him for the moment a false strength. That glare became fixed upon her now, and the head of Billy Angel thrust out toward her a little.

"Is it you, Charlie?" he asked loudly. "And are you ready?"

"It's Sue Markham," said the girl, trembling. "Billy Angel, talk soft. They'll hear you in the street!"

"You're not Charlie?"

"No, no."

"You lie!" snarled out Billy Angel. "I've been waitin' a tiresome time, Charlie. But I got you here now, Charlie, and I'm gonna leave you to rot here, in this cave where no man'll ever find you. . . ."

A hand fixed on her arm with a grip like iron; she was drawn slowly inside the reach of his other hand. Billy Angel had begun to laugh like a devil incarnate.

"Now, Charlie," he said, "what you got to say? I have you here. I can break you to pieces like an orange. Where's your strength, Charlie? Have you turned yaller? Has the nerve gone out of you? You're tremblin' like a woman. . . ."

"Billy Angel!" cried the girl. "Don't you hear me?"

"I'll hear you beg like a coward and a sneak and a cur. Will you beg like a dog for your life, Charlie? Will you beg?" His right hand fumbled at her throat. It was a hand of ice, and it brought the chill dread of death into her soul.

"Billy, Billy," she gasped out, "don't kill me!"

His hand fell away. He sank back on the bed. "I knew all the time," he said, "that you was yaller inside." His voice fell to a mumble: "But if you say you're beat . . . you're safe from me this time. Until one day I'll corner you, and make you . . ." The strength crumbled out of him. He fell sidewise on the bed and lay motionlessly.

After that, half reeling with weakness and with relief, she turned up the flame of the lamp. And then she went toward him as one might go toward a sleeping tiger. He was quite unconscious. His hands, she knew, were icy cold, but his head was fiery hot to the touch. A new fear came to her. If she called a physician, she might make sure of helping him from the fever, but would she not certainly be fitting a rope around his neck?

She sat down by the bed to watch, telling herself that only if the delirium returned would she send for the doctor. And there she watched the hours out. It was a broken sleep. Often he stirred and stared and muttered to himself. Once he sat bolt erect and stared at her with terrible eyes, but he sank back again and slept once more.

It was after midnight, well after, before he settled into a quiet slumber, the muscles of his forehead quite relaxed, and his breathing regular. Then she tried his pulse, and found it firmer and more regular. She laid her hand lightly on his face, and it was no longer of such burning heat. So she stole back to her attic room and slept out the remainder of the night.

But there was little sleep in Derby that night. Men had something to think about in the recent murder, and the northwester had settled to a howling demon that wailed and screamed with double force between midnight and morning. With the dawn it sank in force, but it was still whistling fitfully when Sue Markham awakened and looked out her window upon a dull gray sky stretched across with blacker, low-hanging clouds that threatened more snow. With what had already fallen, the hollows were already filled, although the gale had scoured all away from the highlands and the exposed places. All was stark mud, black rocks, or the crusted snow in the hollows. A miserable world to waken into, surely.

She went down to the lunchroom. It was a grisly sight to her. For some reason the squalor of the place had never struck home in her before. Cigarette butts were everywhere, some mere streaks of ashes and black charred places in the wood where the butts had been dropped by careless hands. Others had been fairly ground into the very texture of the floor by wet, heavy heels. There were new smudges on the counter where the thickly oiled jacket sleeves of the trainmen had rested. There were half-washed dishes, too.

Then there was a trip before her to the woodshed, wading through the gripping cold of the morning and through the snow, drifted knee deep behind the fence. As she came back, her arms aching with the weight of wood, she turned her head to the east and looked down to the great valley below her. There was a break in the leaden color of the sky there to the east. There was a streak of shining sun and gentle blue along that eastern horizon, and in the big valley itself was not the sun shining brightly?

No doubt to those dwellers in a better land, looking out from their cozy homes, old Derby Mountain was a pure and a grand picture on this morning, his white cape lower around his shoulders, and with a wreath of smoky clouds around his brow. How little did they know of the miseries of mountain life.

She built the fire in the stove. It sent up first a fume of smoke, until the draft cleared and began to pull on the flames. In the meantime, she jerked all the windows wide, and with the pure wind scouring through the place, she set to work sweeping and scrubbing with might and main, loathing herself for the work that she was compelled to do, hating the world for the fate that it had unjustly bestowed upon her.

Even while she worked, she wondered at herself. This humor had never come upon her before. She had gone cheerfully to the dull beginning of every day. But now, all was sad effort. She told herself, mournfully, that blue days must follow such a night as the last one had been. But that explanation was not satisfactory. Something had been added or subtracted from her existence since yesterday dawned, and she could not yet tell what it was. But was it not, perhaps, the consciousness of the rift that had come in her old friendship with Jack Hopper?

So, half dreamily, half wearily she went to the kitchen and started to cook breakfast.

V

UNCLE PETE TELLS A TALE

But when the water was boiling and the coffee steaming and pouring its thin, piercing fragrance through the room, a joy came back to her. By the time that she had finished setting out the breakfast on the tray, she told herself that this was a game worth playing more than anything she had ever done before in her life.

She bore up the tray to Billy Angel and found him lying, pale and weak, on the bed, hardly able to lift his head while he watched her out of dull eyes.

"Where am I?" he asked. "This ain't the jail."

"This is my room," she told him. "And I'm gonna keep care of you till you can handle yourself."

She expected a tide of protestation to come from him. But he merely turned a dark red and said not a word. He did not even thank her for bringing the breakfast to him, but worked himself slowly up on the pillows and ate the food that was before him. She was half angered, half amused by his pride, and, with the amusement, there was mingled a sting of fear. As she watched his set and gloomy face she told herself, more than ever, that here was a man capable of anything.

She went back to the lunch counter. Already, about the stove, half a dozen laborers in the yards were gathered, blinking sleepily at her. She served their orders in silence, knowing well that men do not wish to talk in the morning when the steel edge of the curse of Adam is eating into their souls.

In the mid-morning, the wind swung sharply around to the southwest again, and in an hour the mountainside was covered with rivulets of water running down from the melting snow. By noon the report had come in that the fugitive had probably escaped. If he had been able to live through the bitterness of the night, he was now far away. For the horses were unable to make any progress through the slippery slush. The sheriff, to be sure, and three helpers were working rather blindly through the mountains, trying to pick up some sign of Billy Angel. But there was little hope of that. All that remained was that some outlying town might catch a glimpse of Angel as he fled toward safety.

Old Pete Allison, tending the fire in the big stove and vainly trying to make himself useful, offered a target for conversation when the breakfast time was done.

"How long'll it take them to catch this Billy Angel?" she said.

"Not for a long time," said Pete Allison. "Folks can't hope to run down a gent like that right off-hand."

"Why not?"

"Well, we all got something comin' to us. Some folks live quiet lives for a short time. But everything is balanced up. God plans it all, I reckon."

A man must be old and must have passed through great sorrows before he can speak of the Creator as

Pete Allison did, with a sort of gloomy surety and understanding.

"But, Pete, think of the men who simply run into a bullet . . . and that's the end of them!"

"Because there wasn't anything left in 'em," declared Pete Allison with conviction. "When you light a candle, it's gonna keep right on burning until the wax is all used up. Same as with a man. The minute he's born, the wax begins to be used up. If the flame burns high, he's gonna die young. If the flame burns slow, he's gonna die old. Or, if there ain't much wax, he'll die soon. If they's a lot of wax, he'll die late."

"But when a bullet hits . . . ?"

"Every bullet," said the old man, "is sent by the Almighty. Dog-goned if He don't direct everything. The sin of the killin' lies with the gent that pulled the trigger, but the death is by the orderin' o' Him." He made these strange pronouncements in a quiet voice, not as one who prophesied, but as one who was acquainted with the facts of the case.

"There was Sam Lever," said the girl. "Never was such a big, strong fellow as Sam. He fell off the cliff last winter. . . ."

"He was ready to die, then. God was done with him. You can't tell by the outsides of a gent. The wax is on the inside. It's the heart and the soul that counts. The wax must have been burned out of Sam Lever without us knowin' it. Look at this here Billy Angel. He's loaded with wax. Maybe he ain't gonna last long, but he'll make a darned bright light while he's burnin'."

"Do you know him, Uncle Pete?" she asked eagerly.

"Ah," said the old man, "you're took a lot with him, ain't you? Girls is like moths. Them that burn with a bright light attract the calico to 'em. No matter whether the flame is red or white. Well, yes, I know Billy Angel."

"What do you know about him?"

"This was ten years back. I had two arms, then, and I was a piece of a man, anyways. I come ridin' down that trail along Old Timber Top . . ."

"You mean the narrow trail?"

"Six inches of rock for a hoss to walk on, and next to that, hell is only two thousand feet away, air line! I come around a elbow turn, with my mule steppin' halfway out into the next world, and I come bang into a kid ridin' a mustang. Says I . . . 'Son, back up your pony.'

" 'It ain't a pony,' says he. 'It's a hoss.'

" 'Back up your hoss,' says I, 'to that wide stretch behind you, where I can pass, and hurry it up. This here mule of mine is gettin' plumb restless.'

" 'This here mustang of mine,' says he, 'don't know how to back up.' And he adds, givin' me a ugly look . . . 'Nor neither do I!'

"I looks this young brat over. He had an eye like a fightin' dog's eye, sort of bright and sad-lookin', as if wonderin' where he would get a whole handful of trouble in the world. He has an old gun strapped onto him, and he begins to play with the butt of it, sort of beggin' me to start some trouble.

" 'Kid,' says I, 'I'll teach your hoss to back up.'

" 'Old man,' says he, 'this here hoss don't take to nobody's teachin' except mine.'

" 'What d'you aim to do?' says I, sort of wonderin'.

" 'Never give no inch to nobody in the world,' says he through his teeth.

"I couldn't help grinning, and, at that, he got white, he got so mad. Nothin' makes a proud kid so mad as not to be took serious.

" 'Do we have to fight about this?' says I to him.

" 'Are you scared to?' he says to me, sneerin'.

" 'Why, you little rat,' says I, gettin' sort of mad, 'hop offen your hoss, so's, when you drop, you ain't sure to splash yourself all over the bottom of that ravine.'

"He just tucks in his chin and laughs at me. And then I seen red. After all, he was man-sized, and he had a man's meanness. I got hot and grabs my gun.

" 'You young fool!' says I, and jerks out my gun. What I mean to say is, that I jerked *at* it. But the front sight caught in the holster and didn't come free. And, quick as a wink, I found myself lookin' straight into the muzzle of a Colt, and that kid's hand was as steady as murder, lemme tell you! I could see myse'f about an inch from kingdom come. Then, he drops his gun back into the holster.

" 'Partner,' says he, as sweet as you please, 'you had a mite of bad luck. I guess that's a new gun.' And, sayin' that, he backs his mustang as slick as a circus rider over a ledge that wasn't fit for the hoss to walk *forward* on. So he comes to the wide place and waits for me to pass.

" 'There ain't no bad feelin's?' I says, goin' past him.

"He gives me a grin as broad as the moon. 'None in the world!' says he, and I knew that he meant it.

"Well, sir, he was a fine-lookin' kid, straight as a young pine, strong as the devil, quick as a lightnin' flash. I never seen a pair of black eyes that looked so straight and had so much fire in 'em. And that was Billy Angel. Ever since then, I been waitin' for an explosion back in the hills. And now it's come."

She listened to this tale with a painful interest, dwelling upon every word of it. "But what else do you know about him?"

"That's all. That's enough. You could live elbow to elbow with a gent for a year and never know as much about him as I found out about Billy Angel in them thirty seconds. After that I knew he was mean and proud enough to fight a army of giants, and kind enough to jump into a river to save a cat that was drownin'. I knew that he was able to burn a town, if he had a spite at the folks in it, or else he was capable of riskin' his life to keep it from burning. That's enough to know. The rest is only that he was an orphan and that he was brung up by his uncle, Ormond."

"But to have killed his own cousin!"

"Girl, I ain't said that he was a good man. I been sayin' that he was a strong one."

"Stabbin' him in the back?"

"That sort of looks like a stickler for me. But, after all, he looked pretty near ready for anything even when he was a kid. He might have turned sort of sour when he growed up. But what I say is that they ain't gonna capture him none too easy. His wax ain't burned out yet."

"Tom Kitchin is a smart man," said the girl tentatively.

"Him? He'll break Tom Kitchin between his fingers . . . like that. Tom Kitchin? He ain't *nothin'* to a gent like that young feller."

Such was the opinion of Pete Allison. And he was not a talkative old man, which gave the more weight to his ideas. As for the girl, she locked up each one of his words in her breast and pored upon his sayings in her spare moments as if they had been Bible talk.

Those spare moments came few and far between to her. In the days that followed she was extraordinarily busy. For work is slowly accomplished when half of one's mind is on something else, and that was the case with Sue Markham. She could not help thinking of her gigantic protégé in the room upstairs—her own room, brightly touched up with color here and there, an incongruous setting for huge Billy Angel.

For three days he did not seem to gain at all. He grew actually thinner in the face. But then he changed. Every hour, almost, made an alteration in him for the better.

In those days, she found that she was not taking a single step toward a better understanding of him. When she came into the room, he did not speak, and he answered her direct questions with monosyllables. He took the food that she gave him without thanks. He refused the books that she brought to him to pass away the long hours of his imprisonment. Instead, he seemed to prefer to lie flat on his back, staring at the ceiling.

What thoughts went through his mind at such times as these? In the dull, weary hours of the day, was he determining to leave the course of lawbreaking on which he had embarked, or was he resolving more wickedness? In spite of herself, she could not help feeling that the latter was the truth. Silence is always more or less dreadful, and his silences seemed particularly so. She never went through the door into that room without a paling of her cheeks and a quickening of her heart, as though she were stepping into a tiger's lair. A dozen times, when she passed the cheerful face of Tom Kitchin or the thoughtful one of Jack Hopper, the engineer, she was on the verge of calling in the law to take this ominous care off her hands.

Then all her fears were redoubled by a most strange happening.

VI

SUE RECEIVES HOMAGE

Steve Carney returned to town. Steve was the brightest star in the village of Derby. His father had been a fireman of long standing whose wits were a little too dull for him to advance to the trusted post of engineer in charge of a train. However, he was a man full of honest labor, and to the day of his death he had a great compensation for his own lack of brains, and that was the surpassing intelligence of his son, young Steven. In the school, Steve stood at the head of his class, and, when he had finished the grammar school's eight terms, he went on to high school, and, when high school was ended, it was the plan of the honest fireman to send Steve to college. For that purpose he had saved a considerable sum of money, but, in the very summer after the boy's graduation, the father died—a death brought on, to some extent, by the wretched life to which he had condemned himself in order to lay by the more money for the sake of his son.

When that money came into the hands of Steve himself, he decided that he would take the rest of his education by a short cut in the ways of the world.

He left Derby, therefore, in the beginning of his eighteenth year and was gone nearly a twelvemonth, at the end of which time he returned somewhat out at elbow but with a new light in his eyes. The very first night after his arrival, falling into a poker game, he walked away with all the money in the party, and the town of Derby was forced to admit that Steve's year of education had been by no means wasted. The admirable Steven then remained only a short time in Derby in order, as the old stories have it, to recruit his spirits, before adventuring further.

But when he had renewed his depleted stock of money and when he had engaged in a knife fight and a gunfight, in both of which he came out unscathed, something prompted him to leave Derby for parts unknown. He left half an hour after a band of determined men with shotguns under their arms and with lariats handy for various uses called at the door of his father's shack, which Steve had inherited, of course. He was not seen in town again for another year, and this time, when he returned, it was in a condition that made men forget his errors of the previous visit. Money flowed like water from his hands, and he brought a warmth of good cheer with him that penetrated to the farthest limits of the town.

He remained a mere fortnight, and then left as suddenly as he had come. Two years later he was back, this time out at elbow again, with a leaner, harder face, but still with an air of deathless, boyish good nature in his eyes. Even men who shook their heads at him could not but admire him. He stayed in Derby on this occasion long enough to join the sheriff—Tom Kitchin, serving his first term—and run to earth those famous Greening brothers, whose atrocious murders had terrorized the mountains for two years. In their capture, the quick gun and the steady aim and the cool courage of young Steven Carney had taken the leading part, as even the sheriff was the first to admit. Then, after a profitable evening of poker, Steve was away again.

He was gone for a year and a half, and now, at last, he came back, and the noise of his coming was the first news that greeted the ears of Sue Markham when she came down in the morning to clean up the lunch counter and build the fire in the stove.

"He got in around midnight," said Pete Allison, stretching his one hand toward the humming stove.

"Who got in?" asked the girl.

"But he woke up some of the boys and they had a powwow together."

"Who was it, Pete?"

"He's been around a good bit of the world this time," declared the old man, still disregarding her direct question in an irritating fashion. "This time he took a drop out into the ocean. He's seen Samoa. He's seen New Zealand. He's been over to the Solomons, too. Lookin' mighty brown and thin, but handsome and clever as ever."

"Pete Allison, who might you be talkin' about?"

"Wonder to me," said Pete Allison, "that nobody don't marry him. He's the sort that turns the heads of the girls. I guess he ain't found a nobody yet with money enough to suit him. And he'd take a pretty rich one to bring him more money'n he could spend, I reckon."

"Ah," murmured the girl, "you're talking about Steve Carney."

"Who else? You look like you'd sort of be glad to see him ag'in?" queried Allison sharply.

"He'd never remember me," she said, and blushed.

"There it is, there it is!" The veteran sighed. "He

ain't been hung yet, and so all the girls is anxious to throw themselves at his head. If he was an honest clerk in an office, or if he was a conductor on a train, or an engineer takin' Two Forty-Nine over the grade every other day, would they be settin' their caps at him so much? Not they. But he's all afire, and he's all a-burnin' up, so the girls can see him, and bust their hearts out to get to him and burn their wings on the flame."

"Nonsense," said the girl haughtily. "I've looked twice at him . . . and I never will!"

Pete Allison shook his head. He added: "They say that Steve has a roll of bills that would make a meal for a cow."

Steve himself came into the lunch counter at noon. He sat on a stool with his hat pushed back on his head and his mischievous blue eyes laughing at her. And when she asked after his travels, he told her absurd fables.

"What's in the Solomon Islands, Steve?" she asked him.

"They got their name after the king of them. He's an old bronco with a bald head and a white beard that comes down to the fat wrinkles in his waist."

"Wrinkles in his waist?" she cried.

"He's bare to his middle," said Steve Carney. "And he looks so much like Solomon must have looked that people call him King Solomon and the islands are the Solomon Islands."

"Steve Carney!" she exclaimed. "What a thing to say! But what sort of people are there on the islands, really?"

"Cannibals, mostly."

"Steve!" She threw up her hands, and he grinned and chuckled at her. "I don't believe that you were ever near the islands," she declared.

"I was, though. The king and me was pals."

"Did you really know him?"

"Of course I did. He gave me this for a souvenir the day I left." He pulled out a long knife with a blade of beautiful steel, worked into wavy curves, a marvelous and a dreadful weapon. It was fitted with a hilt of antique gold work and set with a multitude of small pearls to roughen the handle.

"Why, it must be worth a lot, Steve."

"He would've given me more than that. He wanted to give me a couple of his wives, Sue. All I would have to do the rest of my life was to lie on the flat of my back under a palm tree while one wife waved the flies away with a branch and the other fed me coconuts."

"Every word is made up. Why should he want to do so much for you?"

"Because I brought in more than any missionary ever did."

"You mean you gave him something?"

"Yep. Something that keeps all the natives busy every evening."

"What was it?"

"Dice," said the incorrigible.

They laughed together over this.

"Did you like it?"

"It was a good place to swim," said Steve thoughtfully. "But I got lonely there."

"You're never lonely, Steve. You make company wherever you go. I've heard a hundred men say that."

"Men are the small half of things, Sue. I was lonely for a girl, d'you see? A girl back here in the mountains."

She was hushed with interest. One did not readily imagine the unconquerable Steve Carney falling in love. It was very, very strange. She lowered her voice as she asked: "Does she live near Derby?"

He thought a moment: "Pretty near," he said at last, nodding.

"Steve! Do I know her?"

"I think you do, pretty well."

"But what's her name, Steve?"

"Sort of an ordinary name. It's Sue."

She started; she stared. But no, this could not be, and his blue eye was fastened upon her with a perfect indifference, a perfect gravity.

"Really? Sue? I don't know anybody else by that name, I think. What's her last name, Steve?"

"Her last name is Markham."

"Stupid!" she cried, growing very red. "I was an idiot not to see . . . you'll never stop your joking, Steve!"

"Does it sound like a joke?"

"A mighty poor one."

"Ah," he said, "*I* think it's a mighty poor joke. But if you'd take it more serious and sort of let it trickle into the insides of you . . . would it be so bad?"

He made no effort to touch her, or even to lean closer to her. There was nothing of the melted calf in his eyes. They were as bright, as cold, as blue as ever. But all of the sardonic mirth was gone from around his mouth. He became, for the moment, nothing of the mischievous boy, but all man, eager, purposeful.

"I've only seen you a few times, Sue," he said. "And still we know each other pretty well, I guess. I know you. God understands that there ain't much that's hard to read in you. It's all clear as a crystal. And you know one half of me. The whole world does. That's the bad half. I never sneaked behind corners and tried to hide myself. I let them see me the way that I am. Well, Sue, there's something in me besides the fool and the cardsharper. I've been playing, you understand? While Dad was living, I had to work hard for him. He wanted to see me get on. He wanted to see me advance a lot. He wanted to see me talk book English and lead my classes and get to be a lawyer or something indoors and soft-handed, like that. His idea of a gentleman was spats and a cane.

"Well, I swallered what was really in me till he died. Then it all busted out. I didn't even know that it was there. But I would have exploded, I think. I had to break loose. I *did* break loose. I've been runnin' around ever since. Well, finally I'm through with my fling. I've made a little pile. A good many thousands, Sue. I got it here with me. Someday I want you to count it. I got enough here to settle down to some kind of business. I don't care what, so long as it keeps me up here in the mountains, you see? Y'understand, Sue? I don't want you to say a thing now. But if you don't mind, put this thought in your pocket and, when I'm gone, take it out and look it over. Maybe you'll take it more serious. Then in a couple of days, I'll come back and talk to you again. Most likely you'll say . . . 'It's a bad idea, I'm afraid. I could never love you, Steve.' Well, I'll not cry. But whatever happens, I know that you ain't gonna laugh at me or talk about me behind my back. That's why I could come straight to you and talk out without no dodging around corners. I'd hate to do that. A fellow has to do what they want. He has to laugh when they want to laugh. He has to dance when they want to dance, and sit down when they want to sit. He pleases them till he gets 'em under lock and key, and, after that, *they* got to do the steppin' around. But, Sue, if you was ever to come into my house, you and me would be partners fair and square. Well, so long."

He stood up; he raised his hat. But presently he came back from the door to where she was tracing invisible patterns on the surface of the counter with the tip of her finger.

"About the way that I've been roaming around," he said. "I've done some pretty bad things. The money I've got in my pocket is gambled money. But I've taken my chances fair and square. I've never beat a man out of a penny with crooked cards, no matter what they say about me. And, Sue, if you was to ask me, serious, I'd tell you every step I've taken since I first left Derby . . . every step!"

With that, he walked out of the lunch counter and was whistling and turning up the collar of his coat as she watched him dimly through the frosted windowpane working his way down the street against a half gale.

He was gone, but his work remained behind him. It seemed to the girl that the four walls of the room had been broken out, and that her eye now roamed across the world through a vast perspective, seeing all things clearly, heart and body and soul. She roamed in spirit as Steve Carney had roamed. She did not know whether or not she loved him; she *did* know that his frank homage made her feel like a queen.

VII

INGRATITUDE

In such times, women cannot think. They can only pass pictures through their minds, and compare them, feature by feature. So it was with Sue Markham. The keen, handsome face of Steven Carney she kept, as it were, in the one eye, and the dark and honest countenance of Jack Hopper arose in the other. But Jack Hopper could maintain that comparison for a very instant only. Then he faded, truly, into nothingness, and never again could his eyes trouble the eyes of Sue.

She knew it with a little shudder. For Jack Hopper, during these recent years, had been looming larger and larger upon her mental horizon, walking big upon her mind, like a figure with a low sun behind it. He had cast the shadow of his presence about her feet like fate, and she had been on the point of surrendering to him, not because she loved him, but because she felt, oddly, that he deserved this and more—that she was honored unduly by the love of such a man. He had a right to a good home. If he chose her to make it, she must not resist his will. For six months, now, she had known that, if he asked her to be his wife, she would have to say yes. She had never seen him without the dread of that approaching moment falling upon her.

But now the danger was gone. Jack Hopper did not exist, and the fire in the clear, steady eyes of the gambler was the thing that had banished him. For that, she was grateful to Steven. She cast about her for a second figure by which she should compare Steve Carney with that which her soul demanded of a man. And of all the scores who had met her and known her and flirted with her, some gaily, some sadly, some sternly, there was only one, she found, who had stepped far enough past the gates of her heart to be worth the counting. To her own astonishment, it was the face and the form of Billy Angel who arose in her mind's eye, now, to be contrasted, little by little, with Steve Carney himself. It was the big man who lay in her room at this very moment.

It staggered her, this revelation of herself. It was as though she had turned the corner of a familiar street and found that a palace or a pit was revealed in the well-known path before her. So was it to Sue Markham, finding this unsuspected thing in herself.

Yes, there was Billy Angel strongly entrenched in her imagination. His bold, black eyes looked keenly back to her, looked cruelly back to her, looked with a scorn and with a mockery, so it seemed, that made a little flush of anger rise to her face. It could not be, indeed. She could never seriously consider this brute.

Yet, in spite of herself, she must. She closed her eyes. If Billy Angel had sat before her at the counter and spoken to her as Steven Carney had done, what would she have answered? She could not tell. But of this she was certain, that she could not have maintained perfect silence, as she had done with Steve. She would have been too much afraid of him.

She went up to her room to see the man face to face, and to convince herself that there was nothing god-like about him—that there was only a great physical strength in the man—that and no more. When she entered, she found that he was seated before her mirror, shaving himself. By that, she knew that he had been prying through her effects until he had come, at last, to the little old chest in the closet where the last mementoes of her father were kept and, among other things, this old, horn-handled razor.

She flushed and bit her lip with shame and anger. As though, indeed, the search of Billy Angel could have revealed something shameful concerning herself—as though that search of his hands could have given him too great an insight into the hidden corners of her very mind.

He was only half shaven. He turned to her, looked at her in silence, and then faced the glass again, intent upon his work. It was as though she were not in the room! There was no apology for the thing that he had done, unforgivable and crude as that had been. He took it for granted—took everything for granted—as he had done since the first moment when she brought him to succor.

She had read, somewhere, of kings who performed their very toilet in public—to whose dressing and undressing great nobles lent their reverent attention and their silent interest. The big-backed man in front of the mirror was like that. He proceeded with his work as though there were nothing better or more absorbingly worthwhile for her to do than to stand patiently by and watch him.

She flushed again; again she bit her lip. He was humming as he worked. Then he paused to wipe some of the lather from the razor blade on a bit of paper. Without turning to her, he said: "D'you know that song?"

"I never heard it before."

"Sam Curran brought it up from Mexico. I dunno what it means, either. But it's a funny lingo, eh? And a funny tune."

She had never seen him so gay and so communicative. *Now,* she thought to herself, *I shall draw from him all of the colors out of which I shall draw a picture of him so black that I shall never again be troubled comparing him with that wild and knightly spirit, Steven Carney!* "What Curran is that?" she asked.

"You must have heard of him. He was pretty well known, I guess, before he died."

"How did he die?"

"Hank Lang got him in a wheat field down in the valley and killed him with a load of buckshot. You remember?"

"I remember. Did you know him, Billy?"

"Know him? I'd tell a man. He was a friend of mine. He taught me how to use a knife." With that, he puffed out his upper lip, and began the critical work of running the razor edge over the curved, stiff surface. But all her blood had turned to ice. That he should have dared to mention such a thing—he the murderer—he the man who had stabbed the son of his benefactor in the back with a knife!

"Curran," she said, "murdered Chuck Marshall?"

The big man nodded. His answer was half stifled, for the shaving still went on. Nothing could have been more noncommittal than his tone. "He done it on a bet. It was easy, I guess."

She went to the window and looked out. She dared not face this man for fear some of her anger and her disgust should appear in her eyes. So she looked forth upon the world, playing with the string of the window shade and aware that Billy Angel had cleansed the blade of the razor again and that he was now stropping it upon the large, pale palm of his hand. How white it seemed—how soft. Yet she knew that hand could be iron, filled with the strength of a giant. And the old fear thrilled through her, the half terrible, half delightful fear.

"Billy Angel!" she cried. And she whipped around upon him. He did not turn. Only, in the mirror, she could see him lift his lordly brows a little.

"Well?" he said.

She swallowed her fury. "Nothing," she said, and turned hastily back to the window.

Now, in a stroke, he finished the shaving. He had been going slowly ahead with it, the moment before. Each bit of the work had seemed to require the utmost care and patience. It had been like sculptor's work when the outer shell of stone is off, and he is working near the very flesh of his subject. But now, at his will, without the slightest hurry, but with a certain large ease, the shaving was finished—in a gesture, so to speak.

He dipped the end of his towel in the pail of water and began to cleanse his face. She had seen him, recently, only through a blackening stubble of whiskers, but now she saw his real self. How like a very god of beauty the man was! Sickness and weakness had refined the lines of his countenance. All was largely and yet precisely drawn. No, compared with this fellow, so far as the mere looks went, Steve Carney did not exist.

"You was aimin' to tell me something," said Billy Angel.

"Nothing."

"I heard you start. You was peeved about something."

"I? Not at all!"

"Well," he said, "all right. I ain't curious."

"You're not fit to get out of bed like this," she told him.

"What I'm not fit for don't count," he told her. "What I got to do is the important thing."

"Such as what?"

"Nothin' but leavin' this house today."

"Billy Angel!"

"Well?"

"You . . . why, it's turning to a storm today."

"Is it? That's no matter."

"Leave this house?"

"I said that."

"For what?"

"A little job that needs doin', that's all."

"Billy, are you crazy? You . . . you can hardly walk!"

"I can walk fine," he told her calmly.

"Let me see you, then."

"Proof, eh?"

"Yes. I dare you to walk across the room . . . without staggering. I dare you to walk straight across the room!"

He shook his head, smiling, and then a little shadow of perversity crossed his face. "Why," he said, "I'll do it, then." He paused for a moment, serious, almost abstracted, and she could almost feel the effort by which he gathered his will, and with that will controlled and summoned the strength of his body. After that, he stood up from the chair, walked with a light step across the room, and stood above her. She was amazed. It was, indeed, like a work of enchantment.

"Now," he said, "what's been worryin' you?"

"Nothing, Billy."

"Speak out true," he commanded. When she turned from him, shaking her head, he took her by the shoulder and made her confront him again. Once again, her anger flamed furiously, and once again, and as always, the anger turned cold in fear. "You come here to say something. You busted in like you had something on your mind."

"I wondered, after I came in, how you happened to find Dad's razor."

"I seen his box . . . I opened it, and I got what I needed. But that ain't what I asked."

"Why . . . there was only a bit of news, I thought you might like to know."

"What's that? Has anything been found out?"

"About you?"

"No, no! Not about me. God knows that I don't matter. But about . . . well, nothing."

Here was a new sidelight thrown upon his mind, and it fairly dazzled her by all of its connotations. There was something, then, in spite of his nature that seemed so purely self-centered that had actually responded to the troubles of another. There was something in this world that he valued more than he valued the safety and the comfort of himself. She would not have believed it from any other lips.

"There's no news about you," she said slowly, and wondering at him.

"Well, well," he said, sighing. "About what, then?" He lowered himself into the chair beside the window. The power in his legs seemed to have gone, first of all. He had gripped the back of the chair with his large hand, and so, the floor creaking under his weight, he had lowered himself to the seat.

She could realize, now, by exactly what an immense effort of the will he had been able to bring himself to do this thing. By such an effort did men rise from the cockpit and rush to work the guns of a sinking battleship. By such an effort the dying avoided death!

"Why," said the girl, with a thrill of admiration and of disarming pity creeping through her, "I only thought that you'd be glad to know that Steve Carney is back. But maybe you don't even know him."

"I know him. Yes, I've heard of Steve Carney."

"He's come back rich, they say."

"Ah?"

"D'you know him well enough to really care?"

"They's money in cards," said the big man grimly. "More money than there is in dynamite . . . or in guns, I guess. How much did he get this time? Do you know?"

"Enough to buy a ranch and fix it up in style. Enough to marry and settle down . . . they say."

"Enough to marry?" said Billy Angel. "Well, for a gent like Steve Carney I s'pose that's quite a lot."

"His poor dad," she said, hastily turning the question, "it's a good thing that he's not alive to see what Steve has become. I remember how he used to stand there . . ."

"Is that little shack . . . the Carney cottage?"

"Of course."

"Well," said the other, and, turning his back on her, he rose, struggled feebly across the room, and lay down on the bed—rather, he fell along with the crash.

She ran to him, filled with terror. "Billy Angel!"

He did not answer her. His face was perfectly white. Utter exhaustion had taken all the blood from it and left him a deadly mask to look upon.

"Billy, do you hear me?"

He made a little gesture with his hand, as though to signify that he heard her, but that he did not wish to be disturbed at this moment.

"Can I get you anything?"

He shook his head a little. "I'm comin' through fine. Only . . . don't bother me now. Lemme be alone in peace."

Such an answer for her kindness. She flung out of the room, but at the door she paused again. No, no matter what happened to him, she would not waste further time and further thought upon such a brute. But when she was downstairs again, her soul melted suddenly. She filled a cup of hot black coffee—it was the dregs of the pot—the sort of coffee that he liked—a brew that would have taken the lining from the throat of an ordinary man. Up the stairs she scurried with the cup until she reached the door of her room, and tried the knob. It was locked!

"Billy!" she called guardedly.

But there was not a sound from the room.

VIII

STRANGE PROCEEDINGS

In the first moment of panic, she felt sure that he had
collapsed along the floor—after locking the door.
Perhaps at that very moment he was dead, for he
was very weak—terribly weak. Nothing but the
most dauntless strength of mind had enabled him to
rise from the bed and do such a simple thing as
shave himself. The blood he had lost from the
wound in his arm had been a far more vital drain
than she had dreamed.

Yet, as she stood there, balancing in her mind
pity for him and fear, there was almost an equal fire
of anger in her. How had he dared to treat her as he
had done, as though she were simply an unneces-
sary encumbrance upon him. She reviewed, little
by little, his actions since she had entered his room
that morning, and she found them all equally intol-
erable. A devil either of impudence or of brutality
possessed the man. Only one genial recollection remained of him, and that was the manner in which
he had vigorously protested and even resisted with
all of his dying strength, when she had first told
him that he must stay with her until he was healed.

What he had said then, however, seemed like a voice from the grave. The living reality of him spoke in far other terms.

In the meantime, there was nothing to do but let him have his own way. If he chose to remain there with the door locked, through some idiotic notion of the brain, she would let him be. Hunger, before long, would make him set wide the door.

Several hours, however, passed, and there was no sign from him. Then she went up to the door again and pounded upon it. There was no answer. Or if there were one, it was so faint that it was lost in the steady roaring of the rain. A southeast wind had brought the rain in the mid-morning, and since that time it had increased momently, falling as only mountain rains can fall. That is to say, it came bucketing down in headlong torrents, one moment; the next, the wind seemed to have eddied to another and opposite point of the compass from which it threw a spray, driving and stinging.

Or, again, the rain rushed down in immense, horizontal drifts, each smashing against the roofs of the town with thunder, then walking away and leaving a moment of comparative silence before the next crashing downpour. The girl listened for a time to the steady progress of this walking storm. But still there was not a murmur from the room. She even squinted through the keyhole, but all she could see, at the farther side of the room, was a flashing bit of the mirror, with nothing before it. She put her ear to the rather deep crack at the bottom of the door. She could hear nothing except the strange and ghostly echoes that the rain sent to and fro in the chamber within, like wandering, senseless steps.

She went down to the main floor of the building,

again, full of trouble. This convinced her that, in spite of herself, she cared a great deal for this Billy Angel. For the sake of the work and the care that she had invested in him, if for no other reason—and she vowed to herself that there could be no other reason—she could not see him cast away without a pang. And the two images had never left her from the early morning. She saw the faces sharply contrasted—the gambler and the alleged murderer. Although all her reason told her that there was no comparison between Steve Carney and this wild man out of the mountains, yet she knew that he had as great a grip upon her as Carney himself. The more she strove to argue herself out of this emotion, the deeper it settled in her.

There was no pause in the rain. Instead, it actually increased, dropping in thick torrents that penciled the air with even lines of gray and turned midday into deepest twilight. When the mist was rubbed from the windows, she looked out upon mountains from which every vestige of the snow was gone. From the windows of the nearest house, she saw the yellow shining of the lamps.

There were half a dozen people in the room, not lunchers, but gossips gathered around the stove— and then the next crash struck Derby. Trouble was about this month. The announcer of this stroke of misfortune was none other than Steven Carney. He came quietly into the lunchroom. One hand was wrapped in his handkerchief. He had a faint little smile on his lips. But his eyes were brilliant with a threatening light.

"Partners," he said in his quiet way, but with his glance going over them swiftly and steadily, "is there anybody here that knows a tall fellow . . .

about six feet three . . . with shoulders big enough for two . . . a fast man with a gun . . . with a very pale face and a sort of a sick look about him?"

"Billy Angel!" cried Sue Markham, the words bursting from her lips of their own force.

"Ah," said Steve. "You know him, Sue?"

"Billy Angel!" cried the others, getting their breath again.

"What about him?" asked Steve Carney.

"He's the man who murdered Charlie Ormond!"

"Murdered?" repeated Carney, lifting his brows a little.

"Stabbed him in the back!"

"It's not the same man, then. This gent don't have to stab in the back. He stood up to me and beat me to the draw . . . and, when he might've sent a slug of lead through my head, he simply shot the gun out of my hand!" He raised his bandaged hand, spotted with significant red. "Then," he added, "he cleaned me out. What I want to know is . . . where can I find him? I want another word with him. My hand ain't hurt too bad to handle a gun right now."

"He robbed you, Steve?" cried the girl.

"Clean as a whistle," said Steve Carney. He set his teeth, but still he forced himself to smile at her.

"The sheriff will be a wild man when he hears about this," said someone. "Get Tom Kitchin now. Tom will nab him . . . he can't get far away through all of this mud."

Three or four hurried out to find Tom Kitchin. The rest drew in a close group around Steve Carney to inquire after more details of the affair. He told them smoothly, without undue excitement.

"I was trying to fix a lamp so's I could read by it . . . the morning was so dark. Something stepped into my doorway. I looked up and seen this big fellow that you call Billy Angel. A fine-looking man, I'll tell you! He nodded to me.

" 'You're Steve Carney?' he says to me.

" 'I'm Carney,' says I. 'Who might you be, stranger?'

" 'The rest of 'em,' says he, 'will tell you my name afterward, if there's any afterwards for you, Carney. I rather doubt it.'

" 'You've got a grudge ag'in' me?' says I.

" 'Ag'in' your pocketbook,' says he. 'I hear it's pretty fat.'

" 'Robbery, then?' says I, and I looked across the room where my gun was hanging on the wall . . . no more use to me than if it had been a hoe. He seen where I'd looked.

" 'This'll be a fair break for you, Carney,' says he. 'You've got your money by crooked cards.'

" 'That's a lie,' says I, making a jump for him.

" 'Maybe so,' says he, flashing a weapon on me. 'I'm here to let my gun do the talkin' for me. Not to argue a point with you. This is a fairer break than you ever give anybody with your cards. Go get your gun. We'll fight fair.'

"He says this with the chimin' of the clock in the McGoortys' house just bustin' in once to say the half hour. I went over to the wall and got my gun out of the holster. I figgered on what my chance would be in makin' a quick turn and tryin' a snap shot at him. But somehow I figgered out that it wouldn't be no use. He looked like the kind that ain't took by surprise easy. I turned around to him.

" 'Are you ready?' says I.

" 'We heard that clock strike pretty clear,' says he. 'We'll wait till it strikes the hour. At the first noise of it, you're free to blaze away, son.'

"He says that, and then he slides down into a

chair and lets his head fall back against the wall. His eyes was half closed. He looked pretty sick, just then. His face got whiter, too. I wouldn't've been surprised if he'd fainted. I sat down opposite him. So long as he wanted to fight fair, when he could've sent a bullet through my back plumb easy a little while back, there wasn't anything for me to do except to stand pat and give him his second chance at me, with an even break.

"That half hour took as long in rolling by as though it had been half a year. Ten times I thought it was strikin', and ten times I made a pass for my gun, but Billy Angel, if that's his name, he didn't pay no attention. He just lay there in his chair, watchin' me with a sick sort of a smile, not sayin' a word, with his eyes only a slit open. Mighty weak and flabby was how he looked just then.

"Then the clock struck, and the sound of it sort of gave me a shock, I can tell you. I jerked out my gun. I'm not slow on a draw. I spend my time practicing the same as most of you boys do, and I've never left off that practice no matter where in the world I might be. But I had no choice ag'in' him. I might as well tell you plain and frank . . . he beat me to the draw as easy as I'd snap my fingers. And when he shot, he shot at the gun in my hand, not at me. It knocked the gun clean across the room.

" 'I certainly do hope I ain't smashed up your hand,' he says as cool as the devil.

"I looked down and seen that there was only a small cut between the thumb and the forefinger.

" 'I'm all right,' says I.

" 'You can hand over your wallet, then,' says he.

"I gave it to him.

" 'Now,' says he, 'there's two things left for me to do. One is that I can tie you hand and foot so's you can't move, and the other is for you to give me your word that you won't make a move out of this shack for five minutes.'

"It sort of took me back, hearin' him talk about trusting me.

" 'Do you mean that?' I says.

" 'I mean it,' says he.

" 'Well, then,' says I, 'I don't hanker to be tied up like a chicken for market. I'll give you my word.'

"I took out a watch and laid it on the table.

" 'All right,' says he. 'In five minutes you can raise a noise. That's all I need for fadin' away.'

"And that was the way he left me. Except that, when he started away through the mud, it seemed to me that he sort of wobbled a mite, as though he found the goin' pretty hard for him. If that's Billy Angel, I'll lay you a hundred dollars to a nickel that he's been sick pretty recent."

Such was the narrative of the gambler, concluded just as the sheriff rushed into the room. He went straight to Carney. "Is this true, Steve?" he asked. "Is this true, that that devil, Billy Angel, went in and cleaned you out?"

"As true as I'm standing here."

"We'll have him in half an hour!" cried the sheriff. "He can't have gotten far. Boys, are you with me?"

They were already in their slickers. Now they stormed out of the room behind the sheriff. In the street they were joined by other voices. The whole town was up to apprehend the criminal. And the girl remained alone, listening, again, to the rain. It would not have been difficult, after all, she decided. Angel had simply climbed out of the window and then down the roof over the kitchen until he could drop from the lower edge of it to the ground. She must get into the room and make sure. She took a hammer and ran up the stairs, determined to batter in the lock to her door, but when she laid her hand upon the knob, it yielded at once, and, stepping into the room, she found Billy Angel in person stretched upon her bed.

IX

IMPOTENT FURY

Impulses of rage and of scorn rushed through her brain so fast that she could not act upon one of them. First she decided to denounce him to his face. Then she was of a mind to run down the stairs and call back the men of Derby to come at once and capture the fellow. After that, she decided to get only one man, Steven Carney himself, to come to the room and destroy the villain.

No, for one man could not do it. She realized, looking down on him, that even limp and weak as he was, he was dangerous, and the steady black eyes looked up to her now without a trace of emotion. He showed neither shame nor remorse. His color, which was a very sick white, did not alter in the least. At this, something of awe came over her.

"Billy Angel," she said to him, "you've robbed my friend, Steve Carney."

He nodded.

"You've robbed him because *I* told you that he had money!"

He nodded again, and his complaisance infuriated her.

"Why don't I call them up here to take you? I *shall* call them in." She turned toward the door.

"Nope," he said, "I guess that you won't call 'em in."

She turned back to hear his reasons. "Why not? I've treated you like a brother. And now you turn on me like a . . . like a traitor! What keeps me from turning you over to the law?"

"About three things, I figger," he said.

"Really? What three, if you please!"

"First, because it would mean a lot of shootin' and bloodshed, and this here furniture would get pretty badly spoiled . . . that's the reason."

"It's no reason at all!"

"Then you ain't so anxious to have folks know that you been takin' care of a murderer all these days."

"Ah, coward!" she cried. "Do you count on my shame and take advantage of that?"

"I take advantage of anything," he said, watching her without emotion. "The third thing is that you've sort of a kindly feeling to me, in spite of what you say."

She was paralyzed with fury. It is odd that one should guard the emotions as such sacred things. It is pleasant to reveal them oneself; it is hideous sacrilege to have them revealed by another. That he should have discovered her weakness for him immediately wiped out any virtue that he might have. She told herself in a white rage that she hated him and everything about him. So, staring at him for an instant, wide-eyed, she hesitated, trying to find words. Words would not do, she decided. She whirled to the door, but, as she reached it, a long arm, thick with muscle stretched before it. Her rush carried her against it. It was like striking against a wall. In some mysterious manner he had managed to slip from the bed and reach the door in a single leap. A noiseless movement, like a cat's.

"Let me go!" she cried.

He brushed her back, gently, irresistibly. He closed the door behind him, locked it, and took out the key, which he dropped in his pocket.

"I'll shout out the window," she assured him, her voice low and earnest with her passion.

"Would they hear you through the rain?" he asked her.

"I'll . . . I'll . . ."

"Well?"

That terse, unsympathetic word broke down all of her strength, for like a rush of light it revealed to her perfectly her own impotence. She broke into tears and leaned against the wall with her face cupped in her hands.

"All right," he said. "I was sort of worried for a moment."

She heard a *jingle* on the floor. Then he recrossed the room and, reaching the bed, lay down on it. She discovered that he had thrown the key at her feet. It bewildered her. Why he should have thrust her back from the door one instant, and the next presented to her the means of leaving the room at her will, was most strange. It was as though he had dared to look into her heart once more and had seen that there was nothing remaining to be feared in her.

And she, looking inward into her soul of souls, saw that he was right. Her fury had changed to sorrow that any man could so repay good with evil as he had repaid her. That the very friend she had pointed out to him should have been selected as the next prey, and that then he should have had the effrontery to return to her very room for shelter!

She had no longer the sharp fury at her command that could make her betray even this evildoer. He had seen it. Perhaps her very tears had been enough to reveal to him all that he cared to know. She looked across at him as he lay stretched on the bed. Wonder and hatred and awe and grief were mingled so inextricably in her mind that she could only snatch up the key and flee from the room. Before she went down, she stood at a window and let the cold, wet air blow in upon her face. Then she went down.

Of course, Billy Angel had not been found, and the trail that had been picked up from the shack of Steven Carney had merely led back into the town, a strange thing that dumbfounded everyone. For, with only five minutes to escape before the alarm was raised, certainly it seemed that every minute was very precious to him and he would try to put a mile between him and the pursuit in that interval. However, as Steve Carney himself suggested, that move back into the village was a mere feint. The instant he was out of sight he had doubled back for the hills. Yet there were some incredulous ones who swore that someone in the village must be playing the friend to Billy Angel and shielding him from discovery.

The sheriff was a desperate man. Never before in his reign had the law been so openly defied. He made the lunchroom of pretty Sue Markham the center. Beginning there, he searched every house in the town for the person of the ruffian. Through every nook they passed, and through every cellar, every garret, and every closet, and every shed, barn, and lean-to. But there was not a sign of big Billy Angel. They came back wet with the rain, chilled with wet and wind, utterly downhearted.

"Well," said the sheriff, and he stood steaming in front of Sue Markham's stove, "he ain't in Derby. That's pretty clear, I guess."

"Have you searched every house?" asked someone.

"Every house in town."

Jack Hopper stood out from a corner, where he had stood gloomily silent. He raised his head. "Every house except this one," he suggested.

The sheriff merely tilted his head and laughed.

Never in the world was there such music to the ears of Sue as in that laughter.

"If Sue," the sheriff said, "wants to keep a man-killer hid, I guess that we'll let her do it. She'd have better reasons for it than we'd have for hangin' him."

He grinned at Sue to give a point to his jest. Half an hour later, he and the others were working through the country around the town, having ridden off with such a terrible zest and eagerness that she almost feared that on the broad, wild breast of the mountain they might find their man—as though he could exist both there and in her room at the same time.

All the rest of the day they labored. And when the evening came, they were still working in the distance when Steve Carney himself came into the lunch counter.

"Steve!" she gasped out at him. "They've found Billy Angel, then?"

"Found Angel? Found the devil, and a black, wet one! Nope, they ain't found Billy Angel."

"But why are you back?"

"Something sort of told me that there wasn't any

use keeping it up. A man has to work by hunches half of the time, you know. That's the way I do, at least. So I turned around and came home. No use riding through mud and wind when they's a fire in town with an empty chair beside it, eh?"

He smiled at her so cheerfully that her heart went out to him with a rush.

"Oh, Steve," she said to him, "there's not a mite of malice in you for all that he's done to you."

He shook his head. "When a gent stands up and fights fair for a thing, I aim to say that he's won it and deserves to keep it . . . unless it can be took away from him by force. I wouldn't've called in the law to help me, except that I didn't want to waste a lot more years tearin' around to get together another stock of coin. Well," he added, "I don't know that the money would make any difference, though, to a girl like you, Sue."

She stamped her foot a little, in the strength of her affirmation. "Not a mite in the world!"

At this, he shook his head, watching her still in his half-smiling, half-derisive manner. "Ah, well, Sue, I'd feel a lot more hopeful if you'd only blushed and said nothing. If you come right down to it, I guess there ain't much hope for me with you, Sue."

"There is!" she said stormily. "I like you more'n I like anybody, Steve!"

He shook his head again. "That doesn't fool me," he said. "It's the sort of thing that doesn't come with waiting. I fool myself thinking that if I stay around a while, maybe you'll get to know me well enough to marry me. But doggone it, Sue, that sort of knowing ain't what counts. The sort of knowing that makes love is rigged up with lightning. That's the way I learned to love you. I seen you a couple of years back, polishing up the top of that counter with a rag in your hand and listening to some lumberman flirting with you, and trying to keep from laughing at him, and only letting the smiles get as far as your eyes. Well, it didn't strike me at the time. But, a year later, when I was off by myself, holding the wheel of a little sloop that was smashing through a crazy head sea and near washing me off my feet every other jump, with a lee shore looking as tall as Derby Mountain and all rigged up with white teeth at its feet, and with one scared nigger to work the ropes for me . . . when I was out there, watching the clouds sashaying across the face of the moon, all at once I remembered the picture of how you'd stood back of the counter, here. And it was lightning, Sue. That let the picture of you into my heart, and it'll never get out again. If that sort of lightning had ever struck you, you couldn't help but talk right back to me when I told you that I love you. You wouldn't have to talk, because I'd feel it before you spoke."

She could not speak. He stood up and went to the window. That window was crusted with mist and framed with sheerest, thickest black of the night. He had not gone there to look out but to cover emotion of which he was ashamed, she knew.

"However," he said, without turning his head, "I s'pose that I'll stay around for a while, and wait to see what my luck might bring. If I can't get you to marry me out of love, maybe I'll get you to marry me out of pity, eh?" He looked at her with a mirthless, twisted smile. Then he went hastily out into the night.

Although she tried with all of her might, she was not able to say a word to him. It was a wretched evening that followed. When the last of the posse came in, at midnight, she had to rake up enthusiasm and interest and shakings of the head over the tales that

they had to tell her. They had not found Billy Angel.
That mysterious fellow seemed to have disappeared
from the face of the earth. She listened with an
aching heart. How happy, she told herself, she
would be if she had never seen that man. And in the
first place of all, if she had never seen Billy Angel,
she would have promised to marry Steve Carney.
She was sure of it now.

She pondered it at the end of the dreary day's
work, when she sat in her room with her chin in her
hand and her eyes sightless with thought. Not that
she loved Billy Angel, instead. Indeed, what she felt
for him was the strangest mixture of loathing,
dread, horror, awe, scorn, and actual sharp-edged
hatred. But the very strength of the emotion that
stirred her when she thought of Billy Angel made
her understand that the thrill that Steve Carney
brought into her life was not real love. It was a pleasant feeling. It was compounded of various elements,
not the least of which was pride that Steve, after all
of his travels and his voyaging around the world,
should have come back to her and offered her his
heart.

But there was something else, something stronger,
she told herself. If she could be so moved with hatred and all the rest toward Billy Angel, there must
be the converse of those feelings tied together in one
soul-stirring harmony—and that thing could be
called love. If there were a man as pleasantly con-
versational as Billy Angel was blunt and terse, if
there were a man as open-hearted as Billy Angel
was secretive, if there were a man as genial and kind
and generous as Billy Angel was cold and self-
centered, then, added to these things, if there were a
man as truly lion-hearted and indomitable as Billy

was, she knew that she would feel for him a true love that would sweep her off her feet.

There, after all, she had been able to put her finger upon the one attractive feature in the character of Angel—and that was his giant will, his giant courage that enabled him to go out, sick as he was, and strike down such a practiced fighter as Steve Carney. This was all.

But the moment she had come to this decision, she shook her head. There was something else in him— but what it was she could not tell.

X

SPYING IN THE DARKNESS

Steve Carney did not wait for his fortune to be recovered from the hands of the mysterious Billy Angel. Instead, he disappeared from the town of Derby for thirty-six hours and came back again, affluent. Sue Markham blushed with shame when she heard of his success. Only the cards could explain it. No doubt, the cards had also explained the money that he brought back from overseas, for no matter in what land he worked, his tools were sure to be the same, always. The gold that he dug was brought to the surface in the same manner, at some silent table circled by grim-faced men watching the fall of the cards. But it seemed more honorable to have brought back his money from strange lands that were filled, perhaps, with strange crimes.

Only the sheriff still retained a hope that Billy Angel would be caught. He had worked himself to exhaustion and become a thin-faced, tight-lipped man. If he met Billy Angel, there would be no attempt to arrest a live man; it would be a swift and bitter battle to the death, and everyone knew it.

In the meantime, the girl watched a constant and

very rapid change in Billy Angel. She had not spoken of the time of departure. Neither had he ever referred to it. But each of them knew that the mind of the other was full of it. It seemed as though, by putting forth an extra effort of the mind, he was able to control the healing of his body, which went on apace. His color changed. His face filled a little. The strain was going from his expression. The wound on his arm had closed and was healing with amazing rapidity. A little longer and he would be himself.

The weather had changed again, for the tenth time in as many weeks. South winds prevailed. It seemed that the last wild rainstorm had drained every bit of moisture from the air. Every morning dawned crystal clear with the pale, blue mountain sky arched impalpably above the head of Derby. The wind was warm and dry, the surface of the ground drained. The riders down the street of Derby raised a little cloud of dust behind the heels of their horses.

It was on account of this still weather that she knew of the next move of Billy Angel. For, in the middle of the night, wakening suddenly, she was aware that someone was stirring in the house. Some noise had sounded. Some noise was sounding now, something felt rather than actually heard. But the faintest of tremors shook this upper floor of the house, as the effect of a soft but weighty footfall.

She waited only an instant. Instinct was working fast in her, not reason. She slipped from bed and dressed like lightning—dressed in time to hear the same sound go steadily down the stairs. Then a *creak* announced the footfall passing down the kitchen steps to the outdoors. She went to the window and craned her neck out to look down. There, below her, clearly in the starlight, she could see the broad back and the lofty form of Billy Angel. He went straight back to the barn. Then she saw him go into the corral.

There were two horses there, the one that had belonged to her father and the dainty little mare that Tom Kitchin had given her from his uncle's ranch the year before, a thing all spirit and speed and no strength. If the criminal wanted a horse, there was no choice left to him. The mare would not sustain his bulk. He had to take the big, strong, slow gelding.

She went down the stairs in haste, and yet softly. From the back door she spied on him and saw him catch and saddle the gelding. No doubt he was merely stealing the horse as a sort of grace note after the selfishness and thanklessness of his treatment of her.

Anger burned with a quiet, deep warmth in her heart. There was no time to call for help. Presently the great bulk of horse and man swept out past the barn and went up the northern trail out of Derby.

She did not pause to consider. She ran out blindly, tossed a saddle onto the back of the mare, and instantly pursued him. If he clung to the northern trail, she would catch him, to be sure. For the mare could run all day at the rate of two to one, compared with the gelding. But she had no hope that he would remain on that trail. He was far too clever for that. Deep in her heart, there was planted a conviction that, no matter how she tried, she could never succeed in overreaching him in anything on which his heart was set.

Yet, a scant mile out of the town, with the wind blowing hard into her face with the speed of the mare's galloping, she saw on the rise just before her the great form of Billy Angel on the tall brown gelding. She drew rein with a gasp of astonishment. Now that she had caught up with him, what would she do about it? What could she accomplish by accosting him? He would simply fail to answer, and, if she chose to rail at him, his calm silence would turn her biting words like the merest water from a stone.

However, she could at least see in what direction he traveled. It would be into the higher mountains, of course, there to seek for a secure cover until the hunt for him should have grown less intense, and she vowed to herself that, if she could follow him far enough and securely enough to make sure he intended to hide, she would ride straight back to Derby and send the sheriff on his trail.

He did not hold on for the upper mountains, however, but turned presently down out of the hills toward the flat of the valley, and there he directed his course straight toward the far-off lights of Three Rivers.

It was wonderful to her; unless, indeed, he possessed in Three Rivers some friend who would give him shelter, just as she had done before. It was not hard to keep behind him with little likelihood of being discovered. The wind blew constantly and briskly from him to her, and, while it would strongly stifle the sound of the hoofs of her horse, it carried the sound of the gelding's hoofs clearly back to her.

He did not go straight on to Three Rivers, but turned off toward a farmhouse on the right of the road. That byroad twisted through a grove of young poplars, all trembling and sparkling faintly in the starlight, and brought the fugitive under the side of a broad, low-built house.

From the edge of the copse, the girl saw him dismount, pick up something, and make a gesture to throw toward one of the windows that gaped open above him. There was a moment of pause. She had been chilled by the ride through the sharp wind, and now, in this sheltered place, her blood began to stir with a grateful activity again. She felt herself growing more and more curious.

Presently a light glimmered through a window above Billy Angel. A head showed for a moment with the light dimly behind it, so dimly that she could not make out the outline. There was a soft-spoken interchange of words, a gasp from above, and the head was withdrawn.

But that gasp had been in the voice of a woman, and the blood of the girl ran cold with disgust and with anger. It was from women then that this great, hulking, handsome brute found shelter wherever he went.

Billy Angel now tied his horse to a young sapling and went around to the back of the house. At the same time another light showed in a lower window. It was enough to tell the girl that the woman in the house and the man outside of it expected to meet one another where that light was shining. She dismounted in turn and went close to the window, ashamed of the impulse that drove her, but over-come with an intense curiosity to see the face of the girl to whom Billy Angel had entrusted his safety.

The shade was not drawn. She could look plainly through the glass and see everything in the room—a big living room, roughly but comfortably furnished, the sort of a room where men would be a good deal more at ease than would women. There were elk and deer horns mounted along the walls. There were big, deep-seated chairs. There was a yawning fireplace in which a few embers of the evening's logs were still smoldering. The man who owned that house and furnished that room was prosperous, uncultured; so much she could read with her active eye.

And the girl? She came back into the room at that moment, and behind her was the towering bulk of big Billy Angel. She looked a mere child, at first, with low-heeled slippers on her feet, and a rose-colored kimono with long, flowered sleeves, swaying about her as she retreated backward before Angel, inviting him in. She closed the door behind him. She turned—and Sue Markham sighed. No, this was not a girl. She was among women what Billy Angel was among men. As he was handsome in a glorious way that raised him above his fellows, so she was wonderfully lovely. And, like Billy, she had black hair, black eyes beneath level, beautifully penciled brows. She was small, but she was full of dignity as she was full of grace. To be sure, she was young, but at nineteen or twenty she had an air of maturity—she was old enough to have turned the head of any king in the world.

The girl, who stood beside the window, made a swift comparison between herself and the other woman. She could not stand for an instant contrasted with the beauty of the girl. She had not the grace, she had not the regal, confident manner, she had not that commanding air that goes with a perfect loveliness. At least, if Billy Angel had been indifferent to Sue and had treated her as he might have treated any man, here was a good reason for it. She did not need an introduction. That delicately lovely face had been photographed a thousand times. Her picture was everywhere in the towns through the valley and through the mountains. It was the daughter of the rich rancher; it was Elizabeth Wainwright herself!

If one is despised, it is a little soothing to have

been despised for the sake of a queen, and a queen was Elizabeth Wainwright!

But what did the queen do now? She flung her arms about his neck; she drew down his head and kissed him! If Sue Markham, red with shame and with scorn of herself for having remained to be spy-witness of such a scene, turned away in haste, she as hastily turned back again.

It's my right! It's my right! she thought savagely to herself. Why it was her right, she could not for the life of her have said. But, in turning back to the window once more and pressing closer to it, she felt that she would have given ten of the richest years of her life to have heard the words that passed between these two. But she could not. The window was closed, and the wind kept up a constant sighing through the trees. Only occasionally she heard a hint of the high, sweet voice of Elizabeth Wainwright, and now and then she felt a tremor of the deep, strong bass of Billy Angel.

XI

CAPTURE

Tears clouded her eyes, although why they should be there she could not know. Burning tears, that blinded her, and, when she had wiped them hastily away and looked again, she saw a thing that stopped her heart with shame and with rage. For big Billy Angel had drawn out a wallet, took from it a whole handful of money, and offered it to Elizabeth Wainwright.

She who stood in the night, watching and wondering, could not believe the thing, but there it was before her eyes, most palpably. She saw Elizabeth push back the money and shake her head—saw Billy Angel persist, speaking gravely, almost with a frown—and at last the girl took the greenbacks in her hand.

Sue Markham could wait to see no more. She hurried back to her mare and swung into the saddle. She reined back among the poplars, wondering what she should do now. There was no question about it in her mind. Billy Angel was a villain and must be destroyed. He had won the heart of this lovely girl by his good looks, and he was bribing her further with money. Oh, incredible thing, that the daughter of the rich rancher, Wainwright, famous for his prodigality, should have fallen so low that she accepted money at the hand of a shameless fellow.

She had no chance to carry on the burden of her thoughts. There was a guarded sound of a door closing; then Billy Angel came back, striding swiftly, mounted the gelding, and rode quickly away. He took the road by which he had come, and the girl only waited to make sure that he was fairly committed to it. Then she herself went back by a different route.

He was taking the upland course. She herself followed the longer road over the easier country, knowing that the mare would take three swift strides at full gallop to every labored stride of the gelding over the rough country. Through the night she flew on the back of the willing horse, and with every stride of the mare she told herself that she would not weaken in her determination. She would press straight on, until she had seen, as a result of her work, Billy Angel locked in strong fetters and in the hands of the law.

Very strange, indeed, that she had known him as a murderer, that she had seen him as a thief, but that it was a tender scene with a girl that convinced her that he was worthless. She thought of everything but this, however. And, with a swelling heart, she rode on, pressing the mare relentlessly until she reached the last long pitch up that carried on to the town of Derby, winding back and forth among the giant boulders.

She gained the outskirts of the village with the horse staggering beneath her, and she went straight to the house of Tom Kitchin. With the handle of her loaded quirt, she banged against the front door. Instantly there was a stir inside; the door was jerked open, and Tom Kitchin was saying hastily: "Well, what's up?"

He changed instantly when he made out, in the dimness of the starlight, who his visitor was. She broke in sharply: "Tom, get all the men you can . . . go down the upper valley road. Hide there and wait. Billy Angel is coming up that way! Billy Angel!"

"Sue, how . . . ?"

"Don't ask me how I know . . . go! Go! Quick, Tom, or he'll get to the mountains . . . he'll . . ."

He turned on his heel without a word and sprinted for the paddock behind his house where he kept four fast, strong horses. Even these were worn down constantly by his unusually hard riding.

She did not wait to see him saddled. She felt that, if she remained, she would have to speak again and say things that should never have been spoken. So she turned the mare homeward. At the corral, she dragged off the saddle and turned the mare into the little fenced enclosure. That tired animal did not even go at once to the watering trough, but stood with her head down, panting hard.

As for Sue, she felt as the horse felt—broken in strength, broken in spirit. She went back to the house. But there she stood in the open doorway, waiting with her heart in her mouth. Then she heard the thing for which she had been waiting. Here, there, and again, voices sounded. She could distinguish the clear tones of Tom Kitchin as he called his chosen men, then a banging of doors. Other voices were calling from windows and doors many inquiries, but those inquiries were not answered. There was only the bustle of saddling and catching horses.

All that while a wild spirit was swelling in her to rush down to them, to reach the sheriff, to tell him that it was only a joke—that Billy Angel was not on that road—tell him anything rather than let him go and set the trap. She saw, as in a painted picture, the bulky outlines of Billy Angel against the stars as he rode calmly, confidently up the path, talking to the gelding, or whistling to the wind. Men started out before him. He drew a gun. Harsh challenges rang across the stillness. Guns began to speak in barking voices. Here, there, and again men fell, and at last the big rider swayed and toppled from his saddle.

She ran out suddenly into the night, crying at the top of her power: "Tom! Tom Kitchin!"

For answer, she heard the rapid thundering of hoofs begin down the street and sweep away toward the hills. They were gone! Tom Kitchin and the rest were gone past her recall.

So she went wearily, slowly back to the lunchroom. She built the fire in the stove, not because of the chill of the night, but because she must have something to do to employ her hands, if her mind were to be kept from maddening her with pictures of bloodshed.

The fire burned hot; it cast a widening circle of warmth through the room, but still she could not be quiet. She went on with the work of cleaning the place—hating the work, hating the place, but forced to be busy.

It was all in vain, for every instant new pictures darted into her brain and made her shrink. She saw Billy Angel once more enter her place, lift his hat to her, and pass on. She saw him collapse in his chair. She saw the struggle by which she had brought him, at last, up the stairs to her room. She saw him in the madness of delirium catch at her and hold her with hands of iron. She saw his gradual progress from day to day. She felt again his silence and his steady, brilliant black eyes fixed upon her.

How slowly, slowly the time went on. Then a new thought struck her. He had broken through the cordon of the men of the law. Long before this, if they had succeeded in shooting him down, they should have returned, bearing his dead body lashed on the back of a horse. But still there was no sign of him. Perhaps he had smashed through them, leaving dead and injured men on either side and had plunged away through the night, his pistol flashing back death at the sheriff's posse.

That thought in her was not a fear—it was a burning hope. She felt that, if she could unsay the words she had spoken to the sheriff, she would have laid down her life, smiling. Not for the sake of Billy Angel. No, not that, but because it was treason, low treachery to spy on a man and betray him in this fashion.

Then, down the street, she thought she heard voices. She went to the door, and leaned there, panting. Yes, they were coming. She heard them more clearly. They came on slowly. Why at such a snail's pace? Because the dead man was with them? Because they were bringing back their own wounded and dead? That was it! A hot triumph shot through her. They were bearing away their injured and their dead, and their slowness was the slowness of defeat, which has a snail's foot.

"Hello!" called someone, for in the pale dawn the town was wakening. "How did it go?"

"We got him! We got Billy Angel!"

She shrank back from the door. She fumbled for a support, and, finding the edge of the counter, she clung to it. Gradually the mist cleared from before her eyes. She was weak and sick with horror. Billy Angel lay strapped on the back of a horse. His great arms hung feebly down the shoulders of the animal. This was the end and it was she who had put out that light.

There was a pause. Then men came to the door and passed in. What a cheerful lot they were, and how she hated them for their joy. Their faces were lighted. They were smiling upon one another. Not one bore the brand of Cain upon his brow. Then they were crowding around the counter. They wanted food. They wanted hot coffee, black, and lots of it. Still they laughed, she thought, like madmen. And still, as they talked, they smote one another upon the shoulder.

But where were the dead? Surely he had not fallen without striking one blow in self-defense. If he struck, it must be fatal. He was not the kind to deal small wounds.

Then two stragglers came in, each fumbling at a bandage on his face. One was plastered across the upper lip. The other had a great patch over one eye and the other was discolored.

She said finally: "Tell me what happened."

"Tell her, Sam," they said to one of their number. "You could talk it up the best."

"Well," he said, "we got him. That's the whole of it!"

"You got him," she repeated with stiff lips. "But how?"

"The sheriff had a tip from somebody. He wouldn't say from who. He got us out on the upper valley road. Then he put up behind the brush. Joe Smythe took all the hosses down the hill and kept 'em there. We waited twenty minutes, and then we seen him comin', lookin' twice as big as a man."

"He did that," broke in a second.

"The sheriff, he gave the word, and we busted out at Angel when he was right on top of us. Somebody just showed himself in front. The rest of us dived at him from behind. It was in the pass, where there wasn't much light, and there was as much chance of hitting one of our own boys as there was of hitting Angel. We didn't use guns. We went at him with our hands."

"He killed . . . who?" she breathed.

"Killed? What chance did he have for killing? There was six men at him from behind before he could say Jack Robinson. They pulled him off the hoss and got him down."

"Ah," she cried, "then who . . . ?"

"He was up again in a jiffy. I seen the boys spill away from him like he was a stone, and they was drops of water. Think of that! I reckon there wasn't one of us that wasn't able-bodied as much as most men. But he shook us off like we was nothin'. In another minute he was jumpin' out of the heap of the men that he'd knocked down. And the sheriff, runnin' in behind with his gun. . . ."

"Ah, heaven forgive Tom Kitchin!" moaned the girl, covering her face with her hands.

"For what? He slammed him along the side of the head with the gun. He didn't have no chance to get his finger on the trigger. And down went big Billy Angel. He was clean out, but by the time we reached him, he was half recovered again. He started for his feet. He took a couple of the boys and knocked their heads together. But after that we hit him solid. Everybody cottoned onto some part of him . . . a couple of us on each of his legs, a man or two on each arm, and the rest catchin' where they could. Well, not even Billy Angel could make much headway with a ton of gents hangin' onto him. Down he went, and in a jiffy we had him tied so's he couldn't move. We strung him on a hoss and brung him back."

"Alive?" she gasped out.

"Sure. That's the best part of it. But say, Sue, d'you know what hoss he was ridin'? The skunk had stole your brown geldin' that your father used to ride."

She did not hear. She was merely saying over and over again in a sort of intoxication of joy: "Thank God! Thank God!"

XII

SUE'S REWARD

All of Derby was awake in a moment. They thronged about Tom Kitchin's house, where the prisoner was kept tied hand and foot, and still under a strong guard. The overflow of the crowd washed back into the lunch counter for coffee and pie to talk over the details as they had heard them and to quiz the members of the posse.

But the girl left them to help themselves and pay as they pleased. She went to Tom Kitchin, and, when he heard her voice, he broke through the crowd of congratulating admirers. He was a made man, was the sheriff. He had done well before, but nothing had been a success as great as this. The county would never have another sheriff so long as he chose to continue running for office.

"I want to talk to you . . . alone," she breathed to Tom Kitchin.

He brushed the others aside and took her into a little front room in his house that served him as a sort of informal office, with saddles and bridles and guns hanging from the walls.

"It's all due to you, Sue," he told her. "If you say

that I can, I'll let the boys know that you get the credit."

"Credit? I don't want it! I don't want it! But . . . tell me what's going to happen to him?"

"To Billy Angel?"

"Yes, yes!"

"Why, there ain't a jury in the mountains that would let him off with anything less than hangin'. A rope is too good for a dog that'd stab another man in the back!"

"You're sure, Tom?"

"Mighty sure of that. A gent that helped to acquit Mister Angel wouldn't lead no happy life around these parts ever afterward!"

"Oh, Tom, mightn't a lawyer help him? Lawyers can do queer things."

At this, he took her strongly by the shoulders and turned her face suddenly to the light.

"Lemme see," he said, "why you're so all-fired particular about what a lawyer could do for him. Why, Sue, heaven help me if it don't look like *you* want to help him."

"I'd never be able to sleep," she whispered to him, "if I knew that I'd been the means of a man's death."

He tried to smile at her and shake his head, but the smile died. "Sue," he said sternly, "what d'you know about this Billy Angel? How come you to care *what* happens to him?"

"Don't ask me . . . but a lawyer . . ."

"He's broke. He wouldn't have a cent to hire a good lawyer. There's no chance of that. Some young kid right out of law school with nothin' much on his hands, he'll step out and try to rig up some sort of a defense. That's all there'll be to it. Just a form, you see, that they'll go through. Then they'll hang him."

She cried out, and the sheriff started a little.

"Sue," he said, "by the Lord I figger that there's something else in your mind."

"I've got to see him," she said. "I've got to see Billy Angel, and see him alone where nobody'll overhear what I have to say to him."

The sheriff flushed. "Sue," he said slowly, "I owe him to you. But I got a queer sort of an idea that if you was to see him now you might. . . ."

"Might what? What could I do?"

"Touch a knife to the ropes, and the devil would be loose again!"

"My word of honor."

"Will you shake on that, Sue?"

"There." She gave him her hand and he took it with a long, firm pressure, looking hard at her, as though he were still full of doubts that he was ashamed to put into words.

"Sue," he said, "will you tell me why you turned him over to me, and now you . . . ?"

"Don't ask me. I'm half mad. I can't talk. But I have to see him, Tom!"

He drew a long breath, and plainly it was much against his will. "Stay here," he said, and left the room.

He came back at the end of a few moments and, opening the door, showed Billy Angel in before him. She half expected to see on the face of the man some sign of the desperate adventure that he had been through that night. But there was absolutely no token. There was not a mark on his face. It seemed that the united force of the posse, although it had been enough to overwhelm him, at last, had not been able to injure him in the slightest. His hands were tied together before him. His legs were secured with irons. He could only move his feet a few inches at a time.

The sheriff closed the door. "Angel," he said, "Miss Markham has asked me to let you come in here for a little while because she's got something to say to you. It ain't regular. I hadn't ought to do it, but I'll let you stay, I guess. She's given me her word that she ain't gonna cut those ropes. Will you gimme *your* word, Angel, that you won't try to escape while you're here?"

Billy Angel smiled. "I'll give you my word about nothin'," he said. "I haven't asked to be brought in here. You take all the chances if I'm left. That's all."

At the brutal curtness of this speech, the color of the sheriff became high. He hesitated, wavering in his angry impulse. But a glance at the girl decided. "I'll trust it all to you, Sue," he said. "I'll stand outside the door . . . if you want me to keep from hearin' your voices, you'll have to talk soft. But the first queer noise that I hear, I'll be back through that door with a gun. That's for you, Angel. Lemme tell you that I brought you in alive because it was my duty to try it. But if they's trouble, remember that you mean as much to me dead as you do alive . . . or a mite more, my friend. Sue, it's up to you." So, curtly, he turned his back and left them.

The prisoner sat down in a chair and leaned his head against the wall. Without embarrassment, he watched the face of the girl. He seemed more interested in her than he was in his own fate. Was he, then, merely a brute?

"Billy," she said, trembling as she spoke, "I want to know what I can do for you?"

"You can make me a cigarette," Billy said calmly.

"I mean . . ." She broke off. After all, no matter what her aspirations might be now, what was there that she could do for him more important, truly, than some such small service as this? She took the sack from his vest pocket, together with the package of brown papers that accompanied it. Then, with clumsy, inexpert fingers, she slowly fashioned the smoke and handed it to him.

"A match," said Billy.

She took his box of matches and lighted the cigarette. Drawing a great breath, he closed his eyes, allowed the smoke to circulate through his lungs, and then blew forth a thin blue-brown cloud.

"I've come to ask if I couldn't do something more than this for you, Billy."

He nodded. "Sure," he said. "Jail grub ain't the best. You might send in some fruit, and such stuff."

It amazed her. Iron-nerved though she knew that he was, still this exhibition of animal disinterest staggered her.

"Oh, Billy Angel," she said, "heaven help you!"

"Heaven's not showed much interest so far," returned Billy. "But there ain't anything else that you can do."

"I can get a lawyer for you."

"Lawyers cost money, Sue."

"I have a little saved up. I could get it from the bank and make a first payment to the lawyer and pay the rest to him little by little."

He raised his hands in protest.

"Why not? Why not?" cried the girl.

He looked fixedly down to the floor. There was no frown of thought on his brow, but she could tell that he was intensely fixed upon some problem. At length he looked up to her with a quick, half-sidelong glance.

"I see," he said at length. "It was you."

"I?"

"That told them where to camp for me."

She was struck mute, striving to speak, although

she knew that her white face and her staring eyes convicted her.

He nodded again. "How did you know?" he went on, thinking aloud, and watching the confirmation of all he said appear in her face. "You saddled the mare and follered me when I left. That was it. And you follered me on until I came . . . by the heavens, you was outside, lookin' in!"

She shrank from him.

"You saw!" he said huskily.

It would not have been a great deal in any other man.

But when he raised his head and looked at her with glittering eyes and with a set jaw, it seemed to the girl that a very devil sat before her.

"I . . . ," she began, and there paused, unable to speak again.

"Then you followed back," he went on, "until you seen me take the upper road, and you cut straight back to town . . . was that it?" He paused, then said: "It was the hoss! You was scared that I'd take the hoss along with me! Why, Sue, if I'd wanted that wooden hoss, I'd never've rode back by that trail, would I?"

"It wasn't that, Billy . . . only . . ."

"Well, there ain't any use talking about it. I ain't complaining. Only, why did you ever put out a hand for me in the first place? Well, I won't ask you even that. I'm through talkin'."

"It came all over me in a sweep, Billy Angel. I had to come back to the town and tell the sheriff. I *had* to tell him."

"For whose sake?"

"For the sake of Elizabeth Wainwright," she whispered.

At that, she thought that his eyes drew to two points of light. He stared at her and said not a word.

"Do you understand, Billy Angel?"

He uttered not a syllable in reply; a cold dread entered her soul.

"Billy, will you speak to me?"

There was not a word.

"Tom!" she cried in a sudden panic.

The sheriff was instantly in the room, a gun in his hand, his faced covered with perspiration—a mute testimony of the agony of spirit and of suspense through which he had been passing. "What's wrong?" he asked sharply. "What's he been doin' to you, Sue?"

"Nothing . . . only, I want to go and . . . and . . . I was afraid, Tom."

"Angel," said the sheriff bitterly, "hangin' is a sight too good for you. Sue, come away with me." He showed her through the door, and, as she fled away, she heard his voice continuing to his prisoner: "Now, you stand up, young feller. Stand up, Angel, and march. Faster! Why God ever made rats like you, I dunno. It sure beats me. It sure does."

She went on as fast as she could, eager to get where that voice would not follow, yet knowing to the day of her death she would never stop hearing it.

XIII

No Hope for Steve

Sometimes conscience has no voice at all. Sometimes it forms itself into a small, dull chant, endlessly repeated. Into such a monotony it framed itself in the mind of the girl, and she went down the winding street saying to herself over and over, endlessly, helplessly, hopelessly: "I have killed a man! I have killed a man!"

She passed the Hinchman place. Oliver Hinchman was in the pasture riding his new cutting horse and trying to work the big roan stallion out into the paddock. A dangerous task, for the roan was a devil, ready to use teeth, heels, or two fore hoofs like steel stamps. Oliver waved cheerfully to her, and she paused to wave back and to watch him, for in some mysterious manner it eased her mind to watch the skill of his horsemanship and the cunning with which he drove the stallion before him. Most of all, the stallion himself was beautiful to see, terrible, useless, but glorious as he was, no man had been able to stay on his back for more than a few minutes at a time. Eventually he would be destroyed as not worth his keep. But she wondered if merely to live and be beautiful was not worth something to the world, even though the heart is wicked.

And if that were true of a dumb beast, was it not trebly true of big Billy Angel? A glorious form among men was his. Herculean strength, lion-like courage was his. And even if his soul was one compact of evil, there might well be a reason for his existence. But she had chosen to slay him, with her own hand. She could not think of it in any other way. The hand that fitted the rope around his neck was hers.

She went back to her place again. It was like entering a dungeon, and like a dungeon it remained all the day. For between her hands and the things she strove to do, shadows arose and filled her with sadness. Before noon she went to Humphrey Wraxall, the lawyer, and carried with her $115. She put it down on his desk.

"Mister Wraxall," she said, "I've got this much to begin paying you. I could save a lot of money by putting it away every week. Instead of putting it away, I'd give it to you. I could give you a share of everything I take in, at the end of every day, if you want it that way and . . ."

Mr. Wraxall took out his old fountain pen that was to him what the marshal's baton is to the general. He began to pass it through his pale fingers. "Now, what's the trouble?" he said. "What's the money for?"

"Billy Angel . . . ," she began.

"Ah!" said the lawyer. "Ah!"

There was something so full of suggestion in the way he raised his eyebrows and looked at her, there was something so sinister, almost, that she quaked and then grew crimson. "I'm only interested . . . ," she began.

"In seeing justice done, of course," said the lawyer.

But still his voice was rich with undertones of suggestion. She hated him. But he was clever. He had a reputation. Such brains as his must be enlisted if Billy Angel were to be saved.

Mr. Wraxall became serious. He tapped the fountain pen against the desk. "If you employ me," he said, "I must know everything." The fox was in his eyes.

"There is nothing to know," she said, "except that I want to see Billy Angel . . . free."

"Because he's innocent? Because you are sure he's innocent?"

She could not answer. Putting the question, in turn, to herself, what was her pushing reason? What did she think of Billy Angel? What was he to her?

"Innocent of what?" asked the lawyer's smooth voice. "Of robbing Steven Carney? Of stealing your horse? Or . . . innocent of murder, Miss Markham?"

She was transfixed. She could not answer.

"Ah," said the lawyer. "Then it's not because you feel he is innocent . . . but because you . . . admire this man? Because you respect him? Is that it? I must know everything, Miss Markham!"

"I'll come again tomorrow," she murmured, and fled from the office with an impression that he was left, smiling and triumphant, behind her.

But the questions that he had put remained in her mind all the rest of that day and all of the morrow, while she worked in a dream at the lunch counter, serving men who talked of one thing only—and that was Billy Angel, his career, and the probable end of it all.

Steve Carney came to her that evening at a moment when the room was empty. "Have you had a chance to think things over, Sue?" he asked.

She regarded him vaguely. It seemed a thousand

years ago and another self that he had asked to marry him. Then she flushed a little. "I've thought it over, Steve," she said gently.

"It's no go," he said. "I could see what was coming. Well, that's done for, then. That's done." He took a breath. He made a little gesture in which he seemed to be casting away one half of his life. "There's no hope of staying around, Sue, I suppose?"

"There's no hope, Steve. I'm sorry."

"You're a kind sort of a girl, Sue," he said. "But, that's that." He settled his hat on his head firmly, as though he were about to walk out into a storm, even though the sun was shining brightly and the air was soft for that October day. Then he left the room, and she knew, as well as though she had heard him vow it, that the town of Derby would never see him again.

XIV

A Mystery Solved

There was no meeting place in Derby except for the lunch counter. And in this time of excitement, there was a greater call for coffee and for pie than ever before since she had opened the place. She was glad of it. The baking, the brewing of the coffee, the endless cleaning of the cups and plates, the serving, the necessity of making some reply to the chatter that went on around her, kept her from going distraught with all that was sweeping ceaselessly through her mind.

She had only glimpses of the sheriff, now and then. He was busy keeping guard over his prisoner, who was about to be removed to a stronger place of safekeeping. Besides, she felt that Tom Kitchin had avoided her since the day of her interview with Billy Angel. Yet Tom was in her place when the revelation came.

He had come in to find his deputy, Jerry Saunders, and, while he was there, conversing heatedly with Jerry in a corner of the room that the loungers had generously left to them, a big man, well advanced in years, but still strong as an oak, came striding into the place.

"I want to see Sheriff Kitchin," he said.

His strong bull's voice brought every eye to him. They saw a rough, red face, beetling brows, a wide, thin-lipped mouth. He was clad in a linen duster, and he was stamping the dust out of the wrinkles of his boots. Plainly he had traveled some distance that day.

"I'm the sheriff," said Tom, turning to him.

"I'm Wainwright," said the big, rough man. "I'm Wainwright, from down the valley way. Maybe you've heard of me?"

"I have," said Tom.

"Most folks have up this way," said the cattleman, running his glance swiftly over the faces of the others, like a politician anxious lest he neglect a vote. "Well," he said, "I've come to see you about this here Billy Angel."

"Billy Angel?" said the sheriff. "If you have a complaint against him . . . if you've found some sort of a clue . . . just step over to my office."

The girl behind the counter listened, unimpressed. So much had fallen upon the head of Billy Angel, that she merely wondered, dimly, why men chose to torment him still.

"I got nothin' ag'in' him," said the cowman. "I got something for him."

"What?" exclaimed the sheriff.

"That's it. Something for him. I'm gonna set him free!"

The sheriff started. Then he smiled. He shook his head. "That sort of a joke don't get many laughs in Derby, Mister Wainwright," he said.

"Laughs ain't what I'm after," said Wainwright. "What I want to know is, first, what's ag'in' this here Billy Angel?"

"Stealing horses, robbery, and murder, that's all," said the sheriff with a very faint smile.

"What hoss did he steal?" boomed Wainwright. "Damn my heart if a gent like him would be low enough skunk to steal a hoss. But I dunno. When his mind is made up, he'd do most things, I s'pose, that stood in his way. Whose hoss did he steal?"

"Hers."

Sue had found her way out from behind the counter, in some way.

Wainwright turned upon her. "He stole your hoss, ma'am?"

"I make no charges against him," poor Sue said.

"Ah! You don't? You ain't steppin' on him now he's down?"

Tears of pity—for herself, for Billy Angel—crowded her eyes.

"Well," said the rancher, "you're Sue Markham?"

"Yes."

He nodded. "He told my daughter something about you. That cuts down the crimes by one. It's only robbery and murder, now. Who did he rob? A gent named Carney, I think. Find Carney, and I got the money here to pay him and enough money to shut his mouth. And that, Sheriff, will leave one charge left."

"Only the murder, I suppose," said Tom Kitchin slowly. "Are you going to buy him off from that?"

"I am," said Wainwright.

"With what, Mister Wainwright? Money?"

"With the blood of my own son!" exclaimed the big man in a voice of thunder. "For it was him that murdered Charles Ormond. It'll be known. It's got to be known. I'm here to talk it out where folks can hear me. It was my fool girl Betty that went out to see Charles Ormond . . . that handsome, useless young rat. It was my boy that went along with her. But she knowed that there might be trouble. She's been engaged . . . sort of under her hat . . . to Charlie. She wanted to break it off. And he was aimin' to be nasty about it. She took her brother along. But she took another man, too. She took along the strongest fightin' man that she knowed, and that was Billy Angel, that she asked to trail the rest and be around handy in case there was bad work on foot. And he done it. Well, there *was* bad work. The end of it was that Charlie Ormond and my boy got to passin' language. And finally Charlie out with a gun. It misfired. My boy had a knife in his hand. He made a pass at Charlie . . . Charlie turned around to get away . . . the knife stabbed him through the back to the heart. There stood Betty and her brother in a mess, but here slips in Billy Angel, tells 'em to hop on their hosses and ride home . . . he knows a way out of this. Life is dull for him. He needs excitement.

"They're too rattled to stop and talk about it. They jump on their hosses and ride for it. When they get home, they find out that Billy Angel has been found on the scene of the crime, ain't stood when he was challenged, and has been hounded through the mountains by a sheriff's posse." He paused, and then he roared: "You blockheads, can't you see that the girl is nigh dead? Get me water for her, somebody!"

He himself caught Sue and lowered her into a chair. Water was brought, but she waved it away. She wanted neither food nor drink, but only more words from the mouth of this homely angel and bringer of strange tidings.

"That was all for a while. Then down comes Billy Angel on a night that some of you can remember. He calls for my girl and talks to her in the house. He tells her that he knows that it's a hard thing to ask, but that, when he took the blame of that killing and got the chase after him, he figgered that he was foot-free, but, since that time, he'd met up with a girl in the mountains and fallen in love with her . . . a girl that had been nursing him and sheltering him since the first day when he was wounded." He pointed. "Sue Markham, was it you?"

What a shout from the men! In a dizzy whirl she made out the grim face of Jack Hopper from a corner, the amazed sheriff, and all the rest gaping at her.

"He wanted to be free from his bargain. He knew my boy had had trouble with his father because he ran through his allowance too quick. And Billy Angel had brought down coin for my son to run away on, if he didn't want to stay and face the music. But first he wanted my boy to talk up and take the blame for the killing of Charlie Ormond. Whatever blame there was . . . and my lawyer is gonna show that there was damned little! Well, sir, that's the story. I've told it brief. But if there was ever a romantic young fool, it's this here Billy Angel. I want to see him. You might have thought that he was in love with my daughter? The devil, no! He was in love with trouble, and that was all that there was to it. A trouble lover! Love of danger for the sake of danger. Well, all I can say is that he got it. But my boy ain't runnin'. He's standin' his ground. He's told all the story to me. Now, what I want is Billy Angel out of your hands, Sheriff!"

It could not be done at once. But it suddenly appeared that there were no charges to be pressed against Billy Angel. The state had nothing to say against him. Indeed, the state was very glad to shut its mouth tight, for Billy Angel had suddenly been borne aloft on an immense wave of notorious popularity.

The wild and improbable tale of what he had done was on the tongue of every man, a story that men could appreciate because of the danger in it, and that women could understand because of Sue.

And Sue?

She did not rush to the sheriff's house with all the others to congratulate Billy Angel on his deliverance. She remained behind in the lunch counter, sick-hearted, crushed. It only remained for Billy, as a free man, to come to her, and pour forth his scorn upon her! But now, as she looked back over all the days he had been in love with her, she could understand. It had been love. Indeed, that chained his tongue and kept him silent. It was more an agony of sorrow than of rage that had burned in his eyes when he had discovered her betrayal. But love, at last, had been killed by her own hand.

There were only two days before the meeting. Two dreary eternities they were to poor Sue Markham.

And then he stood in the doorway, and filled it up from side to side. There were half a dozen other men in the room. Instantly they picked up their hats. They grinned at one another and at Sue. And they walked out.

Oh, fools! Fools! Little they knew the terror and the sorrow with which she looked forward to this meeting with him! Now he was coming straight toward her. She shrank behind the counter. He followed her and loomed, enormous, above her. He took one of her hands and held her fast. She closed her eyes and said through her teeth:

"You bought the right to say what you want . . . you can scorn me and hate me and rage at me, Billy. I got to listen!"

He said: "What I got to say won't take long. I've come to say that I love you, Sue. And I've come to say that you love me, or else you'd never have sent the sheriff for me."

She had no strength to deny it even for a single moment. She let him take both hands and all of her.

BAD MAN'S GULCH

"Bad Man's Gulch" made its first and only appearance in *Western Story Magazine* in the issue dated July 17, 1926, under Faust's George Owen Baxter pseudonym. It was one of twelve short novels published that year, all in *Western Story*. "Bad Man's Gulch" is a powerful story about a reformed gunman, Pedro Emmanuel Melendez, who arrives in the lawless mining town of Slosson's Gulch armed with the philosophy that "the right thing is just to drift, and you'll land lucky or unlucky, just the way that everything was wrote down for you when you was born, or maybe before that." But can he just drift when he meets up with Louise Berenger who, along with her father, has discovered gold and fallen prey to the desperate and predatory miners of the gulch?

I

LAW AND ORDER

If William Berenger had, in the first place, known anything about gold mining and gold miners, he would never have brought his daughter along with him when he joined the rush for Slosson's Gulch. What he knew about mining was connected almost entirely with the works on geology that he had read and mastered. As an amateur geologist he was a very well-informed man; certainly he made a greater picture of a successful man when he was out with a party of admiring friends, chipping fragments off bits of rock, here and there, and telling the story revealed there, than when he went downtown to his office where a sign on a clouded-glass door informed all who cared to look that William Berenger was a lawyer. But as time went on, very few cared to look at that sign. For when a case came the way of Mr. Berenger, he never allowed business to interfere with geology, and he never allowed fact to interfere with theory. Mr. Berenger held a confirmed theory that every man, in his heart of hearts, was perfectly honest, and nothing could wean him away from this belief. When he cross-examined a recalcitrant witness, it was in the fashion of a saddened uncle pleading with a misguided child to be charitable to the truth and his better self. The result was that no lawyer ever succeeded in making men and women feel more at home on the witness stand—which is exactly what a lawyer does not want, of course.

Obviously the proper attitude is that all of one's own witnesses are scholarly gentlemen, and all of the opposition's witnesses are scoundrels, liars, and thieves, if they can get a chance. But Mr. Berenger could not help treating the entire world, not only as though it were his equal, but even a little bit more. He could not so much as tip a waiter without asking the pardon of that gentleman in disguise.

When a jovial and heartless friend of Mr. Berenger suggested that he close a law office that was simply a useless item in rent, and apply some of his geological knowledge by joining the gold rush, Mr. Berenger took the matter instantly to heart. He called in his daughter to help him make up his mind, and she poked her walking stick at the potted geraniums in his library window and listened thoughtfully. She put no faith in the ability of her father to be anything but the kindest of fathers and the worst of businessmen, but she was certain that nothing could be more disastrous than to keep on as they were doing. Knowing that the family fortune had diminished dangerously close to the vanishing point, she felt that, at least, this might be a cheap way of taking a summer's vacation in the Western mountains.

So William Berenger was encouraged to make up his pack as a prospector, and in that pack, of course, his geology books formed the greatest item. He would have thought it absurd to advance upon the practical problem of locating gold-bearing ore without equipping himself with references, page, and paragraph, for every one of his steps. His legal training forced him into this attitude. But, in due time, they dismounted from the train, bought two pack mules and a pair of riding horses, built up two towering miracles of packs, and advanced on the mountains like two children on another crusade.

When they came to Slosson's Gulch, they halted on the overhanging shoulder of a hill and looked down upon the long, narrow town of shacks and tents and lean-tos that straggled along both banks of the creek. Even at that distance, through the thin air, they could hear faintly the noise of the mining camp. While they waited in the rosy dusk of the day, they heard from different portions of the gulch three shots. It sounded to Louise Berenger like three signal guns, warning the newcomers away.

Her father was not dismayed. For a week he mixed in the wild crowd of the camp in the evenings, and spent his days with Louise in tramping along the hill slopes, where thousands of others had already wandered before him. They learned now what they could have read in the papers before they started—no more strikes were being made in Slosson's Gulch. The vein seemed to have been traced as far as it ran, and as for the throngs that still rushed to the mining camp, some were simply blind sheep like the Berengers, and others were the exploiters of the miners. That is always the case in such a town; there are 500 hangers-on for every 100 honest laborers. But there is always a wild, vague hope of fortune lingering about a new-found ledge of gold ore. Mr. Berenger still tramped the hills farther up and down the valley, from day to day, talked with the adventurers in the evening, and then burned his lantern beside his heavy tomes of geological lore.

One day Louise came to him, with her eyes glittering and her face on fire. "I don't think that this is a place for you, Father," she said, "and certainly it is not a place for me!"

"What in the world has happened?" asked William Berenger, looking up over his glasses.

"Nothing," said Louise, setting her teeth like a man about to strike or be struck.

She would say no more, but her father could gather that something disturbing had happened, and, since it was almost impossible for him to resist any suggestion, he agreed at once that they should give up the adventure. He only wanted a single day to try out a little theory that he had just found out.

That extra day was spent in roving far up the valley, leaving the noise of Slosson's Creek behind them. They turned the complete flank of the great mountain and marched up a narrow ravine that, in those days, bore no name whatever.

As the town dipped out of view behind them, the girl asked: "Do you think that there will ever be law and order in that town?"

"Law and order," said William Berenger. "My dear, wherever there are more than two civilized white men together, there is sure to be law and order!"

His daughter stared at him. "There have been *five* known killings since we arrived," she reminded him.

"The dregs of society! The dregs of society!" Mr. Berenger explained easily. "They have to be disposed of in one way or another. Drones must be thrown out of the hive, my dear child. Wine is not good until the lees have settled."

Louise sighed, helpless and hopeless. She murmured finally: "Metaphors are not arguments, Father, except in poems."

"And what could be more of a poem than this

spot?" Mr. Berenger said, waving his hand toward a
blue giant of a mountain in the distance, for a turn
of the ravine had just brought them into view of its
sparkling head and white shoulders. "And what
could be more of a poem ... a living, breathing
poem ... than the strong men who have gathered in
Slosson's Gulch to hunt for fortune in the ribs of old
Mother Earth herself?"

"Or ... the earth failing them ... in the first
handy pocketbook," suggested Louise.

"Ah, child,"—her father sighed—"a rough face
does not make a rough heart. You must learn to look
beneath surfaces ... of men and of mountains! Age
brings a gentler insight."

She knew that it was foolish to argue. If she mentioned the fact that one sheriff and two deputy sher-
iffs had already disappeared from the ken of men in
Slosson's Gulch, and that the same fate had been
promised for the next upholders of the established
law that dared to show their heads near the camp,
she knew that William Berenger would have some
handy explanation. To dispute the goodness of
mankind with him was like condemning the faith of
an ardent priest. He felt that his hands were soiled
even by opposing such mundane theories.

They rested at noon on the upper waters of the little creek that ran through that nameless ravine. As
the western shadows began to come kindly out
across the slope, Mr. Berenger advanced to make his
exploration. He had not worked for an hour before
he paused to consult the pages of his book again.

Louise, weary of idleness, seized the pick and
struck it into an eroded ledge of rock. It struck so
fast that she could hardly work it out. A bit of rock
stuck on the end of the steel when at last it was free.
She broke that fragment off in her hand—and found

that sparkling threads of gold were shining back at her through the mountain shadows.

Even her silence seemed to send an electric warning to her father. He came hastily and saw what she held. Together they attacked the ledge. In half an hour they had no doubt. It was a strike and a wonderfully rich one, if only this were not a surface color that would soon disappear. They hastily staked out the claim and put up monuments.

Then they sat down in the shadow and made their plans. To Louise, it seemed that the whole world had instantly become an enemy, wolfishly eager to snatch their prize out of their hands. But her father had no such fears. When they finally turned down the valley, he, with a rich lump of the ore in his pocket, was already building hospitals and universities, and bringing Rembrandts across the Atlantic.

At their little lean-to on the lower edge of the town, Louise stopped to prepare supper. Her father went on into Slosson's Gulch to file his claim.

She waited until the dark with no sign of him, and then she knew that it would be worse than foolish for her to go unescorted through the streets of the gulch.

In the morning she made her hunt—a frantic search. She made wild inquiries here and there; searched at the claim, everywhere, knowing in her heart that his body lay at the bottom of some abandoned prospector's hole, or perhaps, weighted down with rocks, it was being rolled slowly down the bed of the creek.

II

THE FURY OF NATURE

She went back to her little lean-to and sat down to think. The obvious thing was to find out first whether the claim had been filed in Slosson's Gulch, then to discover a man in whom she could place implicit confidence, and entrust him with working the claim on a partnership basis. But in whom could she place implicit confidence?

She counted her friends, one by one, upon the slender tips of her fingers—a dozen boys and men, all fine fellows, as far as she knew them. But who could tell what they would do when a temptation the size of this was placed in their hands?

With her eyes closed, she tried to weigh them, one by one. In every one, she felt that she had discovered a strain of weakness. Gold supplied an acid test. The men in the gulch were law-abiding like others, when they were at home, but here they became wild beasts!

She heard a clamor of voices and looked out on a group of half a dozen stalwarts, not thirty paces from the door of her own lean-to. They were breaking ground with a wild, jovial enthusiasm, as though they knew beforehand that gold *must* be there. She scanned those men one by one—a giant Negro, a tall, pale-eyed Scandinavian with a bared forearm as huge as another man's thigh, a gaunt Yankee, a red-faced German grinning with effort as he swung the double jack—all young. But, in addition, there was a middle-aged pair who looked enough alike to be brothers, men uselessly well dressed, with pale, savage faces, cursing their own flabby muscles loudly as they toiled. She felt that a cross-section of the gulch had been presented to her.

But she must find an honest man. That was the first requisite. If there were the slightest flaw in his integrity, he would not fail to rob her of her share. Might was right in Slosson's Gulch. In the second place, he must be brave and strong enough to withstand the dangers from others—from six, say, such as yonder group across the way.

Where was she to find such a man? She turned that problem slowly. Never for an instant did she think of flinching from the work. Not that the gold lured her on, but she felt that to abandon the claim would be to abandon her father himself and the one great thing that he had ever accomplished with those theories at which she had smiled so often. So she set her teeth and determined to struggle ahead with her search, feeling that the instant she weakened, tears would be stinging her eyes and dimming them. Loving her father too much to sit and weep for him, she decided to work out her sorrow, not sit and weep it away.

So thought Louise, saddling her horse straightway, and riding down through the gulch. At the claim office she found that her father had left no record of the holding. In despair she turned her horse toward the ravine.

Certainly she was neither a fool nor a sentimentalist, and, if every man she looked at on this day appeared more than half a villain to her, it was simply because each face that she saw was involuntarily contrasted with the image of William Berenger, half wise man, half saint, and perhaps a little of the fool, as well. But, as he was, he had spoiled her for other men.

She passed through the gulch without having made a choice, and rode out of it, filled with a disgust for the whole race of men. Down the valley she rode, with the alkali dust whipping up into her face and stinging her eyes, her jaws clenched, and fury in her heart.

If she had been a queen, she would have ordered her army into the field on this day—bound anywhere, so long as it were for destruction of other men. But she was not a queen; she was simply a twenty-year-old girl with nothing at her disposal but 135 pounds of wiry strength. And this was a man's country in which she was riding.

Passing out of the gulch, at last, she spurred her mustang unmercifully up the last long slope. Here she found herself in a hinterland of ragged lands, neither mountains nor plains, but chopped, wretched badlands, where the spring watercourses ripped and tore for a month or two; where the sun burned or the ice gathered through all the rest of the year. It was just such a place as suited the humor of Louise Berenger, at that moment.

The trail led upwards again, crossed a ridge, and dipped into a great, silent valley beyond. She paused here, for it was peace to the spirit and rest to the vision to let her eye plunge across to the white-topped mountains of the other side, and down the river that twisted and shone through the center. Nothing stirred; nothing lived here except trees, scant, hardy grasses, and a few cacti. There were no men, at least, and she thanked God for the absence of them.

But at the very moment of her thanksgiving, she had sight of a rider coming slowly down from the farther side. Louise bent a gloomy eye upon him. He was no more than a black silhouette, at that distance—even with this limpid mountain air to help the vision. Only, on the white forehead of his horse, the sun glinted now and again. The man was like the rest in the gulch, no doubt. Or, if he were decent enough before he went there, he would be defiled and brutalized like the rest in a day or two, for so she thought of all the men in the gulch.

The whole valley was poisoned for her by the presence of that one rider, and therefore she looked up toward the sky, and so, where the white ridges joined the blue, she made out a little column of smoke rising. It seemed very strange that a fire should be built on the snows themselves. Then she saw that it was no fire, but a rapidly traveling column. It dipped out of view and came into sight again much lower down the slope, traveling twice as fast.

She recognized it, now—the white flag of snow dust that flies at the stern of a slide. Too, she heard a faint rumbling. She guessed that it would be a mighty avalanche before it spent itself against some intervening rock ridge.

It came down with a constantly increasing front, a constantly heightening flag of smoke in its rear. As it gathered weight and speed, it crossed the white snows, leaving a wedge-shaped mark upon the opposite mountain. It was like a thinking thing, a great, blunt-headed snake, winding here and there to follow contours of the ground that she could not make out, at that distance. Then, twisting sharply to the left, she saw that it would spend itself in a thick belt of trees that stretched like a great shadow across the slope.

When it reached the trees she could not mark any abatement of its speed. No, it rushed on through them, and they went down like grass. A huge, raw gash was cut through that forest, and the slide that had entered the trees, as a child, came out as a giant, with a tossing, bristling front. The stripped trunks of pines were flung like javelins high into the air.

It was no longer a white forehead of snow but something like a wave of muddy water, except that she knew the darkness was not mud, but snow, boulders, pebbles, sand, the whole surface soil, and the trees themselves, roots and all, that had been gathered in the arms of the monster. A distant roaring reached her, like the clatter of 1,000 carts across a hollow bridge.

Still the creature gathered power and speed. It was fleeter than a locomotive, staggering down the track, with no train of cars to check its flight. So this heap of ruin lunged down the valley wall. A strong ridge of rocks lay in its way. She waited, breathless for the shock. Then she was aware, again, of the solitary horseman who journeyed down the valley straight in the path of the flying danger. It seemed as though the thundering avalanche behind him had robbed him of power to stir, as a snake fascinated a bird. Yet, he *did* move, although compared to the lightning flashes of fear that fled up and down her nerves, he seemed to be standing still. He moved at the same steady dog-trot of his horse, quietly down the broad ravine.

She looked up again. He had known, evidently, that the ridge of rocks above would check the course of the slide. Probably he was some wise old head among the mountaineers, skillful in these wild matters.

The cataract of rolling snow and rock and soil struck the rock ridge. It flung its head high into the air like water, one hundred feet aloft. Then it crashed down upon the mountainside beneath and rushed on, with all of its train leaping and flowing across the rocks behind—not over them, now, but through them! She saw ten-ton boulders wrenched off and brought leaping like devils with the rest of the wreckage.

The noise sounded nearer. It seemed as if thunder were roaring in the heavens just above her, or that the ground was being torn to pieces beneath her feet. It seemed to her that she felt a trembling of the great rock mountain shoulder on which she sat her horse, and the mustang itself cringed as though a whip was shaken in its eyes.

And the single rider? He still jogged his horse quietly down the slope, heading for the river.

III

The Cruel Snake

The heart of the girl stood still. Of all dreadful things in the world, there is nothing that so paralyzes all the mind of man as the sight of some inexplicable horror. But it was not inexplicable to her long; she decided that the man was deaf. That was undoubtedly the explanation. The thundering tumult behind him was as nothing to him, and he would not be disturbed until the very shadow of that towering river of destruction was above him. Then, one frightened upward glance, and he would be swallowed.

She turned to her mustang, and he whirled gladly about to escape the sight of this thing. But before she had ridden off the shoulder of the mountain, pity and hysteria made her check the horse and turn again.

Straight down the slope the avalanche was careening wildly. It struck and demolished a stout grove of trees.

Still the deaf man jogged his horse patiently downhill.

She snatched out her field glasses and trained them on the spot. What she saw was no old mountaineer, but a young one, riding a little atilt in his saddle, with most of his weight upon one leg, and his attention now occupied entirely by the serious business of—rolling a cigarette! His horse seemed to be nervous and twitching—yet held in check by his master's one hand.

It was perhaps better that the thing should be like this; far better that he should have no serious thought in his mind, and certainly no fear when the blow struck him. For it was now too late to flee, even if he were to be warned.

And warned he was, at that very instant, for she saw his head twist around over his shoulder. Her hands shook so that her vision was blurred a little. Finally she could see that he had turned toward the front again. The horse was not brought to a gallop. It still dog-trotted leisurely down the slope, and its rider was lighting his newly made smoke.

She lowered the glasses to look with her naked eye, as though what she had seen magnified, could not have been the truth. To her naked eye it seemed now as though the great front of the slide was already upon the doomed rider. She caught up the glasses again with a murmured word. One meager hope appeared for the fugitive. Just behind him, there was a deep swerve of the floor of the slope and it might be that this would turn the current of the slide. Stop it, it could not, but ward it into another direction perhaps it might.

The rider had barely ridden across this gully when the storm struck upon the other side. She saw the whole front of the landslide dip, the great head of the monster stagger, turn, and rush wildly off down this new channel.

The mustang, too frightened now to heed his rider, was striving violently to race away from destruction, but his rider merely sat upon his back, pulling strongly upon the reins, with danger showering all around him, for the great rocks that had been picked up by the avalanche were not so easily diverted to a new course as was the more liquid mass of the remainder. Mighty boulders were tossed straight ahead, bounding past the horseman with power and size enough to blot out a whole troop of cavalry, let alone a single man and horse.

The force of a miracle still surrounded this fellow. He rode through the storm unscathed, so far as she could see, until the whole length of the slide had twisted into the gully, which it was plowing deeper and deeper as it went.

It lurched on toward the bottomlands of the valley, pouring like water across them. Not so big as formerly, it reached the river and cleft it in two, with a white leaping of foam. From bank to bank the river's chasm was filled with hundreds of thousands of tons of detritus in which massive pine trunks bristled, no larger in proportion than bristles on the back of a boar. On the nearer side of the stream toward the girl, a huge overwash of the wreckage flowed far out across the land, lodging, at last, even against the foot of her own mountain.

The course of this cruel snake was ended. That its trail would be marked for 10,000 years in the vast rent that was gouged out of the valley slope, that the river was dammed completely, and much of its upper valley probably flooded, did not matter. All that was worth heeding—was that yonder lone rider had escaped from destruction.

She stared at him, aghast. He had ridden into her innermost thoughts. For she had heard of bravery before, but this utter contempt of life was a thing that she could not fathom.

He did not pause in his course to get down from his saddle and, upon his knees, give thanks to God for his deliverance. He simply dog-trotted the mustang along the course from which he had never turned since the beginning of this little tragedy a few minutes before.

He came to the wall of detritus across the river, and he sent the mustang across it, the wise brute working daintily, testing the tree trunks and the rocks before stepping upon them, and so making to the nearer shore again with no mishaps beyond a stagger or two.

The stranger was riding straight up the trail toward her. Louise Berenger waited on the trail, spellbound. He was a young man; she had seen that much in the glasses. But what else he might be, she had been too excited to observe, and now he was hidden under the steep face of the cliff. Presently she heard his whistle rising to her, a sweet, high-pitched whistle that seemed to flow from his lips as easily as the song of a bird. She liked that. He whistled not like a boy, but like a musician. She had never heard that song. But at least it was no cheap, foolish popular song. As he came closer, she heard him speaking to his horse.

"Steady, Rob, you old fool! If you got to have your lunch, jest you aim for the grass on the *inside* of the trail, will you? Because it makes my eyes ache a lot to be hung over the edge of nothing, like this."

Made his eyes ache! Louise Berenger, feeling rather weak and ridiculously happy, found herself chuckling softly. No matter what sort of a fellow he might turn out to be, in appearance she was at least certain that there was not his like in the whole world.

Then, taking her almost by surprise, he turned the next corner of the trail, and she found herself looking into a brown, handsome face and a pair of good-humored eyes equipped with a continual smile. She saw that he was a well-made man, tall, strong-shouldered. To give additional proof of his madness, he had been riding that twisting, desperate trail with his arms folded across his breast and his reins looped carelessly over the horn of the saddle, letting the horse pick his own way and take his own time.

For an example of what chances that meant, even now as the gelding sighted the stranger just before him, he flung up his head and leaped aside and backward, faltering on the very brink of the precipice, or so it seemed to Louise Berenger, who was too startled even to scream a warning.

But the stranger was not perturbed. "Rob," he asked, "is that manners, and to a lady?"

He took off his hat, and Louise saw that his forehead was even as lofty and nobly made as the forehead of her father had been.

"Ma'am," said the rider, "it's a lucky thing that we met here at this good passing place, ain't it?"

There *was* a good passing place on the level surface of the mountain shoulder from which she had turned her horse before, as she was fleeing from the sight of a dreadful catastrophe to the lone rider. But the present diameter of the trail seemed to her not more than wide enough for a single animal.

"If you'll rein back to the wide place and . . . ," she began.

But it was apparent at once that he had not been sarcastic. He sent Rob straight on, along the terrible outer edge of the path.

"Wait!" cried the girl. "There's no sense in taking such a fearful chance on . . ."

She could not complete the sentence. Rob was already beside her, and, as Louise reined her own mustang closer in against the wall of the mountain, it seemed to her that the other swayed out over dizzy nothingness. Then Rob came back into the trail again.

"Will you stop one moment?" called the girl.

He turned instantly in the saddle. Rob paused and, planting his hoofs on the crumbling outer edge of the trail, strained far out toward a tuft of grass that sprouted from the face of a rock.

"Is there anything that I might be able to do for you?" asked the stranger.

"Only tell me this," said Louise Berenger. "Why did you take that last terrible chance in passing me on this trail?"

"Was it a chance?" said the other, leaning from his saddle and looking calmly down the side of the precipice. "Well, lady, I'll tell you how it is. The way this here life is arranged, there's nothing *but* chances, all the time. And if you ain't killed by the chance of falling off a mountain trail, maybe you'll be scared to death by the chance of a bad dream at night. So what's the use of bothering?"

IV

THE THINGS THAT ARE FATED

Of all the things in life that Louise Berenger detested, there was nothing she loathed more than braggadocio. But this was something more than bragging, as she could very easily see. This man spoke as he felt, no more, no less. She was as delighted as she was amazed. And she said, laughing: "Will you please tell me your name?"

"I will"—he grinned—"if you'll tell me why you laugh."

"I laugh because I'm tickled," Louise Berenger said inelegantly, "and I want to know your name so that it'll help me to remember you."

"Thanks," said the brown man. "Would you want to know the whole name?"

"Why, I suppose so," she said.

"My name is Pedro Emmanuel Melendez," he said.

She could not help laughing again; the contrast between his totally Western-American personality and his pale-blue eyes—with his intensely Latin name quite unbalanced her self-control.

"I know." Pedro Emmanuel Melendez nodded, with his usual smile shining out of his eyes. "It

sounds like it was out of a poem in some dago language, don't it? Don't sound like a real name, at all."
He sat sidewise in the saddle, making himself at ease in much the same fashion as when he had been dog-trotting his horse away from the thundering pursuit of the landside.

"I've tried that name backwards and forwards," said Pedro Melendez. "I've tried calling myself . . . Pedro E. And I've wrote myself down plain . . . P. E. Melendez. But it all sounds queer. Even when I worked it up fancy into P. Emmanuel Melendez, it was no good. So, generally, the folks call me Pete, and let it go at that. But why I was hitched up to a name like that, I'll tell you the reason. I was brung up by an old gent that wore that moniker of Melendez. And would I switch from his name back to my own? No, lady. I would not, though that there name has cost me more trouble in the way of avoiding fights than any other one thing."

"Trouble in avoiding fights, exactly," said the girl. "And how many fights that you *couldn't* avoid?"

"The fact is," said Pedro Melendez, "that I'm very much of a peace-loving gent." She smiled, but he insisted: "No, that's the fact. I hate fighting. I just naturally loathe having to stand up and look into the eyes of a gent that is mad at me." He sighed and shook his head. "But I got to be getting on," he said. "This here hoss is needing a feed before long. Ain't you, Rob?"

Rob, at the sound of his name, flattened his ears and reached back to snap at the toe of Pete's right boot; a jab of the said boot made him swing back his head with a grunt.

"Are you going for the gulch?" asked the girl.
"Yes."
"Then I'll go along with you, if I may."

"There ain't anything that I'd like better."

The trail remained narrow for only a little time, and then it widened enough to allow them to ride side-by-side. She looked up out of her thoughts and found him watching her with a frank admiration and interest.

"You're in trouble about something," he suggested, and there was something so extremely frank and open in his tone that she could not help answering:

"Yes . . . about you, just now."

"And how come?" he queried.

"Why," said Louise Berenger, "I have a lot of cousins. I watched them grow up. I played with them, climbed trees with them, and knew them better than I knew any girls. I got to know boys fairly well, and by the look of you, Mister Melendez, I should say that when you were their age, if they had seen you coming, they would have doubled up their fists and said . . . 'Here's trouble coming!' "

"Well," he admitted, "you got a pretty accurate eye, at that. When I was a boy there was nothing but fighting for me." He sighed and shook his head, and then brought himself out of that dim haze of memory into the present again. "I was always whanging somebody and getting whanged, but, after a while, I growed up, and I lost all sorts of taste for fighting. No, ma'am," he said, repeating his thought with a soft emphasis to himself, "when I hear voices raised up loud and high, I just back up right away, and, when you draw a line, you can bet that I don't cross it!"

She studied him. Certainly he would never be guilty of false modesty. He meant what he said.

"No," he said, "about this fighting business . . . but I seem to be talking a lot about myself."

"It's a long way to camp," she said. "And I'm interested."

"So am I," Melendez said, with his unfailing grin, and, as they jaunted down the trail, side-by-side, he told her the story of his life with perfect simplicity, enjoying all that he remembered fully as much as any auditor could have done.

She, turning to watch him from time to time, or looking before her down the trail, heard the tale carry Melendez back to his boyhood. It was easy to summon up the picture of the handsome face of that other self in the old days. No wonder the old Mexican had chosen to adopt this striking youngster. The blue eyes of that other and younger Melendez gleamed out at her from the cool shadows beside a pool on the mountain slope beneath them. There was stamped on her mind forever pictures of Melendez in his story, and pictures of the mountains through which they were riding came home to Louise Berenger.

They had been troublesome times almost from the first, because old Melendez lost almost at once the prosperity that had induced him to adopt a son. He had taken Pedro wandering here and there, and wherever they made a new home there was, of course, a new set of boys to be fought.

"My eyes," he said reflectively, "were always either black or purple, when along would come another fight, and I would get whacked again. And so, you see, when I grew up to be man-sized, I was sort of in the habit of having trouble come my way. Trouble is like a pet dog. It gets used to you and keeps following you around at your heels. It was that way with me. The first time that I got into a serious mess was this." He pointed to a thin, white line that ran across his cheek. "That was Mexican style, with knives," he added. "And then this came, while I was still wearing bandages around my head." He touched a place on his left arm. "And a lucky thing for me that day"—Pedro Melendez sighed—"that it was the left arm that they drilled, and that I could keep right on shooting with my other hand. But after that, it was just the same thing over and over again. There was always some part of me patched with iodine that hadn't yet scrubbed off. I got knives through my right side, and down this here shoulder, and one of 'em jammed into my neck. I got bullets through both legs a couple of times, and one right through me, finally, that laid me up for nigh onto six months, while the doctor every day said . . . 'Maybe he will, and maybe he won't.' And the nurse, every time I looked up, had a tear in her eye. However, I pulled through, but I had a lot of time lying on the flat of my back and studying the ceiling and thinking back. By the time that I could walk, I was sure it was no use."

"That *what* was no use?" asked the girl.

"Why, struggling and fighting your way through," he said. "Not a bit of use at all. The way things is planned, that's the way that they'll turn out. The gent that sent the slug through the middle of me, what was he? Why, a hobo, a tramp, a no-account, yaller-livered hound that just had enough liquor in him to give him the courage to pull a gun. And there was me that had lived with weapons in my hands as long back as I could remember, and that went to bed feeling guilty if I hadn't had my hour or so of target practice that day. But when the pinch came, what happened? Why, the hobo had never hit a mark before in his whole life, I suppose. And me, my gun hung in the holster, and I just stood up and fell down again. Why didn't I die, after lying there for three hours before help come to me? I *should've* died. Everybody admitted that. But I didn't. Because in the place where things is wrote down, it wasn't issued for me to die on that day. And there you are! Staying awake and worrying don't help none. Planning and hoping and praying don't help, either. But the things that is fated for you, those are the things that'll be sure enough to come along. So what's the use of trying to make the bucking horse carry you? No, lady, the right thing is just to drift, and you'll land lucky or unlucky, just the way that everything was wrote down for you when you was born, or maybe before that."

V

A BORN KILLER

It threw a keen light upon one thing, at least, and that was the manner in which he had jogged his horse down the valley in front of the avalanche behind him. Yet the thing seemed incredible.

She asked sharply: "Was that the reason that you didn't try to ride out of the path of the landslide?"

"The landslide?" he echoed with a puckered brow. Then he seemed to remember. "Why, yes. I seen that I might try to get to the high ground on one side of me or the other; but there wasn't much likelihood of arriving. The main thing was to hope that the slide would dodge me to one side or the other. What good was there in trying to guess which way it would dodge? Did you ever notice the way that smoke will follow you around a campfire when you try to get away from it?"

Although she had it from his own lips, it was still hard to believe. She could close her eyes, now, and see the rush of that giant down the slope, the leap of it as it lurched across the ridge of rocks; she could see it, chopping the river in two with foam, choking the valley with ruin.

Melendez was speaking again: "So when I got up and onto my feet, I quit trying. I put away my guns and I've never wore a shooting iron since, except when I went out hunting. The only knife I carry is one with a clasp lock on it that takes about ten seconds to get ready to use. No help at all when the danger is driving at your throat."

"But," cried Louise Berenger, "if they shot you down before when you were fighting in self-defense, what would they do when you had nothing to help yourself?"

"The fact is," he said, "that mostly you don't get into trouble when you ain't all ready for it. You look over the first hundred dogs that you meet. All of the yaller-hided mongrels that don't know nothing about laying hold and keeping hold, they ain't got the mark of a tooth to show on themselves. They live fat and happy and never have to do more than bark, now and then. But when you see a fine bull terrier, made for fighting, and trained for it, with the brains to know where to grab and the nerve to hold on when he's got his grip . . . why, you'll say that other dogs would be afraid to trouble him. It would seem that way, but the fact is that the fine bull terrier has got one ear all chewed off close to his head, the other ear pulled into shreds, he limps on a hind leg, goes light on a foreleg, and he's got a scar in his throat. He's so mottled with tooth marks all over that he looks plumb mangy. He's left a whole lot of dead dogs behind him, on his way, but does that make him any happier? Does that take the ache out of his bones or the limp out of his legs, or does it piece together his ears again? No, lady, it don't! So what's the good of the life that he's lived?"

"The glorious battles that the bull terrier has fought and won!" cried Louise Berenger.

"Aye"—Melendez sighed—"the ladies is always more bloodthirsty than the men. It's always that way with 'em. But the fact is, lady, that besides that one chewed-up bull terrier, there's others of the same breed in the world, and some one of them is just as glorious or even more glorious than the first one, and sooner or later the gloriouser one will get the other fellow by the throat and choke the dog-gone glory right out of him forever! And there you are."

"Well!" she exclaimed. "He will not be forgotten!"

Melendez looked patiently at her, not irritated, as she was, by the course of this argument, but with a smile behind his eyes. Then he pointed to a streak across the mountains. It wandered here and there, dipping from valley to valley, winding up the heights, like a great broad chalk mark, partly rubbed away by time. "Do you know what made that?" he asked.

"It's the old Indian trail, I suppose," said the girl, "and those are the white bones of the animals that died on the way."

"Yes," he said, "the bones of the animals that died along the way, including the men. Plenty of men! The big husky braves that rode south follering the Mexican moon, and the brave Mexicans that rode north again to get the Indians. Why, I dunno that I can name any of those gents that was out after glory along that trail. I dunno that I know even the names of any of their great chiefs. Do you?"

She saw the point and colored a little. Although she had no ready answer at hand to use against this argument, she felt that in some place it was wrong. Her helplessness turned into a greater heat of anger.

"Ah, well," she said at last, "every man has to live his life in his own way, I suppose. And, after all, we're not talking about dogs and Indians. We're speaking of the way a civilized man should lead his life."

"Sure," said Melendez, "but the kind of a life that most of us lead . . . why, you can use a dog's life to illustrate it pretty good. Not meaning you, lady. Only speaking for myself. I say that I've been bull terrier long enough. And now I find out if I let the other boys do all of the loud talking, why, they also do all of the loud shouting. Or nearly all of it," he added in qualification.

"Yes!" she exclaimed. "But now and then you'll admit that simply being quiet isn't enough. And *then* what do you do?"

"Then I take what's coming to me," he answered. "That's all. If a gent comes waltzing up and says I got to beg his pardon . . . why, I beg his pardon. And the fight blows away."

She grew crimson with shame and anger. "It's very hard to believe," she said coldly.

"I suppose it is," he admitted.

"And after you have taken . . . after you have . . ."

"After you have taken water like that, you mean to say?"

"What do other men think of you?"

"Think that I'm a hound, of course."

"Ah, and isn't that your answer?"

"No, their thinking don't hurt me none. Thinking of other gents don't put food in your mouth, or make you sleep better at night, or sew patches onto your old clothes."

"And if a bully tries to take something from you . . . your horse, say . . . this same Rob?" She waited in triumph, with a flashing eye.

"Yes," he admitted. "That's the sort of a thing that would make even a hound show his teeth, you'd say? But not me. I'll tell you that same thing happened to me, once. Gent claimed, after I had backed down and took water from him, that the horse I was riding was really his horse, and he went out to take it."

"And . . . and what did you do?"

"Why, I just begged the gents that was standing around to keep me from being robbed."

She could only gasp weakly. "And didn't they despise you for begging so?"

"Oh, sure they did," he said, "but they kept the other gent from taking my horse, and that was better than having to shoot it out with him, wasn't it?"

"How long did you stay in that town, after that?" she asked him suddenly.

"Matter of fact, I rode along that same afternoon."

"Ah," she said.

"Yes," he admitted frankly. "But then, I don't mind having to move along, pretty frequent. I aim to see a considerable sight of this here country. I been riding and roving a good many years, and still there's aplenty of it that I ain't touched yet."

"And as for the making of a home?" she said.

"Settling down, you mean?"

"Yes, or doesn't that appeal to you?"

"You are thinking me pretty black, ain't you?" he asked, nodding at her with smiling eyes. "Matter of fact, I want just what all the other folks want . . . a home and all of such. But you see, when the time comes along that it's meant for me to settle down, I'll get fixed and rotted down in the soil, and that'll happen whether I plan it or not. Planning don't do any good."

She stared at him, quite hopeless. Yet she had seen him, on this day, demonstrate such a thoroughgoing contempt for danger as she had never dreamed was in any man. Here was the vital flaw—something, she felt, that was even more contemptible than his courage had seemed glorious. It was a veritable philosophy of debased fatalism. There is nothing so despicable as meanness that is carefully thought out and justified in a man's heart of hearts. She tried him with one final test. "And suppose," she said, "that the bully, instead of trying to take your horse, tried to take *you*?"

He merely chuckled. "I've had to do the odd jobs and the cooking and the dishwashing around a camp for a week at a stretch," he admitted, and still there was no flush of shame on his face.

She turned white with disgust. "And if you are backed into a corner, with a gun under your nose?"

"Why," he said thoughtfully, "I'm glad to say that that has never happened yet. But if it *did* happen, I'm sort of afraid that I might lose my temper."

"I think you might . . . forget all of your careful thinking about the easiest way of living," she said. "And then what would you do?"

"Why, ma'am," said Melendez, "in a case like that, I'm afraid that I would kill the gent that held the gun."

"Even when you are out of practice as a fighter?" she asked rather scornfully.

"Yes," he said. "There is some that don't need much training to keep in shape for fighting, because they're natural-born killers."

"And are you one of those?" she asked, flushing.

"Yes, lady," he said, "that's exactly what I am."

VI

NOTHING BUT DEATH

A silence, rather naturally, fell between the two as they came in sight of Slosson's Gulch. She was filled with wonder and disgust and doubt about him, and he—was aware that she was embarrassed. So he jogged Rob blithely down the road and whistled a thin, sweet tune as they went, with the dust cloud rising behind the hoofs of their horses and settling in a white powder on their backs and shoulders.

Once in Slosson's Gulch, they parted—with no questions asked. The girl rode straight on through the town, filled with questions, not only about her vanished father and the mine, but about this new man she had met. In one part, she felt, he must be false, for such anomalies could not exist within one nature. Either he was no such war-like man under restraint, as he would have led her to believe, or else he was, indeed, a rare case of a lion working within a shackle.

But Pedro Melendez sat his horse for a moment and watched her out of sight around the next corner of the street. There was a strange tug at the strings of his heart as he had the last glimpse of her. And this was a rather new emotion with him. Girls had been to him something like cards or music—to be thought of in a careless moment and never to be taken into the life of a man, as horses and other men must be.

He knew, as he watched this girl out of sight, that she would stand in his memory, shoulder to shoulder, with the best men that had come into his life. She had a man's frankness, a man's directness, and yet there was an undiminished femininity about her.

However, he was too much inured in his calm philosophy of living to let a sentimental sorrow master him. He put up his horse at the first livery stable, and then he went through the thronging street to seek amusement, walking with a leisurely step, ever willing to give other men the right of way. In this fashion he wandered through the town of Slosson's Gulch.

Louise Berenger had ridden straight out to her lean-to beyond the fringe of the town, and there she had found trouble enough. The shack had always been small, but now it seemed to her that it was shrunk amazingly. She drew nearer, and then she made sure that the entire wing that she and her father had used as a storeroom had been removed—utterly wiped out. When she dismounted and looked through the door into the place, she found that the goods that had been in the storeroom had been piled in rude disorder in the main section of the little shack that remained standing.

It was a bewildering thing. It occurred to her, with a leap of her heart, that her father might have returned and performed this work, for some reason that she could not understand. But lumber was at a costly premium in the gulch, and if Berenger needed timbers for the mine . . .

She banished the idea from her mind almost as soon as it had entered. If her father, after his strange disappearance, was still among the living and had become free to return, he would not have wasted such time as this in such work. His first great thought would have been to get to his daughter and let her know of his welfare.

So she thought, as she stared at the confused jumble of the pack goods that had been thrown in upon the floor of the shack—not simply thrown in, either. More than one package had been opened. It was not a systematic thievery, but the careless picking and choosing of people who were not really in need.

Stepping to the door of the lean-to again, she looked vaguely about her. The six men who had started working nearby, that same day, had apparently struck pay dirt, beyond all hope and expectation in such well-prospected quarters. They had thrown up a miserable little shack of a house to shelter them and their goods. She looked in wonder at their tiny house and then at them, slaving in their growing hole. Last of all, her eyes rested upon a shining, white Panama hat.

Such hats were not altogether common, and by the pleasant, flowing lines of this one, she recognized it well enough. It was a possession of Berenger himself. With a start of rage, she knew that yonder fellows had been the ones who had taken advantage of her absence to plunder her property.

Tears of blind, helpless rage started into her eyes. She started forward, recognized the very timbers in the stolen lean-to. She knew, somewhere between tears and laughter, the crooked marks of her own sawing, and some of the crumpled nails that she herself had tried in vain to hammer home.

Now she stood on the edge of the pit that the men

were sinking. Whatever else they might be, they were great workers. They had ripped off the surface soil and they were driving their hole steadily deeper. Her feet were level with their chests as she stood there, staring down at them.

"It's the professor's daughter," said one, resting upon the handle of his pick, and panting and smiling as he glanced up to her. "What you want, honey?"

"You . . . ," said the girl. Then her rage choked her, and she could only point.

"It's you, Bill," said one of the others.

He who wore the stolen hat raised his head. "Me?" he asked in much apparent surprise.

He was one of the two middle-aged men who she had noted before. At close range, she could read every sign of viciousness in his face—cunning in the eyes, cruelty in the straight-set mouth, and something ominous, too, in the unnatural pallor of his face.

"Me?" he repeated. "Have you come to see me, young lady?"

"I have come to tell you," she said, "that I know you are wearing a stolen hat."

He took it off and looked quietly down at it. "Stolen?" he said. "Who claims it, if you please?"

"It's my father's hat," she said, trembling with anger.

"Your pa's hat, eh? What's his name?"

"William Berenger."

"I don't see any William Berenger written on this hat," he said, smiling down at it.

"And our timber, that you tore from its place, and used to build your own shack," she went on.

"No names wrote upon any of the stuff that we've used," put in one of the others. "As for what you think, honey, thinking ain't much important in Slosson's Gulch. Not without guns to back it up. If your pa claims that stuff is stole from him, why don't he come and talk for himself? Eh?"

She looked from face to face hopelessly, seeing their spreading grins.

"Besides," put in one of them, "if your pa has made such a rich strike as they say, he ain't the man to worry about a little thing like a hat, is he?"

They knew of the find that her father had made the day before, then she wondered how much more they knew. Words broke from her lips savagely. "I promise you this," she cried. "The things that you've taken will be torn away from you, and I'll find friends to do it for me!"

"Friends?" said he who wore the stolen hat. "My dear girl, you must remember that no man has more than one friend in Slosson's Gulch, and the name of that friend is gold. Now, don't forget that!" And he heaved up his pick with a laugh to make another stroke.

"Ask Pedro Melendez if that is true!" she cried in answer. She regretted the words as soon as she had spoken them. But what other friend had she in camp, if her father was gone? Yet she had no right to name Melendez.

Bill's pick was frozen in place, poised above his shoulder. "Melendez is his name, then?" he asked. "A greaser, I suppose. Why, then, I'll have to look up this Melendez that's to do all the tearing away and restoring." And he fixed his steady, piercing eyes on her.

She was aware, then, suddenly, that he wore a revolver at each hip, even as he stood there in the hole, working. All the rest were armed, also. Suppose, indeed, that they were to start to find Melendez and take him to task?

She turned away toward her shack, knowing that she must find Melendez, if she could, and warn him of the danger in which he stood because of her foolishness. But how could she find him in Slosson's Gulch? How could she go alone into the gambling halls where the men were crowded? There, alone, she could hope to locate him. To go to find one man in that town was like trying to locate one bee in a buzzing hive.

However, she was comforted by the knowledge that, even if she had brought Melendez into some danger, it could hardly be called an imminent one. If it would be hard for her to find him, it would be almost equally impossible for the others. So thought Louise Berenger, sitting moodily in front of her shack.

But all thought of Melendez passed suddenly from her mind. For she saw the sun flashing on the white Panama in the diggings across the way, and the shadow of her father crossed darkly across her mind and remained there.

For twenty-four hours he had been gone from her. Certainly nothing but death could have kept him away so long.

VII

HANS GRIMM'S PLACE

Of those gambling places in the town of Slosson's Gulch, there was one that justly held preëminence. That was the institution of Hans Grimm. There is something about gaming that proprietors usually wish to keep secret, not only because it is illegal, but chiefly because they know in their consciences that they are taking an unfair advantage of their business patrons, so that the other gaming halls in Slosson's Gulch were maintained with a usual air of forbidding privacy, so far as that could be supported. No matter how dense or how eager a crowd frequented the gaming tables, there was sure to be half a dozen forbidding figures scattered here and there—the official bouncers who guarded the place against riots. And besides, a little air of darkness and of mystery surrounded each of the halls—but not in Grimm's place.

Hans Grimm had risen to his present eminence from the gutters of Milwaukee. Starting life as a homeless street urchin, Hans had wandered far and wide, and gradually he had come to know human nature. He had been a trick bicycle rider in a circus for a time, and, when he came to Slosson's Gulch, it seemed as though he was opening a little circus of his own, instead of a gambling house.

First he put up a seven-foot wooden fence in a circle around an ample piece of land. It was a good, stout fence, and it was secured still more by having a ditch run around it and dirt heaped up almost to the top of the boards, all around. This made a wall that shut out every breath of wind, defying the heat of the torrid western sun almost as thoroughly as a massive adobe wall.

Inside of this circular enclosure, Hans Grimm sank lordly pine trees, with their branches lopped off close to the trunk. And over the tops of these huge posts, he stretched a great quantity of canvas that had once been, it was said, actually a part of a circus tent. At any rate, in this fashion he established for himself a great theater for operations.

He kept it all open and free. Around the outer edges of the circle, there were seats and benches and little tables where anyone was free to sit and cool himself from the hot sun of Slosson's Gulch. There would be no questions asked, and no one would ask them either to play at the tables or else to move on. Those little tables could be used, also, for little games of poker that had nothing to do with the profits of the house. Hans Grimm permitted this and never raised a hand to prevent it, although thousands of dollars were frittered away in this fashion, money that might legitimately have passed through his hands. He was contented to let smaller fish swim here and there as they pleased. But all was done so cheerfully, gaily, normally, and happily in the place of Hans Grimm that no man could sit long at the sides and look on.

This was like a circus, to be sure, but it was also a circus in which one need not remain in one's seat. When one saw some lucky fellow standing at dice, taking in chips by the handful, one could go stand by his side, try to fathom his system, and do a little betting one's self—nothing much—only a dollar or two, perhaps. But if one won, it was foolish to stop, and if one lost, it was ridiculous to stop before the tide of fortune changed. Bad luck cannot keep on *forever!* There was no fear of crooked devices in the gambling house of Hans Grimm; there was a sunny surety of honesty in his establishment.

So men found it easier to bet with Hans Grimm. They found it easier to bet high, also, which is the main point. So that, after all, Hans began to draw two-thirds of all the gaming business in Slosson's Gulch into his place. Yet there never seemed to be a tumult in Grimm's house. There was never a jam, a hustling of shoulders against shoulders, except when some exciting piece of play took place at one of the tables, and a throng of spectators gathered. There was never a dense cloud of tobacco smoke, never an annoying sense of guards and bouncers, here and there, to make one feel that one had entered either a prison or a den of thieves.

Now and again a man could be seen carrying a heavy satchel to one of the tables or taking it away again. A continual current of coin was flowing in at Grimm's in order that the winnings of the gamblers might be paid. When such a river of fortune was running away, who would be so foolish as to miss a chance to dip his hand into the golden stream? So thought the people of Slosson's Gulch, and so thought the six men who had commenced their digging so close to the lean-to of Berenger.

They had done enough work for one day. Now they drew straws to see who should seek relaxation in the gulch, and what two must remain to guard the claim. The Negro and the Dane were the unlucky ones who had to remain behind. The other four strode off down the valley, tired, but very happy, with the Panama on the head of Bill Legrain showing them the way like a beacon light. Although the others went eagerly, he went with the swiftness of a hawk to a familiar hunting field. The talents of Bill Legrain were many, but in no sphere was he so much at home as at the gaming table.

Ordinarily he did not waste his time in Hans Grimm's house. He had not much use for Grimm and for the methods that were in vogue there. There was no opening for the talents of an outsider. No matter what skill might be in the dexterous fingers of Bill, Mr. Grimm could not find a place for him in his scheme of things.

But Grimm was apt to say: "There ain't any real use in faking the machines. When a man wants to throw his money away in gambling, he's gonna do it, and he don't have to have any brakes working on the roulette wheel to help in the robbing of him."

This was the opinion of Hans Grimm, and, since he had made a tidy fortune in gambling houses, he was entitled to a viewpoint of his own. But Mr. Legrain leaned more to the old usages. He patronized the other places in Slosson's Gulch, where the proprietors were not averse to keeping a few "outside men" working from time to time and, like lions, allowing jackals to feast on the kills. However, on this day of days, there was too much happiness in the heart of Mr. Legrain. His pals and he had made a strike that might lead on to fortune for them all. When one is digging gold out of the bowels of the earth, one is also willing to risk one's affairs in new fields.

So Legrain led his fellows to the home of Hans Grimm. "We'll take a few thousand out of the pockets of the Dutchman tonight," said Legrain.

Stepping up to the table where poker dice were being rolled, he lost $500 in five bitter minutes. Then he came back and, with his eye, he challenged his friends to try their fortune at this table, also. They lost—with a ridiculous speed and surety.

"The dice ain't rolling for us tonight," said the Yankee as he came from the crowd and rejoined his companions.

"The dice ain't rolling? The dice is crooked!" said another.

"You're right," declared Legrain, white with passion. "It's a crooked game. Too good to use me, the Dutchman is. He keeps his hands clean, he tells me. And here he is running the dirtiest game in the town. I hate a hypocrite. And I'll get Hans Grimm for this. Because, by heaven, I *hate* a hypocrite!" His upper lip furled like the lip of a snarling wolf, and his eyes flashed to this side and to that, as though in search of a victim to be sacrificed to his bitter humor. Just at that moment, there was a little outbreak of applause from the cluster around a table at the upper end of the room.

"Somebody's winning there," said the Yankee. "Somebody's winning big, too, by the sound of things."

"Bah," said Legrain, "do you fall for that stuff, Jerry? They're just playing with some sucker, and they'll trim him, pretty soon, of everything that he ever could call his own. I know this kind of a dive. Crooked and got no heart in 'em. Clean you out in this kind of place, where they're always talking up how white they are, and how straight they keep their games. But it's a dirty dive, boys, and I'm going to let the town know the truth about it."

So said Legrain, with spite swelling poisonously in him, and, just as he finished his little speech, to which his friends listened with gravely nodding heads, there was a fresh clamor from the farther end of the room.

They could not resist the temptation. They crowded together with the other watchers around the roulette wheel. At the roulette table, usually so packed with players, there was now only a single man playing, smoking a cigarette, and placing his bets in heaps here and there about the board.

"A system, and a knock-out of a system, at that," murmured the crowd.

But this player of the "system" consulted no paper covered with figures, before he laid his bets. He staked and staked again with the utmost rapidity, and the intervals between the spinnings of the wheel were short, indeed.

He was a young fellow, very sun-browned, with pale blue eyes, and a scar across one cheek, like a thin, white line. And he took his gambling very lightly. Neither winning nor losing could change his smile. Even as Legrain and his companions looked on, they saw him stake $100 on the number nine, and they saw the croupier push out $3,500 to pay the winner!

$3,500 at a single stroke!

"Who is he?" asked Legrain enviously, as the noisy cheering died down.

"His name is Melendez . . . that's all I know," was the answer.

VIII

THE GIRL'S MAN

An elbow sank in the ribs of Legrain. He turned and saw the lean face of the Yankee beside him.

"It's the girl's man," said the Yankee.

"I'm not deaf," said Legrain. "What if it *is* her man?"

"The one that's going to do the tearing to pieces," said the Yankee insistently. "You know what I mean!"

Legrain scowled. He knew well enough what the Yankee meant, and the same meaning was in the eagerly anticipatory faces of the rest of his friends. They expected action from their leader, and Legrain knew it.

But of all the men he had stood up to in a long and varied career of battle, he had never seen one that appealed to him less as an antagonist. He did not mind surly savagery in another man. He could handle the bitter natures well enough, because usually they were either too sluggish or too nervous. Nor did he object to taking his chances with fellows whose faces showed the animal cunning that was in them, because he would freely match cunning against cunning. He loved to encounter men who were running berserk in the madness of too much whiskey beneath the belt.

But, above all things, he avoided as most dangerous the smiling men, and yonder Melendez at the roulette table was decidedly the smiling type. Having put $3,000 of his winnings on the black—and lost—he merely chuckled. He placed another $1,000 on the same color. It was swept away in due course by the croupier. Still Melendez smiled. And the more he smiled, the more intensely Mr. Legrain was worried.

He looked back to the Yankee and the others, and he found that their eyes were still fixed expectantly upon him. What was he to do? Yonder Melendez had been formally announced by the girl as a prospective enemy; it was up to Legrain to nip his hostility in the bud. By just such exhibitions of his power had he been able to maintain his authority among his followers.

Yet the more he examined Mr. Melendez, the less he liked the affair. Whether it was the long-fingered, strong hand of this young man, the depth of his chest, or the wiry strength of his arms, there was nothing about him that promised an easy foe. Perhaps the worst of all was the fact that no weapon appeared on his person. In this crowd there was hardly a soul who did not wear his Colt in open view, as if to show that he was ready and prepared to defend himself and his rights. But Legrain felt that he knew enough about human nature in the West to be sure that, when no weapon showed, it was because the man who appeared so innocent of guns and gunpowder was in fact so deadly an expert that he knew how to conjure forth a Colt from beneath his coat as swiftly as another could yank his weapon out of a holster.

In places a little less rough than Slosson's Gulch, did not Mr. Legrain himself carry his weapons out of sight? So he felt for Melendez as one expert for another. Under that smile he told himself that there was the coolest set of nerves that had ever been furnished to a human being. Those long, strong fingers would snap out a revolver with the expedition of a cat pawing at a mouse.

Altogether the affair looked most unpromising to Legrain. Again and again the stranger lost, and still his good nature was a fort that was not in the slightest shaken. Finally he pushed back his chair and stood up, nodding to the crowd of sympathetic spectators.

"That's all, boys," he said. "I've had my licking!"

They gave him a hearty cheer of approval for the fine way in which he had taken his defeat after being so near to a great coup. He could easily have lingered, in order to collect their kindness and their respect, easily have remained to let fall remarks about other exploits of his that had turned out more favorably. Almost any man, Legrain felt, must have succumbed to some of these temptations to fix himself in the minds of so many spectators as a hero. For this, Legrain waited and watched. It would be a sign of a human failing, but still it would be a failing that would supply a bit of confidence to him.

Yet none of these things was done by Melendez. He made his way through the crowd, adroitly avoiding those who would have talked with him. Presently it would have been hard to tell where he had disappeared, had not Legrain followed all of his windings and known that the stranger was standing in the crowd that watched at another table. Although, if Legrain had not known, there were others at hand ready to keep him advised.

"He's yonder!" the Yankee said, pointing, with a leer of savage pleasure.

Legrain set his teeth. He knew that these fellows did not love him. They feared him and they respected his accuracy and speed with a gun as well as a certain daring and adroitness of mind that were his. But they had no fondness for him. They followed him, still, as the coyotes will follow the ranging lobo, expectant of cheap food after the hero of the range has made his kill. Now, no doubt, the Yankee and the rest would be fully as pleased to see their leader thoroughly beaten and crushed as they would be to see him defeat the gambler.

Backwards and forwards, Legrain balanced the matter. He was no sentimentalist but, after all, he liked to have his following, his audience, to wonder at his cleverness and his cruel boldness of maneuver. These were his men, and, if he did not down Melendez, their faith in him would be dreadfully shaken. He would be a lost leader in a very short time, no doubt.

Believing that, Legrain felt that there might be a very great danger in Melendez. He determined instantly to put the matter to the touch.

The instant that he had made up his mind, he determined to put his re-resolve into execution before too much thinking weakened it. He went straight across the room, with his followers drifting hungrily behind him. In his heart of hearts he scorned them utterly, and in his heart of hearts he admired his own courage immensely.

As he entered the little crowd at the farther table, there was an end of the gaming that had drawn their interest. All faces turned suddenly toward Legrain, and men shouldered past him. He was very glad of this. For, having made up his own mind in just such a moment of confusion as this was, he might be able to find his opportunity and take advantage of surprise to help him beat Melendez.

So he put himself in the way of the other, weaving through the crowd. As the tall, brown-faced youth came by him, Legrain drooped his shoulder and jarred heavily against his enemy.

With the same instant he spun about on toe and heel, his voice screeching a harsh challenge. "Curse you!" yelled Legrain, "do you own this place and everybody in it? Are we dirt for you to kick around in front of you!"

At the first sound of his voice, the brown-faced man spun around to face him with such instant speed, that Legrain looked for the sparkle of a gun in the hand of the other. His own Colt was out and leveled; he intended to shoot, and shoot to kill, the instant that he spotted a weapon in the grip of Melendez.

But there was no weapon there, and, having the drop upon the stranger, Legrain, vastly reënforced in spirit, poured out the rest of his insulting speech. It was as though a bomb had exploded. A sudden rush on all sides jammed the crowd back, leaving a gaping hole in the center, where Legrain and his opponent stood face to face.

He did not regard the others, however. It was well to have so much attention, of course, and from such men. It would make him a known and feared man in the camp. But it was Melendez in whom he was interested, and he found that for the first time in his life he was standing before a man who did not change color when a gun was pointed at his heart.

It was a staggering discovery to Legrain, opening possibilities in human nature such as he had never dreamed of before. But he made sure that the eye of Melendez was as clear, as bright, and as open as ever, and that the form of Melendez did not shrink back one jot from him. He heard the younger man saying in the most calm of voices:

"Why, partner, what's eating you? You don't mean me, do you?"

"Don't I mean you?" said Legrain. "But I do, you swine. You tried to kick me out of your way just now and you . . ." He hardly knew to what conclusion he could bring this affair, but he stepped boldly forward. Certainly the nerve of this young fellow must have some snapping point.

Melendez did not so much as budge. He merely shrugged his shoulders and stood now at arm's length, looking quietly into the face of the other.

It was a dreadful thing to Legrain. It blasted away all his confidence in himself. The knees of his spirit, so to speak, were bowed almost to the earth. And he knew that he would have to do something desperate to maintain himself.

Just at that critical instant a strong voice called: "Put up your gat, Legrain! Are you trying to do a murder in here?"

Legrain wrote the sound of that voice down in his memory and swore that, if he lived through this trial, he would never forget the speaker as a most deadly enemy, to be brought to account for such an unseasonable remark.

If there had been only one voice behind the suggestion, Legrain would never have listened. He would have been deaf, indeed, to half a dozen such remarks. But now there was a roar from 100 strong men, calling upon him to restore his gun to its holster and to put the fight back upon even terms.

But did he dare to do it?

IX

No Fight In Him

With an eye most quiet and yet most calculating, as of one who reads an interesting book, Melendez was looking his antagonist up and down. It seemed to Legrain's evil heart that the younger man was glancing over a tale more than twice told. Standing so boldly and so steadily, it seemed as though Melendez was simply waiting for the instant when that leveled revolver was put away before he snatched out his own gun and fired from the hip. Or, perhaps, he would simply rely upon the power of his long, strong right arm. That clenched fist promised to go' through another's body almost like a leaden bullet. Mr. Legrain vowed that he would almost as soon be shot outright as struck by such a man, with such a heft of shoulder behind the punch.

He balanced the question in his mind and found the scales just even, until another universal roar from the crowd advised him to put up his gun at once. There was no denying those voices. He had heard it roaring before, on sundry occasions. Once he had been glad enough to have the walls of a jail, and the guns of a sheriff, between him and just such a roaring crowd. Now Legrain decided that obey he must, dangerous though he felt it to be, when he was in arm's reach of this man.

He dropped the Colt suddenly into his holster—although as his right hand came a little clear of the holster, it hung there quivering above the grip, ready to snatch out the weapon again with one convulsive movement of wrist and fingertips.

Yet as fast as he knew he could make his move—and with the stranger's handicap in having to extract a gun from beneath his coat—the cold certainty arose in Mr. Legrain that his was a losing cause, that, at the command of this youngster, there was such blinding speed that his own cunning would avail him nothing.

So he waited, tensed. The whole crowd waited, also, pressing back on either side so as to leave a narrow channel open through which bullets might be free to fly.

But bullets did not fly. There was no swift reaching forward of the right hand of Mr. Melendez. Neither did one of his hands flip up under his coat to make the draw. He remained as he had been before, with his arms hanging patiently by his side.

Legrain snarled, although he could hardly believe the thing as it snapped into his own frantic mind: "You're yaller!"

Even that crowning insult, although it wrung a groan of expectancy from the crowd, could not force the hand of Melendez. His smile did not waver. His pale-blue, thoughtful eyes continued to gaze at his foe.

"You yaller skunk!" screamed Legrain. "It's a *mask* that you're wearing, and, inside, you're shaking in your boots!" As he spoke, he reached out swiftly and struck the other lightly across the mouth with his open hand.

Striking with his left, his right hand was free to make his draw, and he snatched his Colt out, ready to split the heart of young Melendez and send his spirit on a distant journey. But Melendez did not stir to defend himself.

Another universal voice rose from the crowd, but this time it was one of purest disgust. "Leave him be, Legrain. There ain't any fight left in him."

"Leave him be?" repeated Legrain. "No, curse him, I ain't gonna leave him be. Not when I'm kicked around by a yellow dog that wants to bully people that he hasn't the nerve to stand up to in a fair fight . . . knife them in the back." He struck out savagely as he spoke. The other stepped lightly back, and Legrain floundered as he missed. He dropped his revolver into his holster, furiously greedy for the work by this time; his hunger was razor-edged.

Now he heard Melendez saying—although in a voice not trembling with fear: "Fellows, I'm not a fighting man. Will you take him off?"

There was a veritable gasp of disgust.

"No," shouted someone fiercely, "let him take what's coming to him . . . the cur!"

Sweet, sweet music to the ears of big Mr. Legrain. He laughed through his set teeth as he strode upon Melendez.

"And you're the hero, are you?" he panted. "You're the one that's going to tear six of us to pieces if the girl asks you to?"

For the first time a tremor was struck through the body of Melendez. "Girl?" he echoed faintly.

"Aye, and I wish that she was here to see what I'm going to do to you!" snarled Legrain. "I only wish for that. Because I'm going to break you up, Melendez! I'm going to. . . ."

He had broken through the calm of Mr. Melendez at last. The color indeed ebbed from the brown cheeks, and the lips of Melendez were suddenly pinched.

"Did she tell you that I'd tear half a dozen of you to pieces for her?"

"Yes!" Legrain grinned. "And so . . ."

He struck again, and this time the other did not leap back; an arm of steel rose and turned the blow of Legrain. He found himself staring, scant inches away, into glittering, terrible eyes.

"Back up, Legrain!" said the younger man. "I've been holding myself hard, but now I tell you that if you so much as stir a hand, I'll kill you, man. Do you hear me?"

"Hear you? You rat, will you still try bluff? Go for your gun. I give you your last chance before I salt you away, Melendez!"

"Gun? The devil with a gun. I don't need a gun for trash like you." And he surged forward.

Legrain should have killed him, perhaps. His own Colt was already in his hand as he sensed the change in this odd enemy. But, strangely enough, he could not tip up the muzzle of the weapon as fast as the left hand of the brown man darted out and gripped his gun wrist.

The gun roared, but it merely plumped a .45 bullet deep in the hard-packed dirt floor of Hans Grimm's gaming house. The next instant a clenched fist, as hard as a rock, clipped the chin of Legrain. He felt his knees buckle under him, his head jerked back under the impact. But when he strove to tear his gun free, it seemed to him that his right wrist was encircled with four bands of biting fire. He saw the second blow coming and strove to lurch inside of it, but it went home, and Legrain fell limply upon the ground, face down.

Even then there was enough fighting instinct in him to make him reach for the gun that had fallen from his fingers. A hard heel stamped down on his hand, and he screeched with pain.

The Colt was scooped into the hand of Melendez. "Get up, Legrain!" he ordered. "Get up, do you hear me?"

A bullet knocked the white Panama from the head of the gambler. And suddenly he had the strength to rise to his feet.

"Now get out!" commanded the tyrant. "And get fast, Legrain. If I lay eyes on you again in this camp, I'm going to wring your neck. Move!"

Legrain did not have to be told again. Indeed, he would almost rather have faced a dozen guns than look for an instant into the changed face of Melendez. He lunged forward unsteadily, took a sudden strength from his very panic, and raced blindly for the entrance. Melendez turned back upon the stunned crowd, and his face was not pleasant.

"You, there!" rang his voice. "You in the black hat with the two guns. You wanted the fight to go on. And it's started. D'you wear those guns for ornament, you fat-faced swine? Step out and let's see what you're made of. He don't step. He backs up. He ain't so set on fights when *he* has to take a hand in 'em. Boys, I've gone for years without a gun or a knife. I've lived like a lamb. But now a gun has been shoved into my hand, and I'm aching to use it."

He turned closely around to face the circle, and the circle widened before him. There was a slow movement toward the door. Following them, he clipped his words, each with a ring like a falling coin.

"Or a knife, if you like. If there's any talented greaser in this lot, let him step out and talk turkey. Or if you don't like that, bare hands. I tell you, I need action and I'm gonna *have* action. Or else I'm gonna have room! Why, you look like men . . . you stand like men, and you talk like men . . . but you *ain't* men. You're all hollow. Did you hear me talk? I need action or I need room. I need lots of room! I need this whole place to myself! Move!"

They moved. Most shameful to relate, all those brave and hardened men, good warriors most of them, felt the craven spirit of the crowd master them. They started more swiftly for the door. They turned their backs. The blindness of panic that instant seized upon them. They lurched forward with shouts.

The gun roared from the hand of Melendez and blew a neat little eyelet through the top of the canvas roof of the house, but it seemed to every man in that crowd that the bullet had whistled a fraction of an inch from his ear, and so they stormed, screeching, for the door. They fought and clawed and wrestled their way out. The weaker went down with groans; the stronger stamped upon them and pushed on for the safety of the open.

In a moment the great, round room was empty, except for a few prostrate forms by the entrance, crawling feebly toward the street.

But Melendez had sunk down in a chair and buried his face in his hands.

X

A PROPHECY

The house of Hans Grimm had become as silent as a cave. All the noise was removed to the street. Only Melendez remained at the table with his head in his hands. Coming toward him now was the last survivor of the crowd, a broad, rosy-faced man, whose cheeks seemed all the pinker because they contrasted with the tuft of white hair at either temple.

When the noise of the man's soft footfall came closer, Melendez looked up with a fierce snarl and reached for the gun that he had taken from big Legrain. But although that gun was pointed at Hans, the muzzle presently wavered and declined again.

Hans Grimm sat down in an opposite chair. "Are you smoking, mine friend?" he asked.

"No," said Melendez.

"Are you drinking?" asked Hans, waving an inviting hand toward the bar.

Melendez, following the gesture, shook his head with a shudder. "No." He groaned. "I ain't drinking! Not any more. For three years or so I've been able to do as I please, take life easy, never worry, and have one drink or ten, just as I pleased, but that time is ended. My vacation is plumb over."

He sighed as he said it, and Hans Grimm nodded.

"Very well," said Hans, "I understand this all pretty good."

The glance of Melendez fastened itself more intently upon the other. "Who might you be?"

"I'm Hans Grimm."

"Ah, you run this joint."

"Yes."

"I've busted up your games for today," said Melendez.

"It was a good show," Hans Grimm said. "I don't mind it, if I have to pay. You don't get something for nothing."

"Not even at a gaming table?" asked Melendez.

"No," said Hans Grimm.

"Not even if you win?"

"If you win," Hans Grimm said, "you make other people think that *they* beat the game. They think that the luck is running. So they start playing big. But there ain't any such thing as luck in this world."

"Nothing like luck?" exclaimed the younger man. "Why, Grimm, luck is all that there is."

"There is no luck," Grimm repeated, shaking his head with such a perfect conviction that he could afford to smile.

"Not even at cards?"

"No, you can work all the chances out with mathematics. Not very hard. There is no such thing as luck. She's a ghost, but most people chase her. They come here most of all to find her. There is no luck in the world, Melendez. Only brains."

It was a philosophy that tore to shreds the innermost convictions of Melendez, and he fought against accepting it.

"What was it but luck," he said, "that kept Legrain from backing me out of this here place and making me look as yaller as a rag?"

"Two things," Hans Grimm explained, counting them off on the pudgy tips of his fingers. "First place . . . you are a fighting man . . ."

"That don't go," interrupted Melendez. "I tell you, old-timer, that for three years I been making it a rule to take water rather than have to fight. And only the bad luck of Legrain . . ."

"First place," Grimm insisted mildly, "you are a fighting man. You held yourself in for a long time, but sooner or later you had to break out. If you keep a fire under a stopped-up boiler long enough, it will bust. It *has* to bust. Same way with you."

"All right," said Melendez, "I won't argue."

"Second place," continued the proprietor of the gambling house, "Legrain, like a fool, didn't stop where he should have stopped. He spoke about the girl."

"Ah?" grunted Melendez. "How could you hear that?"

"Because I was close," said the other. "I'm always as close as I can get when there is trouble here. Besides, I have very sharp ears. I tell you, mine friend, when the other players hear nothing, I hear the groans of the people who lose around my tables."

Melendez stared at him as at some enchanter.

"And so I heard what he said," finished Grimm. "This is not a place to speak of women . . . not to a man like you. Legrain was a fool, and therefore he had a fool's reward. He should have left Miss Berenger out of it."

"Now curse my eyes," said Melendez, "how did you guess at her name?" He frowned with wonder.

"It was not hard to guess," Hans Grimm said, still smiling.

"Ain't there more than one woman in camp?"

"There are others. But there is only one that would make you fight."

Melendez drummed upon the edge of the table. "You're smart, Grimm. Dog-gone me if you ain't among the smartest that I ever seen."

"Not smart," said Grimm. "It is only simple . . . like adding numbers. You put together the little things that you know, and they add up to some big thing that you didn't guess that you knew."

"All right," said Melendez. "I ain't gonna argue. You know a bit too much for me. You know enough, old-timer, to make me ask you for your advice. What'll I do now?"

"Take your horse and ride out of Slosson's Gulch as fast as you can. That is exactly what you ought to do."

"*Humph!*" exclaimed Melendez. "You mind telling me why?"

"I can tell you why. It is to get away from the danger here. You have shamed a great many people today. When a man has been shamed, he is always dangerous."

"It's a fact," admitted Melendez.

"So what you should do is to ride away as fast as you can go. That is what you should do, but what you won't."

"Hey, Grimm, what makes you so sure that I won't?"

"That is still simple. I add up the figures. They tell me that you will not go."

"Old son," Melendez said, leaning forward and

scowling with the intensity of his conviction and determination, "I'll tell you that you're wrong. I'm gonna go right out from here and saddle up my hoss and ride right out of Slosson's Gulch."

"You may start, but you ain't going to finish."

"Will a bullet stop me? Is that what you mean?"

"Not a bullet. They are not ready to shoot, just yet. But you will not leave."

"Will you be reasonable?" asked Melendez. "Tell me what makes you guess that."

"It is not guessing. I never guess. Either I know, or else I don't know. There is nothing mysterious. When Legrain mentioned the girl, I didn't know who it was until I saw you begin to fight. But after I saw you fight, I knew that you would have to see her again before very long. You are thinking more about her, right now, than you are about leaving Slosson's Gulch."

Melendez stood up. "Old-timer," he said, "you're smart. You're terrible smart. I see that. But this time, you're wrong. I'm thinking about her, sure. But, also, I'm gonna think still more about leaving. I'm saying good bye, Grimm!"

"Good!" said the other. "I like to see a man fight against himself. If you can get away from here, you will have a chance to live a happy life again."

"Meaning what?"

"Why, meaning that you could go back to drifting . . . no fighting . . . taking things easy . . . never worrying. That was what made you very happy, Melendez."

"Aye," said the younger man, "you seem to know me pretty well! And if I stay here?"

"You'd have to be on your guard every moment of the day and of the night. You'd have to have your head turned to look over your shoulder, never knowing when a bullet would come at you from behind. You'd have to sleep light and wake early. And it would be work. Hard work, Melendez. You don't like work very well, I think?"

"Are you still smiling?" Melendez asked gloomily.

"Why not?"

"Meaning," said young Melendez, "that you think that I *ought* to stay here?"

"Well?" said the other.

"And get a bullet in my back, as you say?"

"Perhaps a bullet in your back . . . if you ever dare to grow sleepy."

"And tell me this, old-timer . . . what's to be gained for me if I *do* stay here? What's to be gained, outside of a fair-sized chance of dying with my boots on?"

"Why," Hans Grimm said, "I suppose that there are things to be gained, too. There is one thing *always* gained by hard work and hard fighting."

"Eh? Hard fighting? Ain't that the thing that preachers all howl against?"

"Fighting? Why, Melendez, if men wouldn't fight for what they thought was right, this wouldn't be a world. It'd be a dog kennel. As for what's gained by work and fighting . . . why, Melendez, it teaches a fellow how to be a man."

"I ain't a man, then?" snapped Melendez, his muscles tensing along his arm.

The eyes of Hans Grimm lost their kindness. All of the gentle good humor faded from them and left them wonderfully cold and dead.

"No, Melendez," he said. "You are only an overgrown boy. But after you come through this fire, you'll either be a man . . . or dead."

XI

IT JUST HAPPENED

It is proverbial that prophets are not regarded when they cry aloud in the street. Yet one would rather expect to find a prophet in the street than the proprietor of a gambling hall.

When young Melendez came out into the air, he merely shrugged his shoulders and drew one breath of pure air, scenting the pine-laden wind that came down the valley—mixed with the fragrance of frying bacon, not far away. He breathed of this and he said to himself that Hans Grimm was a very clever fellow, no doubt, but that he, Melendez, could not waste time thinking of such nonsense.

If he were to arrive at manhood, he would try to accomplish it in some other place than this mining town, unless he could find a bulletproof suit to wear while he had to remain here. Only one thing was real—and that was the danger in which he stood.

When he started down the street, men drew aside to let him pass, and their faces turned to stone as he went by. It seemed as if every soul in the gulch had been driven out of the gambling hall by him that same day, and hated him most cordially for it. As he went by them, he could feel the sting of their glances of anger following him and resting coldly in the small of his back. With every step that he made, he knew that he would never regard the advice of Mr. Grimm for an instant. No matter what else was to be found here, at the end of the rainbow would be death.

He went straight to the stable, where he had put up Rob, saddled him, paid the bill, bought some crushed barley to take along with him, and started straight out of Slosson's Gulch. In his pocket there was the revolver that he had taken from Legrain. There were still three bullets in it, and, if he could once get free of the town without having to use up those remaining cartridges, he swore that he would throw the weapon into the nearest nook and go on again, with his hands washed clean of the dreadful temptation to battle.

He chose byways and alleys. Most of all, he wished to avoid a glance at the face of the girl, by any chance. Yet he could not help wondering at the strange cleverness with which Grimm had penetrated his secret. Indeed, he himself had not really known how deeply the girl was lodged in his heart. Certainly she had not been overkind to him. But she had been something utterly new—a sort of food to which he was not accustomed. He felt that, even by thinking of it, he could come to need her more than he needed the breath of life in his nostrils.

So, hedging about the long, narrow town by the alleys and the byways, he passed half a dozen lean-tos. He gave Rob the spur and let him speed down the road. He rushed past the first lean-to and the second. But glancing at the third, he saw Louise Berenger swinging an axe to subdue a refractory stump that she was converting into firewood. Instinctively he leaned a little over the pommel of the saddle and drove the spurs home again. And at that instant she lifted her head and looked down the road.

He told himself that it would be the act of a guilty hound to slink out of her sight in this hasty fashion. So he sat back in the saddle and drew rein. The horse came to such a swift, sliding halt that he felt the cloud of dust that he had raised overtake him and beat, like the hot, soft wing of a moth, against the back of his neck.

She rested the axe on the stump and stared at him, so what could he do but ride up?

"You're not in trouble, I hope?" asked Louise Berenger.

"Oh, no."

"You seemed in a hurry to leave," she said gravely. "And I thought . . ."

She stopped sharply, and he rescued her from embarrassment by saying, with his smile: "Why, you thought that perhaps I'd slipped out from under a fight again?"

She looked down, her face rather flushed. Then she said: "I think that I was rude to you, as we were riding in. I didn't mean to be. Only . . . I didn't understand."

"I knew it." He nodded. "It sounded bad, too. Only . . . would you mind telling me . . . do you approve of fighting?"

"I?" she asked, as one who would like to dodge a question. "No, I don't think so . . . only . . . why, I can't imagine turning one's back on trouble." She added in haste: "But I'm not giving advice! I'm only . . . why, you understand your own affairs much better than I can. But I should think that your heart would burn in you, sometimes."

"Sometimes it does," said Melendez. "Sometimes

it burns in me, right enough. And . . . look here, are you keeping house?"

"Yes."

"Might I ask," he said grimly, "who would've invited you to come up here to a camp like this?"

She smiled faintly. "We didn't guess what the place was, my father or I. Because Father is a good deal of a dreamer, you see . . . such a dreamer that he's disappeared completely. He has been gone over twenty-four hours. He may have found a book and sat down to it. He's that kind." She kept up her smile, but it was obviously a hollow effort.

"He's disappeared?" echoed Melendez, opening his eyes.

But she hastened to change the subject. "I have something to apologize for," she said. "That is, perhaps I don't need to mention it if you are really leaving the gulch?"

"I was figuring on leaving it, but, just lately, I've changed my mind," he said firmly. He thought of Hans Grimm. The very devil was in that fellow; he had seen the future so clearly. But a man's work, certainly, was opening before him. If he should stay here to take up some of the burden of this girl, there would be enough to fill his hands.

Her father gone for over twenty-four hours! He thought of Slosson's Gulch and all that was in it. Not that he had had a chance to see a very great deal, but he had been in other mining centers before, and he knew what was to be expected from them. When strange things happened, one could be justified, generally, in putting the very worst possible construction upon it.

As to Mr. Berenger, Pete had not the least doubt that the man lay somewhere dead, that he would never return to his daughter, no matter how long she waited here, keeping the shack awaiting his coming.

"You have changed your mind?" the girl repeated rather ruefully.

"Yes," he said, growing firmer and firmer in his decision. "I'm staying in Slosson's Gulch."

"Then," she replied, "I have to tell you. You see that little lean-to down the way . . . where that pit is opening?"

"Yes," he answered.

"I had trouble with the men there . . . six of them . . . very rough fellows . . . and one of them a gambler named Legrain who is a real desperado, I've heard since. In the midst of an argument with them . . . when they seemed to taunt me with being a woman and alone . . . why, I'm dreadfully ashamed to admit it . . . but I used your name." She was flaming. And she could not go on.

"It's all right," he said soothingly. "There ain't any need of you worrying about it."

"No, you don't understand," she insisted. "I used your name to *threaten* them."

"Ah?"

"Yes, and, as a matter of fact, I want you to know . . . that these men are *dreadfully* dangerous! I don't have foolish frights about people . . . but when I remember all their faces, I have to beg you to forgive me for getting you into such danger with . . . only your name just slipped into my mind. I was reaching out to find something to strike them with. I do hope that you understand and pardon me."

"Hush, hush, hush," he said, raising his hand as though he was putting a child at rest. "Now there ain't anything in all of this to bother you at all. There ain't a measly thing, Miss Berenger. As a matter of fact, I'll tell you that I've met up with Legrain already, and that him and me have settled things up fine. Really friendly."

"Ah, you knew him, then?"

"Why"—he dodged—"I met him right after I got into town, and so there's nothing, you see, for you to worry about."

She sighed a little, and then laughed a little. "It is very good to hear you say it," she said. "And then, if that's true, I'm tremendously glad that you're to stay a while in Slosson's Gulch." She did not give a reason, but her eyes misted a little as she looked toward the deepening evening that was settling over the mountains.

"Yes," he said, "I think that I'll stay." He reached for the axe and took it from her hand. And thinking of Hans, he wondered if the gambler could be right? Could this be arrived at by mere calculation? Was it not the purest chance that he should have blundered into sight of her as he was fleeing from the town? He whirled the axe. At one powerful and dexterous blow he cleaved the root in twain, at which she had been drudging helplessly.

XII

HOPE

Seated on a rock before the lean-to, he heard the story of the coming to Slosson's Gulch and the disappearance of her father.

"But," said Melendez, "what was his idea in taking the chunk of gold quartz along with him when he went to file his claim? Did he want to raise money to work the mine?"

"No," said the girl. "But he took it . . . simply because it pleased him, I suppose."

Melendez stared helplessly at her.

"Was it wrong?" she asked.

"No, not wrong, but sort of childish. I'd as soon show raw meat to starved wolves as pay dirt to this gang in Slosson's Gulch." He became silent, turning the idea in his mind. "The people in the gulch know that your father made a pretty rich strike. He must have showed the ore to everyone he met." He paused again, frowning.

But she said: "I think I've guessed it. Someone saw the ore and found a way of taking it . . . and disposing of my father! You need not be afraid of telling me that."

He looked straight into her face and saw that she did not flinch. "In a town like this," he admitted gravely, "when a man disappears, it always means that there's a chance the worst sort of a thing may have happened. But you can't be sure. They'd do murder for the sake of getting a rich claim. But they *wouldn't* do a murder for the sake of a piece of rock with some streaks of gold in it. When does the claim office say that he filed his holding?"

"He never reached there."

He started. "Very well." Melendez nodded. "Tonight, I start on through the town and find out what I can about where he was last seen. Are you afraid to stay here alone?"

"No," she answered. "I have a rifle and I know how to shoot."

He looked up and down the ravine. It was growing dim and the yellow faces of campfires showed here and there; the scent of wood smoke came through the windless air.

"If there is any sign of trouble," he said, "while I'm away, the thing for you to do is not to trust to weapons. In a pinch, you holler as loud as you can. There is hounds in this place, but there is a pretty large and liberal sprinkling of real white men, too. They'd come through any sort of a storm if they heard a woman calling for 'em. But leave the rifle be. You understand?"

She nodded.

"There is three or four camps within earshot of you. Remember that and you can feel safe. As for Legrain and his gang, they're rough, but I don't think that they'll bother you . . . not after the understanding that I've had with 'em. You can rest easy about that."

"I feel like a child," she admitted, "since you have

taken charge of everything. It is all in your hands, now. And. . . ."

He stopped her, as a tremor crept into her voice. "Here is a crew that means some sort of mischief . . . and who to?" he murmured.

Up the road came a compact throng of men. As they neared the shack, they increased their pace. Then they gathered in a loosely flung semicircle in front of the place. Louise Berenger stood bolt upright and clutched at the shoulder of her companion.

"What *does* it mean?"

As though to answer that question, a voice from the crowd called: "Melendez, come away from the girl and step out here to talk for yourself!"

Then she saw that there were naked weapons in every hand in that crowd, not revolvers only, but terrible, broad-mouthed shotguns and repeating rifles, all carried in positions from which they could be swiftly slung into action.

"You won't go?" whispered the girl.

But she felt the arm beneath her hand turn into quivering iron, and like iron was the voice that answered her: "I'll just have a few words with 'em."

He stepped from her and stood before them.

"Melendez," said the spokesman—who nevertheless, as she saw, did not step out in advance of the rest—"we've decided that the gulch has had about enough of you. You slide out tonight and you keep going. You hear us talk?"

He made a pause, and in that silence the head of Melendez turned slowly from side to side. He seemed to be studying them with a grave intentness.

"Gents," he said, "are you all errand boys for Legrain?"

It brought a snarl from them. "We've had enough of gunfighters and wild men in these parts," said the spokesman hotly. "This here town has decided to settle down and we're the vigilance committee that's been appointed to take care of law and order. We're beginning on you, Melendez. You talk turkey or you hang, do you hear?"

"Sure," said Melendez, "I hear what you got to say. I hear it all fine."

He spoke so mildly, that the spokesman of the crew now boldly advanced. "You could herd some of the boys out of Grimm's place," he said, "and you could mop up the floor with Legrain, but we're different from them. . . ."

"One minute," broke in Melendez. "It seems to me that I remember how you dived for the door and got stuck there. You was one of the first to run, if I remember right."

The spokesman obviously winced. Half of his strength was stolen from him by this unlucky remembrance. "You lie," he said weakly. "Now let's hear what you intend to do about leaving, Melendez? And let's hear quick!"

Melendez took another step forward. "I'll tell you all about it," he said gently. "I was aiming to get out of this town right quick, because I was afraid that there might be some men in it. Now I see that I was wrong. There *ain't* any men in it. There's only swine! As for the lot of you, why, sons, I laugh at you. Except that you raise a dust right in front of me. And I'd rather have you raising a dust farther up the road . . . back toward town . . . you understand? Now break and scatter!"

A gun was in his hands as he said this—a gun poised and leveled at their heads. And in reply there was a quick flashing of weapons all around the circle.

It seemed to the girl that if any man in that crowd

had had the courage to fire a shot, no matter how blindly, the rest would instantly have turned loose a flood of bullets that would have swept Melendez to an instant death. But no bullet was fired. The guns that were half raised, wavered down again. Two or three men in the front side-stepped and pressed back. Those in the rear gladly turned with them. The remaining front rank felt that it was being deserted under the cold eye and the steady gun of this man-slayer.

They turned, also. A little panic broke out in them, as well. Some weaker nature shouted with sudden fear and bolted to the right. Others followed—some scattered straight down the road. Others fled to the left-hand field.

Presently there was nothing left as a token of their coming except a stinging scent of alkali dust that trailed through the smoky air.

It seemed to the girl the sheerest sort of a miracle. Yet she did not wonder that they had fled. Even from the back of Melendez, as he stood threatening the others, she had felt, as it were, the shooting of lightnings.

He whirled about on his heel. "I'm gonna ride to the ravine," he said gruffly. "I'll take a look at the spot where you say that your father spotted the vein. If there's people on that claim, now, you can lay to it that your father is a dead man. If there's nobody on it, you can lay to it that somewhere in Slosson's Gulch they're trying to squeeze the information out of him as to where that claim of his might be, and where he got his ore sample. Good night, Miss Berenger."

Very brutal talk, it seemed. But when he started up the road, on Rob, she followed him wistfully with her eyes. He was gone, taking her worries with him. For, although reason told her that he was only one man, and that this was a trouble too great for one man to solve, still she could not resist a blind belief that all would be well. As steel is sure, such was his surety. She could not believe that he would fail.

She cooked her own supper and then waited, until a voice called to her loudly through the night: "Melendez is gone, and, if he comes back, you can tell him that he's coming back to trouble!"

She could not see through the blanketing darkness more than a dim form in the roadway, but she thought that she recognized the voice of the man who had worn the hat of her father, and been called Bill. That was Legrain, then. And what did Legrain know? Her very blood went cold.

Another hour went past, and then the sharp ringing of the galloping hoofs of a horse approached down the valley. They paused before the shack, and she heard the low, steady voice of Melendez saying: "No one is on the claim. I got down and looked. Why, even by match light I could see that the stuff is richer than all telling. No wonder your father disappeared, if he showed such stuff around this town. But keep your heart up. This here thing will turn out well."

He hardly waited for a word of answer, but was gone again. Listening to the strong, steady sound of the galloping as it died away, toward the gulch, her hopes arose and happiness came back to her.

XIII

A LITTLE INFORMATION

He went first of all straight to old Hans Grimm and found that gentleman not in his gaming house, but outside of it, in his own shack, seated at the doorway, with his long pipe between his teeth, smoking with a calm enjoyment. The tuft of gray hair at either temple made him seem, in the starlit night, like a horned satyr at the mouth of its cave.

"Well, Melendez," he said, "I'm glad to say that you took my advice."

"It was luck, after all," insisted Melendez. "I seen her just as I started out of town... just as I was *streaking* out of town, as a matter of fact. I saw her and I stopped and so I'm still here. I've come back to you for a little advice."

"Thanks," Hans Grimm said. "Some folks come back to me for coin. But none of them ever come back to me for advice. Now, what do you want?"

"Someone in this town has grabbed old man Berenger. He's disappeared for over a day."

"I heard that he was gone."

"And what I want to know is... who might have taken him?"

"I dunno that I can tell you that."

"You might put me on the right road to finding out about it, however."

"Berenger is gone, eh?" murmured the other, shaking his head. "Why should they have nabbed him?"

"He had a quartz sample so rich that it would have broken your heart to see it. They must have spotted it and got him before he could file his claim."

"For what are they holding him?" asked Hans Grimm.

"To put him in torment," Melendez said. "Then they'll get out of him where he made his find. That's simple, isn't it, Hans?"

"Aye, and after he's told him?"

"Then finish him off and put him where he'll tell no tales afterwards. Of course, that's it."

Hans Grimm stood up from his chair with a grunt of violence. "I understand," he said. He walked back and forth, his head bowed in thought. "Do you know the man without legs that begs in front of the general store . . . Higgins's General Store?"

"Yes, I've seen him."

"He has a camera eye. He never forgets faces. *He's* likely to have noticed your man. Can you describe him?"

"His daughter gave me a photograph."

"Go find that beggar. He's a mean devil, but, if you can make him talk, he might turn the trick for you."

Melendez turned and hurried up the street. He walked very closely to one edge of the sidewalk, and, as he passed each gap and crossroad, he kept his eyes alert for either side. It was well that he did so, perhaps. A block from the store, two shadows slipped softly up behind him. When he turned, they skulked to either side of him and disappeared in the rollicking crowd of miners. But he knew that they had had their eyes on him. How many others were waiting for a chance at him, he could only guess. And bullets through the back counted as much as bullets fired face to face.

At Higgins's store there was no sign of the beggar without legs. He went inside to make inquiries. Higgins himself sat on a box at one end of the counter with a sawed-off, double-barreled shotgun in his hands—a little red-faced cockney with a determined eye.

Melendez's words brought an impatient scowl to Higgins's face. While the little cockney answered, his eyes wandered over the crowd in his store, reading faces, guessing at danger. His till would never be captured by thieves, unless his body were first salted away with lead.

"You go up first road on the left. Find Jack's shack at the top of it . . . straightway."

Jack was the beggar, and Melendez waited for no more. He found a little covert, composed of scraps of timbers, canvas, and a mound of dirt. The beggar sat in the doorway of this cave, and Melendez put a dollar in his hand.

The dying embers of the beggar's cook fire threw enough light to let the taller man read the expression of universal bitterness with which the deformed creature looked at him.

"Jack," he said gently, "have you seen this face?" He laid the photograph before the other.

"Maybe I have and maybe I ain't," snapped the cripple.

"I'm only asking you," said Melendez.

The other tilted his face once more. The dust of the street had not been wiped from it. "You're Melendez. You fight your own fights," he growled.

It was plain to Melendez that the other knew something. So he sat down on his heels and thereby brought his face to a level with Jack's.

"Do you really know me, Jack?" he said.

"I know you enough," said Jack.

"Then you know that when I talk business, I mean it. That dollar was only a promise. There's more behind it." He held out a $5 note. To his genuine astonishment, Jack dragged out the dollar that had already been given to him and threw it into the lap of Melendez.

"Now I'm clear of you," he said. "So get out. I've done enough talking for today!"

"Listen to me," said Melendez, "the day before yesterday . . . it was probably along in the late afternoon, Berenger . . . this is his photograph . . . came into Slosson's Gulch. He had pay dirt in his pocket. He had a chunk of it. Jack, he's disappeared, and I want to know if you saw him walking with anybody. Did he go by you?"

"The whole town goes by me," said Jack. "How can I remember everybody?"

"Because you're one man in ten thousand, or more," Melendez said calmly. "That's why I've come here. You can tell me what nobody else is apt to. Did you see Berenger walking with anyone?"

The lips of Jack parted to something that was almost a smile under this flattery, but they set again at once, and he shook his head. "I've done a day's work," he said. "And I'm tired. I ain't talking, Melendez. I don't want no part of your game, whatever it is."

The hand of Melendez darted out like the striking head of a snake and fixed upon one of the bulky wrists of the cripple. His other hand laid the blunt nose of his Colt under the chin of the little man. "Jack," he said, "you ain't more than half an inch from Hades. Will you change your mind about talking?"

In all his life—and he had been in strange places and among rough men—he had never seen an expression of such concentrated venom as that which appeared on the face of Jack. A cat, cornered by a dog, spits back at it with just such poisonous and devilish rage.

"They'll run you out of town for this!" he gasped.

"You've heard me," Melendez said. "Now do you talk?"

Still Jack hesitated, his eyes burning into the face of the other, but at length he snarled: "Get to Judge's shanty. Hun and Sam Myron was with this dude. And I hope you're cursed forever!"

"Where's Judge's shanty?"

"Up Leonard Creek on the left side. The second shanty. I hope that he gets you . . . and he *will* get you, greaser!"

There was so much respect for this bit of deformity in Melendez, that, when he stood up, he backed away from the little man to a distance, then turned and hurried away. As he went, he heard a shrill whistle break behind him, a whistle that was swiftly repeated. Unless he was very generously mistaken, that was a signal from the cripple to friends. When they came to him, they would learn that Judge was apt to fall into trouble quickly, unless help were sent.

So Melendez dropped into the saddle on Rob and sent the good gelding flying out of town and down the valley. He was directed quickly enough to the creek. It wound down out of a rough ravine, joining Slosson's Creek with a white rushing of waters that sounded, at a distance, like a waterfall. So up the left-hand side of the creek he galloped the horse. He passed the first shanty. The second was removed a little distance between two hills.

Rob, he left in a little grove of poplars in the hollow. Then he went on, on foot, working his way carefully through the shrubbery. When he came nearer, he could see the silhouette of a big man sitting with his back against a tree, twenty yards in front of the shack. Beside this watcher there was the glimmer of steel that made Melendez know that the sentry kept a rifle nearby.

Working still closer, he finally lay behind a rock and stretched out at full length. Then he saw a second man seated at the door of the shanty, taking the cool of the evening, with a pipe between his teeth.

"All right, Judge," said a voice from inside. "He's come to."

"You and Bert try your hands with him," said Judge. "I'm tired of manhandling the old fool!"

XIV

RESCUE

This was proof enough to Melendez that he had not followed a false trail. Yonder in the house was old Berenger, beyond any doubt, but how was he to get the man out? Here were two armed men watching outside the house, and two more within it. Fellows engaged in such work as theirs would be sure to fight desperately. He thought of this as he lay behind his rock and he decided at last on a plan that was as simple as it was bold. Here and there across the clearing in front of the shack were fallen logs and standing rocks. He began to work softly around them, creeping from one to the other, until he came silently up beside the door of the lean-to, and the man who sat there.

At the last moment, it seemed that some premonition of evil stirred in Judge. He stood up suddenly and made a step straight toward Melendez, where he lay behind a jagged boulder. It was the very vaguest of instincts that moved in him, however, for when Melendez rose like a shadow from behind the rock, Judge was frozen in his place, unable to lift the rifle that he carried under his arm. He saw the glim-

mering revolver in the hand of the stranger and he
knew that it was pointed at his heart.

At the same instant, there was a groan from
within the house that wrung the heart of Melendez
with horror. Melendez beckoned, and Judge
stepped still nearer.

"Walk straight ahead," whispered Melendez.
"March for the trees, yonder, and make no noise.
And walk soft, Judge!"

Judge, without a word, stepped gently ahead and
made for the trees. There, in the heavy shadow, he
paused. The nose of a revolver was prodded into the
small of his back.

"Have you brought me out here to murder me,
stranger?" whined Judge.

"Hand back the butt of that rifle," said Melendez.

It was done, and Melendez received it with his
free hand. He weighed it, sighing with satisfaction.
There were fifteen shots in the chamber of this gun,
and a rifle is a hundred times better than a revolver
for work by a dim light, where a bead must be
drawn with care. He shoved the revolver back into
the pocket from which he had drawn it. The rifle he
carried in the cup of his right arm, with a finger
upon the trigger.

So, with the muzzle of that gun still pressed
against the back of Judge, he went through his
clothes with his other hand. There was a Colt and a
long knife. This completed the arms of the miner.

"Now," said Melendez smoothly, "we can talk
business. Turn around."

Judge turned obediently.

"Ordinarily," said Melendez, "you'd think that
this here was a time to start killing. But it ain't that
for me, old son. You need killing terrible bad, the
four of you, but I want something out of you. I make

a dicker with you, Judge. You turn old Berenger over to me, and I let you go."

"Berenger?"

"Most likely you dunno what I mean?" Melendez said sarcastically.

Judge was silent. At length he muttered: "You have the low-down on me, stranger. But I would like to say something. The old fool would never've got himself hurt, if he'd talked up right off, the way that I told him to."

"He wouldn't squeal?" Melendez asked.

"He looked as soft and as foolish as a woman," complained Judge, "but when you come to bear down on him, he was like iron. Seems like he'd rather die than talk."

"All right," said Melendez, "tonight I ain't saying what you should get for this little job of yours. I'm just saying . . . turn this here Berenger over to me and do it quick."

"There ain't any way," Judge said, "without calling in the other boys. And if I do that, there'll be a flock of trouble. The whole three of them is fighting fools."

"You think of a way," said Melendez. "By the way, I might tell you that, if the worse comes to the worst, I'd finish you off right here, and then start on the rest of them . . . unless you can work out a scheme for getting him out to me. I ain't soft-hearted, Judge. Not a bit!"

"Look here," growled Judge, "if you want your share of this stuff, we're pretty willing to let you come in on equals."

"You are, eh?"

"Yes, or if you want more, why, we'll give you *two* shares. Does that sound good to you?"

"It won't do," Melendez said. "You cursed set of leeches!" The last words were torn from him involuntarily as a stifled cry of agony broke from the house.

"Who are you?" panted Judge.

"My name is Melendez."

"Melendez!"

"Now, Judge, if I hear another yap from poor old Berenger, I'm going to kill you, man, and then start in on the others."

Judge waited to hear no more. He turned hastily and called in a loud voice: "Hey, boys!"

An instant of pause, and then a sharp answer: "Now what the devil do you want?"

"I got a new idea. Come along out here and bring the old goat with you!"

"For why, Judge?"

"I tell you, don't you start asking questions. Just bring him along. Pretty quick, will you?"

"Well, we'll make a try. He's a dead weight, though."

Presently Melendez saw, by the starlight, two men issuing from the cabin, one carrying the head and the other the feet of a limp burden. Blind rage overwhelmed Melendez.

"Hello!" sang out the voice of the first look-out beneath his tree—half lost in the distance. "What's up now?"

"Tell him to stay where he is!" commanded Melendez.

"You stay put, Jerry," answered Judge. "You stay right where you are. That's where we need you most. We're gonna finish this job."

"That's spoke right," Jerry said complacently. "Finish the old fool, if he won't talk. I'm tired of this dirty job. He ain't got the *only* gold in the valley!"

"He's a heavy old goat," said one of the bearers, as they came nearer.

There was a faint groan and then: "I can walk, if you wish. . . ."

It made the heart of Melendez stand still. It seemed to him that he recognized something of the voice of Louise Berenger in these weary but courageous tones.

"You stay put," said one of the bearers harshly. "Now what's the game, Judge . . . and who the devil is that?"

As he spoke, he dropped the weight he was carrying. His companion did the same, and they found themselves looking at the long, steady barrel of a rifle held with the butt snuggled comfortably into the deep shoulder of Melendez.

"Are you double-crossing us, Judge?" cried one.

"It ain't me," the Judge moaned. "This here is Melendez. He got the drop on me, and now he has it on you."

"You face around," Melendez ordered calmly. "I would like to drill the lot of you, and I got more than half a mind to do it. But if you'll face around and march straight back toward that shack and go inside of it, I ain't going to harm you. You hear me?"

They showed that they heard by turning solemnly around. Judge joined them, and the three slunk slowly across the clearing, walking as though they feared the rocks would crumple beneath their feet. They entered the door of the shack.

Then the voice of Jerry sounded from beneath his tree: "Now what the devil is this song and dance, partners?"

There was no answer for Jerry until the last man had entered the lean-to. Then there was a loud yell of rage: "It's Melendez, Jerry! Cut across behind him. We'll come back down his trail. The hound has got Berenger!"

There was a wild yell of rage from Jerry, the outpost. Immediately afterwards, the worthy Bert leaped from the door of the shack, rifle in hand, to follow the trail of his enemy. He received a bullet through both his hips that toppled him back into the house, screeching in agony.

For just such a sortie, Melendez had been waiting. Now he drew the father of Louise to his feet. The older man staggered with weakness, like one just out of a sick bed. And he whispered: "Who are you? God bless you, my lad! You have taken me out of Hades."

"Walk steady," said Melendez. "You can rest some weight on my shoulder, but leave my arms free. We have to go slow . . . but we'll try to go sure."

They had not taken half a dozen steps when Melendez paused and left his companion leaning against the great trunk of a tree. He himself sidestepped softly through the brush, and presently, by a dim shaft of starlight that struggled down through a break in the trees, he saw what he had expected—the form of a man creeping along on hands and knees, shoving a rifle before him.

A bullet would have ended him quickly, but a devlish fury rose in Melendez at the sight of the other. He leaped like a tiger and struck down with knees and fists. A shriek of despair and fear rose beneath him. The fellow writhed about and lay face upwards, striking a knife at the throat of Melendez. The knife hand, however, was seized by the wrist, and, straight into the upturned face, Melendez smashed the butt of the rifle, once, twice, and again.

The screaming ceased. The man lay inert. Melendez rose to his feet and raced back to Berenger.

XV

AT THEIR MERCY

Neither of the unwounded pair in the shack had attempted to leave it, yet. But by the noise they made, Melendez guessed that they were breaking through the flimsy wall of the side farthest from him and his rifle. Then they would hurry out and skulk down his trail—carefully, oh, very carefully—after the things that had happened to Jerry and Bert. For all the world he would not have been in the shoes of Judge, who had indirectly brought all these disasters upon them.

He went on with Berenger. The older man was weak, very weak; he walked with one hand clutching the shoulder of Melendez's coat. His head was thrown back, his teeth were set, and his lips grinned in the agony of his effort. What the four devils had done to their victim, Melendez would not even guess, but he longed to turn back and crush the remaining two—Judge in particular! Surely there was no justice under heaven if that consummate villain were allowed to carry his life away freely. But he had other things to think about than mere vengeance.

Up the valley he could hear the drumming of hoofs, as horses galloped hotly toward them.

Perhaps they were coming in response to the noises of shooting that they had heard, or to the sounds of screaming. Yet men around Slosson's Gulch had heard shots and screams before, and they were more apt to remain all the closer beside their own campfires when they heard such sounds.

It was no riding of open-hearted preservers of the peace. On the contrary, these must be friends of Judge who had been sent to help him in time of danger by the cripple. They had not taken long to get ready and ride. Surely Melendez had come fast, and he had not remained long seconds in front of the shack. Yet the rescue was nearly here—rushing up from the trail, turning straight toward the lean-to of Judge and his companions.

At the same instant Berenger crumpled up like a loosely hinged thing, across the arm with which Melendez turned to catch him. There was no time to ask questions and to offer sympathy. He merely slung the older man across his shoulder like a sack of wheat and ran with all his might through the trees, toward those poplars where he had left Rob. If only the rescue party did not spot the gelding in the shadows of the poplars.

They did not seem to be waiting, or approaching, with any caution. They came in a single, storming volley—half a dozen hard riders, it seemed to Melendez, as they crashed through the underbrush and hurtled up the hillside.

Above them, frantic voices were screaming: "Go back! Block the down trail! Melendez is clear!"

The jangle of the screeching voices and the sound of their own pounding horses kept them from understanding. They rode on, and Melendez offered a gasping thanks to God and gained the side of Rob. There he had to pause again. He pried the teeth of Berenger apart and poured a stiff dram of moonshine whiskey, 100-proof, down his throat. It brought the older man back to his senses, coughing and spluttering.

Melendez swung his helpless man into the saddle, mounted behind, and urged Rob into a gallop. He was a stout horse, built not so much for speed as for the patient bearing of burdens, but this double load was too much to expect anything more than a cart horse at a walk. He ran stoutly, but his forehoofs rose high and struck hard, his quarters sagging a little at every stride. Moreover, fast as he might go, at his gallop, it was nothing compared with the rush of the avengers who would soon be at his heels.

Presently Melendez saw them coming—the six who had newly arrived from Slosson's Gulch, together with Judge and his remaining companion from the shack. He could thank the kind heavens now for the night that was covering him, for otherwise their bullets would be humming about him. They gained fast; they gained with a terrible speed. He saw that he could not keep away from them for another half mile.

Perhaps he could have kept them back a little by using his rifle, had he been alone, but he could not handle the sagging body of old Berenger and his own, at the same time, so he saw that one part of the game was surely lost.

Straight ahead of them hung a wall of shadow, where the sides of the gulch drew close together. Through this narrowed mouth, the waters of the creek went crashing onward toward Slosson's Valley. The throat consisted of the white waters of the

creek, and just ten feet of trail in a ledge at the foot
of the next slope. In the black mouth of the narrows,
Melendez called to Rob to stop. Then he quickly
dismounted.

Straight behind him came eight black shapes,
streaking through the night. Melendez dropped
upon one knee, drew a true bead, and fired. The
rider pitched silently, headlong, from the saddle.
His companions swirled, screeching to one side or
the other, breaking for shelter from before that
deadly rifle.

If heaven would only send that horse with the
empty saddle straight on through the narrows,
where Melendez could catch it, and then whirl on
again with redoubled speed for Slosson's Gulch. But
the horse feared the crouched figures in the darkness. It wheeled about, also, and went up the hillside
with jack-rabbit jumps.

Melendez saw what remained to him to do.

If he mounted again behind Berenger and tried to
make Slosson's Gulch, he would be hopelessly lost.
Both of them would go down. He stood at the shoulder of the horse and tied the legs of Berenger hard
with the dangling saddle straps.

"Do you hear me, Berenger?"

"I hear you," said a weak voice.

"I've got you tied on. You can't fall off. Now ride
straight ahead. There ain't any chance of missing
the trail. It runs straight down the valley to Slosson's
Gulch. All that you got to do is to keep flogging the
horse along. Do you understand that?"

"I understand," whispered the other.

"When you get there, ask for Hans Grimm. Do
you know his place?"

"No."

"You don't?" Melendez groaned. "Well, ask for

Hans Grimm. Everybody else knows him. Tell Hans that I'm up here. He'll send help."

"I can't leave you, lad . . . ," began Berenger.

"Do you know better than me what to do? Ride on, and ride fast! Now, get out!"

He stood back and slapped the gelding. The protest of Berenger was torn off short at his lips by the lurch of Rob as he fled down the road. There remained to Melendez only the dark of the night, with the cold, distant faces of the stars, and the departing rattle of the hoofs of the mare.

That sound raised a fury in the seven men who were still here to press the attack.

The eighth lay flat on his face in the deep dust of the trail, and he would never again ride in any hunt. But the others swarmed toward the narrow pass, shooting from behind every covert. It seemed as though the torrent of their bullets must surely sweep Melendez away and aside and let them through. But Melendez lay in the angle between two rocks. Partly the darkness sheltered him, and partly the stones were his shields. However he had his chance to strike back at them almost at once, for on the hillside above him and to the left, he saw the silhouette of a rider dimly against the stars. He fired quickly and heard a yell of pain, and then a steady stream of cursing as the rider scuttled back toward safety.

After that, they could know that Berenger had galloped on toward safety. Their whole effort was not to reclaim him but to exact a sweet revenge upon the head of Melendez. For that purpose they pressed steadily up toward the pass.

Now and again he saw the flash of red fire that indicated that a rifle was speaking to him. But he was contented to lie quietly, only firing now and again, as he shifted from his central little fort. For the distance was saving him.

In the meantime, he saw a film of silver descending over the upper portion of the valley. It brightened rapidly. The rocks stood out in white and black. The brightness of the creek that foamed beside him became a flashing thing, and every moment the light increased. The moon had risen, and in a very brief time the watchers who were crowding toward him were sure to spot him. How long would it be, then, before they were able to strike at him with a sharply angled shot?

He looked about him, but he could see no better way of fortifying himself. When he attempted to break for a loftier stone, whose sheer side might shelter him from a bullet from above more entirely, his break was greeted with three rifle shots, and he shrank back to cover. A moment later, a bullet splashed from the rock on his right side and thin splinters of liquid lead drove like needles into his flesh.

They had him almost at their mercy, now. They could swarm above him at a safe height, and eventually, by the brightening light of the moon, they would be able to shoot with almost as much surety as under the light of the sun.

He had no hope to advance or to retreat. There was only the chance, very remote, that old Berenger could send help to him in time.

XVI

IT ALL ADDS UP

The people of Slosson's Gulch ran toward the limp figure that feebly hung on to his horse. They cut the leather straps and placed old Berenger on the pavement. Water was thrown down his throat, and, in the meantime, strange discoveries were being made.

Someone shouted: "What's happened to this old man's feet? Has the fool been walking on fire?"

And another snarled: "His back! Did you see his back?"

"It's Berenger. It's old Berenger that they say made the great strike. Will he live?"

"He's dead now! Look at his glassy eyes!"

For the eyes of Berenger had indeed opened and rolled up, and they stared above him with no expression and with no feeling.

"Try his pulse."

"There ain't no pulse, and his hand's dead cold already!"

"Listen to his heart, will you?"

"Aye, now I hear something. Stand back, half a million of you, and let's see if he can get some air. No, he's had enough to drink."

The lips of Berenger parted and whispered: "Hans Grimm."

"He wants Grimm. Go get Hans. Get him quick. Here's a dying confession, or something. Somebody gimme a blanket to slide under him. This gent is about to die, boys!"

They made the bed for Berenger down on the sidewalk and stood about half brutally curious and half genuinely moved. Someone had gone to find Louise Berenger and tell her that she was sadly needed.

And then came Hans Grimm. He came in haste with men about him and he dropped to his knees beside the form of Berenger.

"Are you Grimm?"

"Yes. Where's Melendez?"

"Up the valley. Men . . . ," Berenger quietly whispered, and closed his eyes.

He had fainted away, but the wits of Hans Grimm were applied where the voice of Berenger had ended. He was told how this man had come to town, tied on the back of the mare that stood panting nearby. He recognized that horse as belonging to Melendez. He made up his own mind about the rest of it. Melendez had sent Berenger on ahead in this desperate plight; Melendez himself must be either dead or in sore straits somewhere in the rear. And Grimm's influence made itself felt. The men were suddenly ashamed of their treatment of Melendez; they were incensed by the suffering the old man had undergone.

A score of men tumbled into saddles and followed Hans Grimm as the gambler rushed up the valley. They were hardly clear of Slosson's Gulch when they could hear the dim crackling of rifles in the distance.

Like a good general, Hans Grimm headed for the point of heaviest firing, and so he turned up the valley of the creek with his men riding hard behind him, their guns ready. As they approached the narrows of the pass, they could see the flame spurting from the mouths of the guns.

It ended suddenly as they came near, and then, as they drew rein in the throat of the pass, they could hear the departing roar of hoofs up the valley.

At the angle between two stones they found Melendez, his rifle still at his shoulder and five bullets through his body. But there was still life in the body of Judge, found not a dozen paces away up the hillside.

They brought them both back to Slosson's Gulch and they brought, also, Bert and Jerry, who were found at the shack. The others of the party were gone, except for the unknown dead man who lay, facedown, in the trail. Him they buried beneath the neighboring rocks.

Then the citizens of Slosson's Gulch who were in the vigilance committee were given free rein to handle the prisoners. Judge and Bert and Jerry were driven out of town. Then the people of the gulch sat down to learn what was happening to the two men who lay in one room of the house of Hans Grimm, with Louise Berenger ministering to them.

For a week the doctor could not return a sure answer, but after that the reports were all favorable. As the doctor said, each of them had too much to live for to allow himself to die at this moment. As for Melendez, there was the girl waiting. As for Berenger, there was the mine that hired men were opening for him now—finding the vein widening and deepening every moment, pouring forth riches.

The most frequent visitor to the sick man was, of

course, Hans Grimm. And when the brain of Melendez had cleared, Grimm sat by his bed and asked one day:

"Can you see it now, partner? All adds up . . . fact to fact . . . and no chance in it at all. A man came out here to dig gold with a book, and no guns. Had to have a gunman to help. So his daughter goes out and collects the right fellow. Meaning you. Now what chance was there in all of that? Nothing but logic!"

"Hans," the sick man said, grinning, "I'm tired of arguing. Besides, I can afford to change my mind."

And he looked between him and the door, where Louise Berenger was waiting, and smiling patiently toward him.

ABOUT THE AUTHOR

Max Brand® is the best-known pen name of Frederick Faust, creator of Dr. Kildare, Destry, and many other fictional characters popular with readers and viewers worldwide. Faust wrote for a variety of audiences in many genres. His enormous output, totaling approximately thirty million words or the equivalent of 530 ordinary books, covered nearly every field: crime, fantasy, historical romance, espionage, Westerns, science fiction, adventure, animal stories, love, war, and fashionable society, big business and big medicine. Eighty motion pictures have been based on his work along with many radio and television programs. For good measure he also published four volumes of poetry. Perhaps no other author has reached more people in more different ways.

Born in Seattle in 1892, orphaned early, Faust grew up in the rural San Joaquin Valley of California. At Berkeley he became a student rebel and one-man literary movement, contributing prodigiously to all campus publications. Denied a degree because of unconventional conduct, he embarked on a series of adventures culminating in New York City where, after a period of near starvation, he received simultaneous recognition as a serious poet and successful author of fiction. Later, he traveled widely, making

his home in New York, then in Florence, and finall
in Los Angeles.

Once the United States entered the Second Worl
War, Faust abandoned his lucrative writing caree
and his work as a screenwriter to serve as a war cor
respondent with the infantry in Italy, despite hi
fifty-one years and a bad heart. He was killed dur
ing a night attack on a hilltop village held by th
German army. New books based on magazine seri
als or unpublished manuscripts or restored version
continue to appear so that, alive or dead, he has av
eraged a new book every four months for seventy
five years. Beyond this, some work by him is newl
reprinted every week of every year in one or anothe
format somewhere in the world. A great deal mor
about this author and his work can be found in *Th
Max Brand Companion* (Greenwood Press, 1997) ed
ited by Jon Tuska and Vicki Piekarski.

MAX BRAND®

HAWKS AND EAGLES

Though constantly dodging bullets, Joe Good refuses
carry a gun. His weapon of choice: a supple blacksna
whip capable of splitting a hair or slicing open a wi
gash of flesh with just a deft flick of his wrist. Using
the skills and cunning at his disposal, Joe plans to ta
out the ranchers who killed his father, one by one. B
the Altons are a powerful family who own most of t
land—and the men—around Fort Willow. If Joe does
act fast, he won't live to see his vengeance.

ZANE GREY®

CABIN GULCH

In a fit of anger, Joan Randle sends Jim Cleve into the untamed mining camps of Idaho Territory to prove his grit and spirit. Then she regrets their quarrel and sets off after him to bring him back. But she crosses the path of Jack Kells, the notorious mining camp and stagecoach bandit, who captures her and intends to keep her as his woman. He is willing to kill two of his own men to have her all to himself, so how can Joan hope to escape? Her hopes will fade even more when Jim Cleve shows up—and joins Kells' gang....
